ROAD KILL

A TOM ROLLINS THRILLER

PAUL HEATLEY

Published by Inkubator Books
www.inkubatorbooks.com

ISBN (eBook): 978-1-915275-35-6
ISBN (Paperback): 978-1-915275-36-3

For Aidan

PROLOGUE

The girl has been on the run for three days now. She's tried to stay on the road for the most part, thumbing rides. First vehicle she got on was a bus, using up all the money she was able to take with her, only to get four towns away from Belleville. All the cars that have stopped to pick her up have been driven by men. She's been wary of them. Pressed herself up against the passenger door while they drove. None of them tried anything. None of them were able to take her very far, either.

Her escape comes in frustrating increments. She's not trying to get far, not really. It's not like she's trying to get to California. It's just one state line she needs to cross, that's all. North Washington down into north Oregon.

She stays away from the roads at night. Travels through the trees. It's spring. The nights are clear. They're cool, but not so cool she's going to freeze to death. She sleeps beneath Douglas firs, lying on beds of their fallen needles.

By the third day she is exhausted and hungry and frustrated at how long this is all taking. She just needs someone who can take her all the way. Enough of this short-journey bullshit. She needs to find a trucker, someone doing a long haul, someone who can actually take her where she needs to be. She can't stay in Washington. The longer she's in Washington, the more likely it is that the Ogre will find her.

He's always found her before. This is the furthest she's ever got. It's not the first time she's tried to run away. Sometimes, it's like he knows where she's going to go before she does. He gets there ahead of her. Toying with her. Smiling his horrible, Ogre smile. Then he takes her straight back to where she's run from.

She walks by the side of the road, looking back whenever she hears something loud enough to be what she's waiting for. Sticks her thumb out. The trucks don't stop. Nothing stops. She tries not to look into the cars, keeping her face turned away, lowered, her long, dark hair hanging into it to cover herself up. She's a good-looking girl, a beautiful girl – she's had enough men tell her so – and flashing her face would likely get her a ride. But she doesn't want a ride from the kind of person who would stop for a pretty girl, especially regardless of the girl's age. She walks with her hood up, though she doubts this meager disguise could do much to hide her from the Ogre. She lives in fear of seeing him. Of looking up and finding him looking straight back at her, smiling.

The day is a bust. It's getting dark, and no one has stopped. One truck blared its horn in acknowledgment of her raised thumb, but that was all. Her stomach is twisted and pained, crying out for food. She slips back into the woods, close to angry tears, and looks for somewhere to sleep.

The ground is hard. It hasn't rained for a few days. She can't get comfortable. She twists and squirms, trying to settle. A persistent root stabs between her shoulder blades. She's able to ignore it, eventually. Around the same time, the sky darkens fully. It's a clear night. There are many stars. The girl stares up through the trees. The glow of the rising moon is off to the side. Soon she'll be able to see it. Around her, in the trees and the bushes, are the sounds of small animals. Of birds calling intermittently. The scurrying of rodents through and up the trees.

Then a branch snaps. It's heavy. It's loud. Too loud to be an animal.

A pause follows. She pushes herself up on an elbow, head turned, listening. Looking to where she heard it come from, the darkness through the interlocking branches there. She holds her breath. She stares. There isn't any further movement. No more branches snap.

But she isn't stupid. She knows what she heard.

She pushes herself up, and she runs.

The bushes burst behind her. Her instincts were right. Someone was there. He's found her again. The Ogre. The Ogre always comes.

She runs as fast as she can. Doesn't look back, but she can hear her pursuer. Hears him gaining. Hears the pounding of his footsteps, feels his breath on the back of her neck, and then she's caught. Tackled to the ground, weight on top of her. Crushed. She can't breathe. Can't move. Can barely turn her head to see the face of the Ogre leering back at her.

Then she's hauled off the ground, broken twigs and moss sticking to the front of her, to her face. She's able to see now. Able to turn her head. Sees that the Ogre is not here. He hasn't come, though she knows he has sent these men.

This time, it's a different kind of monster that has found her.

1

It has been a month since Tom Rollins left Alaska. It's springtime now. The snow has faded from the sides of the road as he's travelled. The skies cleared. The sun grew brighter as he made his way south through British Columbia. Staying in a motel a couple of days ago, he buzzed his hair and shaved his beard in preparation for the warmer weather. His stubble's already coming in. He scratches an itch at the corner of his jaw and hears his fingernail scrape through it.

He's in the northwest of Washington State now. There is no destination in mind, but Tom is taking his time. Eyes open, looking for potential work. Something in logging perhaps or construction. He has money saved, though it's not all with him. Some is secured in various safe-deposit boxes in banks, mostly in the South. Money saved up from his past. But they are not bottomless coffers. Money runs out, even when living as frugally as Tom does.

The gas is running low in his pickup. He's kept his eyes out for a gas station for a few miles now. It's a long road without much on it. Tall trees line either side, reaching high, the sun's rays battling to get through the branches.

There aren't many other vehicles around, either. Tom has had the road to himself for the last ten minutes. He knows, soon, perhaps after he's got gas, that he'll need to get onto a main road if he's hoping to find work. There won't be much to find around here, except for maybe a greasy backwoods diner. Working a grill and pouring burnt coffee doesn't appeal to him as much as the idea of working outdoors.

He sees traffic up ahead: Finally, some signs of civilization. Sees the various vehicles pulling into and out of a forecourt. A gas station, at last. He pulls in, up to a pump. There's a diner next to the gas station, and most of the vehicles Tom saw pull in ahead of him are going there. It's getting toward midday, lunchtime, and Tom feels a familiar pang in his own stomach. Pumping gas, he looks toward the diner. There's a Help Wanted sign in the window. He grins to himself, shakes his head a little. Notices, behind the building, there's a sign for another diner a couple of miles down the road. It's brazen enough to carry the slogan, '*The best meal for* miles *around! Worth driving just a little further for!*' The sign looks old, but undamaged, and Tom is surprised the proprietors of the diner in front of him have not taken exception to its claims and attempted to tear it down.

A sound off to his side, one of the other pumps, catches his attention, snaps him from his daydream of warring rival diners. He looks. There's a black minivan. It's pulled in after him. The sound he heard was a sharp intake of breath, like someone had been hurt. He doesn't see anyone nursing a wound. He sees three men stretching their legs. One of them pumps the gas, watching the rolling meter as it fills the tank. He sees movement, though, at the back of the vehicle, walking away from it. A fourth man and a girl. Can only see the back of them, but from behind the girl can't be much more than a teenager. They walk toward the station, down the side of it, to where the bathrooms are. The man has his hand on the girl's shoulder, in the crook of her neck and trapezius. Tom sees the way her skin is crinkled. The way the man is holding her tighter than is necessary, like he's guiding her and holding on to her at the same time.

Tom watches the scene out of the corner of his eye while the tank fills. Watches the three men still remaining. They don't see him looking. They wear jeans and sweaters – dark, old clothes. Dirty work clothes. One of them stands by the pump, watching it. He inspects his fingernails while it fills. He's the biggest of the men, broad in the shoulders. His stomach sticks out, but it looks solid, like a keg. The other two are talking. They laugh about something, glancing toward the bathroom where the man and girl have just disappeared. The man went inside with her. Tom feels the skin prickle on the back of his neck. There's a knot in his stomach. The situation feels off.

Tom's tank is full. He goes inside to pay, taking his time. Is careful not to look back over his shoulder, to alert them to his watching, but he listens as he goes by. They lower their voices as he nears, wary of strangers getting too close, overhearing. Inside, Tom hovers by the drinks. The girl and the other man haven't returned yet. He picks up a bottle of water and joins the line. At the front, while he's paying, the two reappear from around the side. Tom pays and steps back out.

The girl has been roughed up. The flesh under her right eye is reddening, perhaps on its way to being blackened. She's looking around, trying to catch people's eyes. No one acknowledges her silent pleading. The man is holding her by the side of the neck again, dragging her back to the vehicle. The three men have finished filling up. They've paid at the pump. They're inside the minivan, waiting.

The girl's eyes lock on Tom's. They hold. Hers are wide.

She tries to tilt her head back toward the man guiding her, but he tightens his grip, pushes her forward.

"Hey," Tom says, addressing the girl.

The man turns, eyes narrowed, but Tom doesn't look at him. He looks at the girl. The man has to loosen his grip enough for her to turn her head.

"Everything all right here?" Tom says to her.

"Everything's fine," the man says.

Tom shoots him a glance. "I'm talking to her."

"Why d'you wanna talk to my daughter?" he says, pulling her back, stepping in front of her.

"Because she looks upset," Tom says. "And she looks hurt."

Tom notices the three men have gotten back out of the minivan. The biggest of them strides up, stands the closest, arms and legs spread, fists balled, in an effort to look more intimidating. The other two stand close by his heel. Tom doesn't look at them straight on. He keeps his eyes on the man and the girl.

"He's not my dad," the girl says, her voice hoarse.

The man who's not her dad clamps a hand over her mouth, pushes her back. His eyes dart around the forecourt, seeing who else might be around, might be looking. He leans toward Tom without getting too close, hisses his words. "Listen, buddy, just mind your fucking business, okay? You don't need to worry yourself over a runaway. I'm just trying to get her home. You keep sticking your nose where it doesn't belong and you're liable to lose it."

Tom taps the side of his nose and grins. "I'll take my chances." The grin fades. "Let go of the girl. Whatever your relationship to her is, I don't like how you're handling her. Now, let go of her and take a step back, so me and her can talk without you interrupting."

The man doesn't do as Tom says. "You've got nothing to

say to each other." He looks at his three buddies. "Deal with this asshole," he says, then pushes the girl on, bundles her into the back of their vehicle. He doesn't follow her in. He slams the door shut, then turns back around. He doesn't stride up to join the others, to enforce their ranks. He stays by the minivan, at a safe distance.

"You heard what he said," the big guy at the fore says.

Tom looks at him, looks him over. The big man is used to intimidating people. Scaring them into giving up without a fight. Tom isn't scared. This man, with his scarred knuckles and brow, strikes Tom as a street fighter. He's not a professional. Tom doubts he has much skill or technique. He has power and reach, nothing more. Tom smiles at him, and it's clear that this unnerves the big man. He's unaccustomed to people not backing down.

"And you heard what I said," Tom says. "Now, who do *you* want to listen to? Choice is yours."

The big guy blinks. He hesitates, looks back over his shoulder to the two nearest him.

"Shut him up, and let's get out of here," says the guy by the vehicle. "We're done talking!"

The big guy nods, resolved, then turns back. He grabs for the front of Tom's shirt. Tom moves faster. Grabs his hand, twists his thumb. The big guy's body contorts as Tom wrenches him to the side. Tom controls his arm with just one hand. The big guy takes a desperate swing, but Tom catches it under his left arm, holds it tight.

The two behind the big guy make their move, one coming from either side. Tom swings the big guy to his right to block the one coming from that direction. The one on the left gets close, reaching, but Tom kicks out, his boot connecting with the side of his knee, blasting it out of joint. He goes down screaming. Tom head-butts the big guy next, his forehead crunching the bridge of his nose. The big guy stumbles back, but doesn't go down. His nose is bleeding. He clasps at it. His eyes will be streaming now, blinding him. He has to wipe them clear. It gives Tom a chance to deal with the one the big guy's bulk was blocking. A swift blow to the midsection doubles him over, then a shot to the temple puts him down.

The big guy is moving in again. Tom prepares for him. Plans out a few quick, hard, strategic blows to vulnerable areas to put him down and be done with him. Before he can strike, he notices out of the corner of his eye that the man standing by the vehicle is gone. Sees, then, how the big guy glances over Tom's shoulder. Tom spins before the man behind him can move into place. Tom raises his elbow, catches him in the chest mid-lunge, drops him from the air.

The man presses both hands to his chest and writhes on the ground, winded, gasping, looking like a landed fish. Tom turns back to the big guy. The big guy jabs. Tom ducks it, plants a left into his ribs. The big guy crumples, attempting to defend himself against a blow that has already landed. His arms drop to it. Tom throws a right into the big guy's throat. It puts him down. He stays there, coughing, hands wrapped around his neck.

The four men are down. They're not getting up in a hurry.

Tom goes to the back of the minivan, the door the girl was pushed through. He opens it. She's not inside. Tom leans in, looks. The vehicle is empty. The door on the opposite side is open. She's slipped away during the fight.

Tom looks around. There's no sign of her. There are trees surrounding the forecourt, at the back of the gas station and the diner. She could have escaped in there, disappeared through the foliage.

What Tom *does* see, however, are the people who are looking his way. The people who have witnessed the fight. Some of them are reaching for their phones. Some of them already have them out, recording the battle that has just occurred. Tom sees the attendant inside the gas station, making a call, watching him through the glass. Probably calling the cops. Tom doesn't hang around. He isn't going to wait for them to arrive, to explain to them what happened. The girl is already gone. There's not much more Tom can do for her if she hasn't hung around. If he comes across her hitchhiking down the road, then he can get the full story from her then. But, for now, his priority is getting away.

Tom goes to his truck and he drives, the four men still writhing on the ground as he leaves.

2

Ken Arnett pushes himself off the asphalt, rubbing his chest and sucking down air. He can already feel a bruise forming. He has to use a nearby gas pump to drag himself up all the way off the ground, coughing and gasping while he does. He sees vehicles waiting to pull into the forecourt, wanting to fill up, but they can't get in. All the pumps are blocked. He sees the people at the other pumps with their phones out, videoing what has just happened, making no effort to get moving and clear out. None of them tried to get involved, either. None of them tried to help. They just wanted to record it, like jackals.

"Who the hell was *he*?" Donald says, still on the ground, holding his throat where the guy punched him. Donald, the biggest of them, and handled like he was nothing at all.

Ken ignores him and gets to the minivan. The back door is already open, and he knows what he's going to find – nothing. There's no one inside. Taylor is gone. He notices the other back door is open, too. She found a way to get it open from inside. Ken had snapped the inside lock's handle before he went to join the fight, for all the good he did. She's smashed through the plastic interior, likely with her elbow, and pulled on the cable inside.

"She gone?" says Donald, stumbling over to join him.

Kyle and Gil are still on the ground. Kyle is clutching at his no-doubt-dislocated knee. Gil is knocked out from a blow to the temple. Ken looks over the damage the stranger has caused. Shakes his head.

"You're gonna have to call Bill," Donald says, rubbing his throat, his hand never leaving it. It looks like he keeps trying to swallow, but he's struggling. His voice is hoarse.

"You think I don't know that?" Ken says. He grits his teeth, snarls. The last thing he wants to have to do is call Bill. He sighs, waves Donald away. "Tell him to shut up," he says. He doesn't care if Kyle's knee is dislocated. All the screaming is getting on Ken's nerves.

Donald lumbers away. Ken pulls out his cell phone, his stomach turning as he flicks through to Bill's number. He blows air through his nose, steeling himself before he hits dial.

"Ken," Donald says.

Ken rolls his eyes, annoyed at the interruption. "*What?*"

Donald kneels by Kyle, clamps the hand not rubbing his own throat over Kyle's mouth to shut him up. "You hear that?"

Ken listens. Sirens, getting closer. The cops have been called. Ken raises his eyebrows. He slips the phone back into his pocket. The police could be an opportunity. A reason not to have to call Bill after all.

"Leave the cops to me," Ken says. "I'll do the talking."

3

Tom keeps his eyes on the mirrors as he goes, watching for pursuit. He's down the road now. Has put a couple of miles' distance between himself and the gas station. His adrenaline is still pumping from the fight. He has to remind himself to stick to the speed limit. Doesn't need to give anyone a reason to pull him over.

There's no one behind him, not yet. No one speeding to catch up. The road is clear behind and up ahead.

He takes deep breaths. Both hands are wrapped around the steering wheel. He's barely bruised his knuckles. They've been in much worse condition before. They have the scars to show it.

He looks to the mirrors again, and movement catches his eye. It's close. In the flatbed of his truck, directly behind him, trying to conceal itself beneath some tarp.

Tom pulls to the side of the road, keeping an eye on the mound, on its movement, should it try to break and run upon realizing the vehicle is stopping. It doesn't try to run. It freezes, tries to flatten itself. Tom gets out of the truck, goes to it. Reaches over the edge of his flatbed and pulls the tarp back. The girl, crouching, looks up at him. The girl from the gas station.

"Hello," Tom says.

The girl doesn't speak, not right away. She stays where she is, crouching, like a deer caught in headlights. One of her eyes is blackening. Tom can see how her teeth are clenched tightly, can see how her gaunt cheeks tremble with the pressure.

"Do you want to ride up front?" Tom says. "It'll be warmer. And more comfortable."

She looks back down the road, the way they've come. Checking, the way he was in the mirrors when he first spotted her. There's hesitation in her form, the way her shoulders are bunched, the way she maintains a sprinter's pose. Ready to bolt at a moment's notice. Finally, she looks back at him. Still hesitating. She speaks. "Fine," she says. It's all she says.

They get into the truck. Tom takes a good look at her as she climbs inside. She's a teenager, but a young one, and she looks younger still from how thin she is. Her clothes cling tight to her slight frame – black jeans with tears in the knees, and a hooded gray sweater that looks as if it has dead leaves and twigs clinging to the back of its sleeves. Bits of them crumble and fall off when she moves, strapping herself in. On her feet, she wears Converse sneakers, and the sides of them look caked in dirt and more dead leaves. Driving, Tom watches her out of the corner of his eye. He sees how her teeth are still clenched, how her jaw and cheeks continue to tremble. Her hair is dark and scraped back into a loose ponytail. It looks as though it has not been washed in a few days.

As if feeling his peripheral gaze, she pulls up her hood, covers most of her pale, bruised face. Only the tip of her nose and her lips continue to show.

Tom doesn't try to talk to her. It's clear she doesn't want to speak. If she changes her mind, she'll make the first move. Tom can engage her then. Can find out her name then.

He turns his attention back fully to the road. To the mirrors. The way ahead is still clear, and behind.

"Thanks," the girl says, her voice low. She doesn't turn to look at him when she speaks, and it's hard to be sure she's spoken at all. Her demeanour remains cold, standoffish.

"For what?" Tom says.

"Back at the gas station," she says. She reaches into her hood, scratches her neck. She pushes the hood down, twists her head to the side, winces as she digs her fingernails into the itch at the back of her neck.

"You looked like you needed help," Tom says. "I'm sure anyone else would've done the same."

She grunts, drops her hands into her lap. "Nobody else did. *You* did." She falls silent again. Her eyes look straight ahead, never leaving the road. She hasn't looked at him since she got in the truck.

"So," Tom says, wondering how much he can question her now that she's talking. How far he can push it. "You got a name?"

"Do *you*?" she says, biting.

"Tom," he says. "Tom Rollins."

His name hangs in the air. The girl's hands fidget in her lap, her fingers tugging at each other. More of her earlier hesitation. "Taylor Hendricks."

"Nice to meet you, Taylor."

She grunts.

"So now I know you," Tom says. "And you know me. So who were the men back at the gas station? He said he was your father –"

"He's *not* my father," Taylor says.

"You said."

"I don't know where my father is. *That* guy was my stepdad."

"*Was?*"

"My mom's dead, so as far as I'm concerned, he's not my step-*anything* anymore."

"What about the guys with him? Friends of his?"

There's a pause before Taylor answers. "Friends," she finally says, nodding agreement.

"Looked like they were handling you pretty rough. Stepdad particularly. What's his name?"

"Ken," she says, "Ken *Arnett*." She emphasizes the name with disgust, as if to illustrate how their surnames are different. She doesn't respond to anything else. She scratches the back of her neck again. Tom wonders if she has a tick from sleeping rough. The leaves and twigs indicate she's spent a few nights outdoors.

"How old are you, Taylor?"

"How old are *you*?" she says with a sneer. She's defensive. Like a cornered animal. She's been hurt. Mentally and physically. She has trauma. Tom can see it. It's apparent in the way she holds herself, in the way she speaks.

"I'm thirty-one," Tom says.

Taylor grinds her teeth. She pulls on her fingers. Tom hears a knuckle pop. "Fourteen."

"Fourteen, huh? And your mom died? That's rough. I'm sorry to hear that. My mom died when I was young, too. I know how tough it is."

Taylor reacts to this. She turns to him a little, looks his way just briefly before turning back to the road. Her mouth works, about to ask a question. "How..." She has to clear her throat. "I was thirteen when she died," she says. "It was eight months ago. Right before my birthday. How – how old were you?"

"I was nine."

"Oh."

"My brother was five. I don't know if it was tougher for him or me. I felt like I had to be strong for him, as the older brother."

"How'd she die?"

"Cancer. She was young when it happened. I figure your mom must've been young when it happened, too."

"She was young," Taylor says. She doesn't say what happened. She changes the subject. "What was your mom called?"

"Mary. Yours?"

"Amy. Amy Arnett. She took Ken's name. I wish she hadn't..."

"What happened to your dad?"

"*Walter*." She snorts. "Who knows? My mom said he was a deadbeat husband, then he was a deadbeat dad, and then he was gone. Deadbeats, ha. I guess she had a type." She falls silent suddenly. She was grinning, just briefly, but it fades just as quick. She's said too much. She's got too comfortable, bonding over dead mothers. She grits her teeth. Gets her edge back.

"Okay," Tom says. "Let me see if I've got this worked out. Your mom died not so long ago, and you don't get along with your stepdad. So you've run away from home. He roped in his buddies to help get you back. They caught up with you, got rough, hence those bruises on your face. I mean, I get it. Your stepfather – *Ken* – he seemed like a real asshole. But what was your plan? You can't keep running indefinitely. Where was the destination? What's the endgame?"

"I'm not going back there," she says, seizing up like she's worried he might turn the truck around. "I'm not going back to him."

"I'm not saying you have to," Tom says. "We're still driving away from them, right? My question is, where do you want me to take you?"

She's silent, thinking. Hesitating again. Tom thought he'd almost got through earlier. They were conversing. She's clamped back up. The defenses have returned. "My friend lives just down the road here," she says. "About ten miles, maybe. The next town."

"That where you were trying to get in the first place? Before Ken and his buddies caught up to you."

"Yeah, that's right. She knows I'm coming."

"Uh-huh. You planned your escape in advance. That's smart. Sounds like you had a destination in mind all along. But I still feel like the endgame might need some work. At fourteen, you're gonna need a guardian. You're gonna have to go to school. Are your friend's parents aware of what's happening?"

"I'll deal with it," Taylor says. "I know what I'm doing."

Tom has his doubts about this friend's existence. Taylor has been cagey so far. She opened up, told him about her dead mother, and he could see how she regretted her momentary lapse. She wouldn't tell him the truth now, not again, not so soon. "What's your friend's name?"

"Sam," she says. She says it fast. Too fast. "Samantha."

Maybe she does have a friend called Samantha, but Tom doesn't believe that she's ten miles down the road in the next town. "All right," he says. "Let's take you to Samantha."

4

Taylor sits. She can't get comfortable. Won't let herself get comfortable. Earlier, she almost did. Started slipping up a little. Telling this stranger more than he needs to know. That was a mistake. She won't make it again.

He helped her, sure, but that's not enough. He's giving her this ride, true, but she was already on his truck when he found her, having sneaked away from Ken and the others while he was handing them their asses. This guy – Tom – he's done her a favor. He's helped her get away from Ken and from the Ogre, and maybe even for good this time now that she has a pair of wheels, but she knows better than to trust a stranger. Knows better than to trust anyone.

She'll take advantage of his help. Of course she will. It'd be stupid not to. She won't tell him where she's really going, though. Can't. He's been seen. She needs someone Ken and the rest haven't seen. An anonymous, long-range truck driver. That's who she's been hoping for. Instead, she's got the guy who beat them up. Showed them his face. Likely got caught on security footage. Plus, she told him all that stuff about her mother, and that was stupid. She didn't tell him *everything*, but it was enough. Should've kept her mouth shut, her teeth tight together like they are now. So tight they hurt a little. Her jaw cramps. She squeezes her fingers to distract from the pain. Hears how her knuckles pop until they can't anymore. Until they're all popped out.

With Tom, she'll cover ground. She'll get far – further than she might have thought possible just yesterday, when it seemed like no one wanted to stop for her. The next town – that's some good distance. She'll tell him to drop him off at the entrance to the first street she sees, and then wait until he's gone. Wait until he's out of sight. And then she'll continue on. On to Oregon, as originally intended. It'll still be a far way to go, but she doesn't want to push her luck with Tom. He might start asking too many questions. Questions she doesn't want to answer. Questions he has no business knowing the answer to. No one needs to know. Not until she reaches Oregon.

She scratches the back of her neck. A localized itch she can't seem to get rid of. A bug probably bit her while she was sleeping in the woods. It might've even burrowed in there. That's an awful thought, and she wishes she hadn't had it. She runs the tip of her finger over the skin. There's a little lump there. She tries squeezing it. Nothing comes out. Nothing changes. She scratches again. It's driving her crazy. She doesn't have much in the way of fingernails, though. That doesn't help. She's chewed them all down. Down to the quick. They used to hurt, but they don't anymore. They've gone numb over time. She never feels it anymore, even when she makes them bleed.

Her scratching hand falls back into her lap. She balls both hands into fists. Clenches her jaw, grinds her teeth. Can hear them scrape together in her ears. Can hear how her blood pumps, too.

"You hungry?" Tom says suddenly.

Her stomach gurgles at the thought of food. "No," she says. "I'm all right." He doesn't have any food in the truck with him. She's already looked around. There aren't any wrappers. She can't even see a bottle of water. Just a bag on the ground between them. There could be food in there, she supposes.

"I'm getting hungry," he says. "We could try to find somewhere, stop for a bite before you get to Samantha's –"

"No," Taylor says. No time to stop. No time to rest. She needs to keep moving.

"Your stomach says otherwise."

"I'll eat at Sam's. They know I'm coming."

"They know you're coming today?"

"Yes."

"When'd you get in touch with her?"

"Before I left."

"How long ago was that now?"

He's asking too many questions. She doesn't like it. "Why? What's it matter?"

"It doesn't matter," Tom says, raising his hands on the steering wheel. "I just can't help but notice you look like you've been sleeping rough. In woodland, judging by the leaves and the twigs. So that means you slept outside at least last night. Could've been longer. So I'm wondering if you got in touch with your friend Sam, that must've been at least yesterday, right? She's gotta wonder where you are right now. Because I know you haven't been in touch with her since you've sat up front here with me. I'm just curious is all. I just wanna make sure she's not worried about you. Why don't you call her?"

"I don't have a phone."

"You don't?"

"I lost it."

"You could use mine."

"I don't know her number. Not by heart, I mean. It was saved in my phone."

"That's a shame."

Taylor sees the holes in her own story. She hopes Tom won't pick up on them. "Look, she knows I'm coming, all right? She won't mind if I'm a little late. You don't have to worry about that." She sits, silent, grinds her teeth. There's nothing up ahead of them. Nothing on either side of the road. Just trees. "Listen, if it's too much trouble for you, just drop me off here. I can make it the rest of the way by myself."

"According to that sign back there, we've still got about ten miles left to go, and this is a quiet road. That'll be a lot of walking for you. And it'll take a lot longer than in my truck."

"Fine – but can we stop talking? I – I have a headache."

Tom glances at her, turning his head just a little. "All right," he says. "But if you change your mind about food, let me know."

"Where are *you* going?" Taylor says. She knows she should stay quiet, keep communication to a minimum – she knows she's even requested it – but she wants to turn the tables. Tom has already asked so much. Now it's her turn.

"I don't know yet," he says.

"You don't know?"

He shakes his head. "I don't set out with a destination in mind. Rarely do. I go where the road takes me. Right now, I guess I'm hoping it'll take me to somewhere I can find work."

"Find work? Where do you live?"

"Nowhere set," Tom says. "I like to keep moving. I spent some time up in Alaska, and I liked it there, but inevitably the time comes when I feel like I need to move on."

Taylor frowns. "You don't have a house? Where are you from?"

"New Mexico."

"New Mexico? You're far from home."

"It's not my home. It's just where I'm from."

"You *looking* for a home, that what it is? You drive around the country, looking for a place to settle down?"

Tom grins. "I've never thought of it like that. I just –" He stops abruptly. "*Shit.*"

Taylor doesn't understand. She follows his eyes. He's looking in the mirror. Taylor looks in her own. She sees what he sees. There's a vehicle coming up behind them. It's coming up *fast*. A state trooper. The car's lights are flashing. It gets on their tail, and it stays there. It wants them to pull over.

Taylor feels her breath catch in her throat. She can't take another. Her chest is tight.

It's *them*. They've sent this trooper. She feels like she's going to be sick.

They've caught her again.

5

Tom pulls to the side of the road. He keeps both hands on the wheel, watching in the mirror as the trooper takes his time getting out of his vehicle, then approaching them with one hand at his hip, resting upon the handle of his weapon, a 9mm M&P 2.0 Smith and Wesson. Tom looks behind him, behind his cruiser, checking to see if Ken's vehicle from the gas station has followed, prepared to take advantage of the situation. They aren't there. No one pulls up after the cruiser. They're alone on this road.

The trooper looks the truck over as he approaches. Comes around the side, toward Tom's window. He turns his head to the side, spits.

Tom winds the window down, glancing at Taylor as he does so. She's staring straight ahead, lips pursed, breathing hard through her nose. "There a problem, sir?" Tom says.

The trooper doesn't respond straight away. He does the tough-guy thing. He needs to go through his act. His hands are on his hips, his right still close to his gun. He's wearing aviator sunglasses that hide his eyes, and his face is in shadow from the brim of his hat. His closely shaven jaw works, like he's chewing either gum or tobacco. He takes his hands away from his hips momentarily, long enough to adjust his bow tie.

Tom stares straight back into his reflective aviators. He doesn't back down. He never backs down. He stays calm, confident. He has nothing to hide. Acting scared, worried, meek – that makes it look like he has something to be concerned about.

The trooper doesn't ask for license and registration, as Tom is expecting. He doesn't mention the fight back at the gas station. Instead, he leans forward, looks beyond Tom, toward Taylor in the passenger seat. Having seen her, he straightens back up. "Who is this female to you, sir?" he says.

"She's my passenger," Tom says.

The trooper arches an eyebrow high enough to be seen over the top of the aviators. "Are you trying to be smart with me, sir?"

"Just answering the question."

"Then how about you answer it the *right* way."

Tom sees how the trooper's fingers start twitching on the handle of his gun. Tom opens his mouth, about to lie, to tell the trooper that Taylor is his sister, when she speaks first.

"I was hitchhiking," she says. "He picked me up."

The trooper grunts. "Little young to be hitchhiking, aren't you?"

She doesn't answer.

The trooper looks at Tom. "She's coming with me," he says. "I'm taking her home."

Tom opens his mouth, but Taylor places a hand on his arm. He looks down at it, questioning, and Taylor snatches it back.

The trooper walks around the front of the truck, keeping his face turned to them through the windshield, watching. While he's gone from the open window, while he can't hear,

Taylor speaks in a low voice. "He'll always catch me," she says. "He has people everywhere."

Tom frowns, but before he can ask whom she means, the trooper opens the passenger door. He doesn't reach for Taylor. Doesn't put a hand on her. Just waits for her to step outside. She does so, keeping her face lowered. She pulls her hood back up.

When she's out, the trooper leans back into the truck, addresses Tom. "Maybe leave the jailbait where you see it next time, buddy, huh?" He closes the door.

Tom doesn't move. Taylor's words, as quietly as they were spoken, ring in his ears. *He?* Her stepfather? He doesn't think so. The way she said it, it didn't sound right. Like she was talking about someone else. He looks back, still frowning. Sees how the trooper leads her to the cruiser. He doesn't touch her. Doesn't put a hand upon her arm to guide her. She doesn't let him. When he does reach for her, she twists away. He gives up trying. He holds open the rear door of the cruiser and waits for her to get inside.

Tom turns back around. In the mirror, he sees how the trooper looks his way. Tom starts rolling down the road, but he takes his time. He's not planning on getting far. He's not looking straight ahead. He's watching the mirrors again. Nothing but the mirrors this time. He sees how the trooper starts his engine. How he turns the cruiser around, then starts heading back the way they came. Back in the direction of the gas station.

When it's rounded the corner, out of sight, Tom pulls the truck over. He turns it around, and he follows.

6

Ken and the others left the gas station shortly after dispatching the state trooper. His name is David Mackenzie. Ken knows him well.

What he *doesn't* know is whether Taylor and her mysterious benefactor left the gas station together. All they know for sure is Taylor got out of there fast – just as fast as the guy in his truck. Chances are – and their *hopes* are – that they went together. Ken has gone the opposite direction than the stranger did. Ken's turned off the road, travelled through the trees a way, found a picnic area to park in. They told David this is where they'd wait for him. There's barely anyone else here. Only one other car, parked all the way on the other side, a family sitting on one of the aged wooden benches. There's plenty of space. They've parked near the back, near the trees. Out of the way.

Kyle is in the backseat. He's whimpered the whole way, holding onto his knee. It's dislocated, no doubt about it. The most they've been able to do is wrap it in tape, keep it tight. It's stretched out in front of him, though he keeps squirming. "I need a hospital," he says.

Ken ignores him. Donald, however, is getting frustrated with his whines. "Shut up, will ya?" he snaps, his voice still hoarse. He rubs his throat. "We've all got problems."

"Yeah, well, none of you have got a broken fucking leg!" Kyle says.

"It's not broken," Donald says, turning back around. "Stop being such a baby." He starts coughing, gasping, his throat in protest at how much he's spoken.

If Bill were here, Kyle wouldn't be complaining so much. He wouldn't dare. Bill would have popped his knee back into place and expected that to be the last of it. Any complaints after that would have been met with a steely stare.

But Bill isn't here, and none of them know how to fix a dislocated knee.

"Nobody said this would happen," Kyle says, rubbing his thigh like this might help. "She's just a kid. Grab her and get back. No one said there was even a chance of us getting beat up."

"Yeah, well, shit happens," Ken says. "We're just lucky one of our troopers came along, or else I'd be on the phone to Bill right now, telling him how we screwed up."

Kyle falls silent at the thought of this. At the mention of Bill. He's finally understanding how much worse things could actually be. He can't resist a final whine, though: "I wish we had some painkillers with us, that's all I'll say."

Gil, next to him in the back, grunts his agreement. He's nursing his head. He, at least, has been silent.

Ken has been watching the road, waiting for the trooper's return. He watches the clock, nervous. He doesn't like how long it's been. In his head, he's working out the route. How long it should take. How long getting Taylor back should take. Is she with the guy, as they hoped? Is he protesting, putting up a fight, refusing to let her go?

"Why'd he get involved at all?" Ken says, not realizing he's speaking out loud.

"Some people just gotta stick their noses in," Donald says, then swallows.

Ken nods. "Nosey assholes."

"Exactly."

Whatever way Ken tries to calculate it, he thinks they should be back by now. Unless the guy *has* put up a fight, and David has had to call backup to the scene. The guy was like a force of nature, after all. He tore through the four of them – tore through *Donald* – like it was nothing. Maybe Taylor has slipped away again. He supposes that isn't the worst thing if she has. They can always find her again. It's just frustrating, is all. Time consuming. Time he'd rather not waste.

"Here he is," Donald says, nodding ahead. "Spotted his colors through the trees."

Ken looks, eager, sees the trooper round the corner, come fully into view. He squints, trying to see if Taylor is in the vehicle with him. Light reflects off the glass. He stays tense. "You see her?" he says.

Donald grunts, and it's hard to tell what this means.

The cruiser pulls up in front of them, and Ken spots her. In the backseat, head lowered, hood pulled up, covering her face. He breathes a sigh of relief.

"Well, look at that," Donald says, turning to Kyle. "Here she is, practically gift-wrapped. Nearly time to go home."

"I don't wanna go *home*," Kyle says, belligerent, "I wanna go to the *hospital*."

Donald chuckles, turning back around.

"Yeah, laugh it up, big man," Kyle says. "I'll keep all your sympathies in mind if ever you break something."

Ken gets out of the vehicle as the trooper does the same. Ken can't help his face splitting into a grin. The relief is still pulsing through him. David nods, steps to the back door where Taylor is, but he doesn't open it yet. Ken steps up to him, reaches out, shakes his hand. "Mr. Morgan will be *very* pleased to hear how you've helped us out today," he says.

David smiles. His whole face softens. He's pleased. "Thank you very much, sir," he says, almost gushing. "It's a pleasure to help out in any way I can."

Donald steps up next to Ken. "Was she with the guy?"

"She was, yeah."

"He give you any trouble?"

The trooper shakes his head. "Just some lip, but nothing major."

"What did he try telling you?"

"Girl did the talking. Said she was hitchhiking, he picked her up."

"He didn't try following you back here, did he?" Ken says.

"No. Made sure of it. He was already heading off when I started on my way back."

Ken could have told David to arrest him. It would be easy enough – they already have reason. But Ken is trying to keep things quiet. Leave the stranger free. Leave him to move on. Out of their hair, and out of their lives. They have Taylor back. That's all that matters. She's nothing to the stranger. There's no reason for him to come after her.

The trooper opens Taylor's door. Donald stands close. He reaches in, takes her by the arm. She tries to twist away, but he's holding tight. He drags her roughly from the cruiser, pulls her off to the side. The trooper closes the door. He shakes Ken's hand.

"I'll see you Sunday," David says.

"I'll see you there," Ken says, smiling, still feeling the relief.

David gets back into his cruiser, pulls out of the picnic area with a wave. Ken waves back, watches him go. He turns to Taylor, still held by Donald. Kyle remains inside the minivan, but Gil has gotten out. The three men surround Taylor. Ken takes a deep breath, blows it out. "There she is," he says. "Daughter dearest. You've had Daddy worried."

She sneers, and Ken grins. He steps closer.

"You could have got me in a lot of trouble, Taylor," he says. "You could have got *all* of us in a lot of trouble. All because you don't know how to behave yourself. You should know by now, you can't escape us."

"Fuck you," Taylor says. She struggles against Donald. "Fuck all of you."

Ken raises a finger, wags it side to side. "Such a potty mouth. What would your mother think, Taylor?"

"Don't talk about her," she says, eyes blazing.

"Why shouldn't I talk about my own wife? My own dearly departed Amy –"

Taylor spits at him. Most of it lands on his chest, but he feels some of it spray on his face. He winces, then reaches out for her, for her face. He's about to grab her, tired of her disrespect, ready to teach her a lesson before he takes her back home to Belleville.

A voice comes from the side.

"Don't touch her."

Ken looks at Donald. Donald is looking beyond him.

Ken turns toward the nearby trees. The man from earlier, at the gas station, emerges from them. His face is dark. He doesn't look happy.

7

Tom followed the trooper, expecting him to return to the gas station. He didn't. He went further. Down the road, then took an obscure turnoff. Tom stayed back, kept a safe distance out of view. He crawled along by the roadside, just barely keeping the cruiser in sight up ahead. He saw it turn off. Disappeared into a clearing in the trees. A picnic area.

Tom stopped the truck. He pulled it into the trees, concealed it, and continued on foot through the woodland. He got near to them, behind them. Through the branches, he saw the cruiser. Saw the minivan from earlier. He arrived late, but he's seen the reunion between Ken and Taylor. Has seen the trooper leave. From where he is, he can't hear them, though. Picks out snippets of words that don't make sense, carried on the breeze. He notices there are only three men out of the minivan. The fourth is likely still inside, unable to stand. Tom remembers the sound his knee made when he kicked it out from under him. He shouldn't be too much of a concern unless he's armed. They weren't armed at the gas station, though, not so far as Tom could see. If they have any weapons with them, they're inside the vehicle. He keeps this in mind.

He watches Ken and Taylor. She's held by the bigger man. Tom can see the redness at his throat where he was struck. He keeps swallowing, too, and wincing every time he does. Ken says something to Taylor. She spits at him. Ken isn't pleased with this. Tom can see how this is going to go. He steps out of the trees, tells him to back off.

All eyes turn to him. Tom stands his ground. Out of the corner of his eye, he looks to the minivan. He sees the fourth man inside. The fourth man sees him, too. He scrambles to the open door near him, slams it shut. He looks terrified. Tom doesn't think he has a weapon. That was not the reaction of an armed man.

"Let her go," Tom says again.

"You just don't know when to quit, do you?" Ken says.

"I could say the same to you." Tom looks at the big man holding both of Taylor's arms. "Let her go. I have to ask again, I'm going to hurt you worse than before."

There's the sound of an engine starting up. At the other end of the picnic area, the family who were sitting at the table there are done. They haven't noticed the altercation taking place not far from them. They're back in their vehicle. They're pulling out of the trees, getting back on the road. Everything pauses until they're gone.

The big man snarls. Ken grabs Taylor, tears her from his grip. Taylor cries out, her arm almost wrenched from its socket. Ken tilts his head at the big man and the other. "Deal with him," he says. "And don't fuck it up this time."

The big man looks eager for another round, but the other is more hesitant. Tom ignores them as they approach, speaks to Ken. "Let her go, or I'll break your arm."

"Fuck you," Ken says, spit flying from his lips. "She's my daughter – she's nothing to you. I'm taking her home. So get the fuck out of here before you get yourself in some serious trouble."

"She doesn't want to go home."

"What do you know about it?"

"Why don't we ask her? I figure Taylor gets a choice in what happens next. She wants to stay with you, go back home, then fine. I'll walk away. But if she *doesn't*, if she wants to come with me – well. Then things will get bad for the three of you real fast." He looks Ken in the eye. "And I notice you haven't let go of her arm, like I asked you to. You're holding her real tight there, Ken. You've already left a mark, I'm sure. Taylor says she wants to come with me, then I *am* going to break your arm."

"You talk too fuckin much," the big guy says, but he and the other have paused in their approach, waiting for what happens next.

Tom grins. "I don't think anyone's ever accused me of that before." He looks at Taylor. "Who do you want to leave here with, Taylor?"

Ken squeezes her arm harder. She grits her teeth against the pain, but refuses to cry out again, defiant. She looks back at Tom. "You," she says.

Ken rolls his eyes. "Big surprise, right? Donald, deal with this guy."

Donald, the big guy, comes on strong. He takes a swing that Tom easily ducks. As he maneuvers, he sees how Ken drags Taylor away, back toward the minivan. Tom understands. Ken doesn't expect Donald and the other man to beat him – he just needs them to slow him down. Slow him long enough so he can escape with Taylor.

Distracted, the other guy is able to dive in and wrap his arms around Tom from behind. "I've got him!" he cries excitedly, prematurely. "Donald, I've fucking got him!"

Donald grins, straightening back up after his missed shot. "You sure do," he says, dark intentions on his mind.

Tom pretends to struggle, like he can't break free. Lures Donald in. Donald rears up a big right. He swings it, and Tom ducks. Donald's meaty fist smashes into the face of the man behind Tom. His grip loosens, but Tom keeps hold of his arms as he straightens up fast, the back of his head catching Donald hard under the jaw. Donald stumbles back with the force of the blow. Holding onto the man behind him by the arms, Tom judo-throws him, slams him down hard on the asphalt. He steps over the fallen man as he curls into a ball, coughing and holding his ribs, and goes straight for Donald. He laces his fingers together on the back of Donald's head and drags his face down into his knee. He holds him there after the first impact, then brings his knee up again and again until Donald has gone limp. He lets him fall.

Tom turns as the door to the minivan slams shut. He runs toward the driver's side, managing to tear the door open before Ken can push the lock down. In the back, he sees Taylor struggling in the arms of the guy with the dislocated knee. When he sees Tom standing at the open door, he lets go of her, raises his arms in surrender, his eyes wide. Taylor drills her elbow down into his sternum, and he crumples in on himself, blowing air. She pushes the door open and falls out of the minivan.

Ken is frozen in the driver's seat, both hands on the steering wheel. His lip trembles as he looks back at Tom with fear etched across his features. He remembers what Tom said he would do to him. He knows what's about to happen.

Tom grabs him by the front of his shirt, hauls him out of the minivan and dumps him down onto the ground, onto his front. Out of the side of his face, Ken begs as Tom wrenches back on his right arm. "No – don't, don't do this!"

His pleas fall on deaf ears. Tom looks back at Taylor over

his shoulder. She's looking down on her stepfather, sneering. "You might want to turn away," he says.

Taylor looks back into his eyes. She shakes her head.

Tom doesn't try to force her. He turns back to Ken, places his knee into his elbow, his right hand wrapped around his wrist and his left pressed down flat into the back of his shoulder, pinning him to the ground. Ken is already screaming in anticipation. Tom breaks his arm.

8

Bill Lindsay is aware that Taylor has run away. It's not the first time she's done it. At this point, it doesn't come as a surprise anymore. Ken or Laurence – depending on whose fault it was this time – should watch her closer. Double-check the locks on the window before they go to sleep. Make sure the keys for the doors are hidden. Tie her to the fucking bed if that's what it takes.

He's entrusted recapturing her to her stepfather. Bill is tired of hunting her down. She never gets far. It's impossible for her to do so. Recapturing her isn't a big job. It shouldn't take long. Yet, as expected, it has taken Ken and the others far longer than it would have himself. Bill is used to disappointment by now. They always let him down, even with the easiest of tasks. He'll talk to them, soon, after they've gotten back to Belleville.

Right now, he has other things on his mind. Foremost, the new girl. She was hired as an administrative assistant, but she's basically been relegated to the role of Laurence's secretary. Right now, she's in the diner Bill frequents almost daily.

Her name is Danny, though Laurence insists on calling her Danielle. Bill knew, from the first time he laid eyes on her, he'd like to get to know her better. To know more than just her name and her job description.

She's young, early-thirties. Worked as a waitress out of high school before she got the administrative job. Bill saw her picture, and he took a hand in getting her hired. She has blonde hair tied back, and a tiredness in her eyes that he assumes comes from back when she was waitressing. All those double shifts.

"Well," he says, sliding into the booth opposite her, his coffee in hand. "Imagine running into you here."

Danny gives a start as he sits. She hadn't noticed him. "Oh," she says. "Hello." She smiles, but it's not genuine. It's as forced as the one the waitresses here in the diner give, thinking of their tips. She probably picked it up the same way. This particular diner, however, wasn't on her resumé.

In front of her, for her lunch, she has a green smoothie that looks like someone threw it up, and a salad. She's scribbling in a small notepad, like something a journalist would carry, but she closes it when she sees him and slips it into her handbag. "What's that you're writing?" he says. "Poetry?" He grins.

"Shopping list," she says. "Nothing quite so flowery."

Bill knows what she thinks when she looks at him. She doesn't look and see Prince Charming. No one's ever looked at him and seen that. Bill has no illusions about his appearance. He owns a mirror. He knows he has a major underbite. Always has. His chin juts out, his lower teeth sit over his top. His head looks too big for his body, and is misshapen from the various lumps and bumps he's taken over the years. He looks like a gargoyle, he knows. It's his underbite people notice most, though. When he was young, it was worse.

Before he filled out, before the rest of his face grew into his chin. Kids were cruel. He was bullied relentlessly. They called him the troll. *Troll boy*. Bigger kids would force him under a tunnel they made of desks, call it his bridge. Tell him it was where he belonged.

When he thinks back, he has to admit they were at least creative.

But then Bill *did* get bigger, and he *did* fill out. Bill learned how to use his 'deformity' to his advantage. Realized that the reason all those people taunted him was because they feared him. They feared what he could become, so he'd allowed himself to become it. They were scared of him, and he made sure to keep them scared. All those bullies who pushed him around, they didn't grow up like he did. He got stronger – they stayed the same. Bill got the revenge he'd always wanted against them when he was smaller and weaker. He didn't just put them under desks or bundle them into lockers – he almost put them in the ground.

No one fucked with him. He's made sure to keep it that way.

Bill embraced his face. So he knows that when Danny looks at him, she sees a troll. Or perhaps an ogre. But it doesn't worry him. Because once he accepted it, accepted who he was, nothing has held him back. Nothing has stopped him from getting what he wanted.

And now, he wants Danny.

"You been here long already?" he says. He looks her over. He's subtle about it. She's wearing a white blouse beneath her blazer. He imagines her clothes on the floor of his bedroom.

She picks up her fork, starts poking at her salad. "About twenty minutes. You?"

"I just got here. You come here often?" He wonders what she looks like naked.

"Not really," she says, putting a cucumber in her mouth. She swallows it before she speaks again. "Thought I'd give it a try."

"It's far from work." He imagines fucking her.

"I guess it is."

He nods at her food. "You'd best be quick. You don't have long left for your lunch break. If you've been here twenty minutes already, and factoring in the fifteen-minute drive here and back, that leaves you ten minutes to finish up. How long'd it take them to bring you your salad?"

"It's not them," Danny says. "I've just been distracted."

"With your grocery list," Bill says. He imagines finishing on her chest. Or her face.

"It's a pretty long list."

"Uh-huh. Well, if you end up running late, I'll vouch for you. Tell the other girls traffic was a bitch, and the service was terrible." He winks. Imagines pulling on her hair.

She doesn't react to him. It's hard for Bill to get a gauge on her.

"So how do you like the work?" he says, changing the subject.

"I like it," she says. "It's a good job."

"How do you like Laurence?"

"Mr. Morgan? He's a nice man. I haven't spoken to him much, but he's always very...pleasant."

"You haven't spoken to him much? Don't you sit right outside his door?" He pictures himself taking her into Laurence's office after hours, when everyone else has gone home, lifting up her skirt and fucking her from behind over the top of Laurence's desk. She's not wearing a skirt, though. He's never seen her wearing a skirt. She always wears trousers. In his fantasy, she's wearing a skirt. He's sure she has good legs. He imagines them thrown over his shoulders.

"We haven't *conversed*, I mean," she says. "We exchange pleasantries, and Mr. Morgan always asks about my weekends and my evenings, but mostly we talk about work."

Bill takes a sip of coffee, then smiles. Smiling twists his jaw to the side, he knows. Makes his underbite look bigger. She doesn't react to this in any way. Her face is impassive. It never changes.

He imagines her lying beneath him. Imagines the ways her face would change then. Can almost hear the way she'd gasp in his ear.

"Is that all you're having for lunch?" Danny says, indicating his cup.

"I had a big breakfast," Bill says. He grins and goes to take another sip. Before he can, he feels his phone begin to vibrate in his pocket. The only call he's expecting is from Ken, to tell him it's done. To tell him that they have Taylor back.

This *should* be what he's calling about.

Bill pulls his phone out, sees that it *is* Ken. "I just need to take this," he says to Danny.

"Sure," Danny says. She eats, barely looks at him. Takes a drink from her disgusting-looking smoothie.

Bill presses the phone to his ear. "Speak to me."

Ken is breathing hard, his breath hitching, and already Bill knows something has gone wrong. "She – I mean, Taylor – she's, she's –" He stops talking, sounds like he's wincing. He's in pain. Something has happened. Bill's mind is already racing. There were four of them – Taylor is just a girl. A teenage fucking girl. Fourteen years old. How could she hurt them? And it sounds like they don't have her. How could she get away?

Bill glances at Danny. She's too close. He doesn't want her hearing any of this. He stands, steps away from the booth, toward the entrance. Goes where there's no one else sitting in the diner. "Take a deep breath, Ken, and tell me what went wrong."

Ken does as he says. Bill hears how it shudders.

"Taylor got away," Ken says, his voice shaking. "This guy, he – he came out of nowhere, helping her out –"

Bill decides to step outside, for fear he may start raising his voice. "A guy?" he says. "What guy?"

"I – I don't know – we don't know him, none of us do. He came out of nowhere. Kicked our asses. He's – he broke my arm –" Ken sniffs hard, right in Bill's ear. "And he's dislocated Kyle's knee. And he went through Donald like he wasn't even there – we couldn't even land a shot on this guy, none of us."

Bill frowns, scrapes his bottom row of teeth against his top. "And he's got the girl?"

There's a pause before Ken responds. "Yeah..."

"And you don't know where they are?"

"No..."

"And you're not in pursuit?"

He hears Ken gulp. "We're not...we're not in any condition to go after them..."

Bill lets this hang in the air. "I'm disappointed, Ken." He knew he would be. Deep down, he always knew it would end like this. "I should have handled this myself."

"I'm – I'm sorry, Bill. We're all – we're all sorry..."

"Uh-huh. How long ago did this happen, Ken?"

"It was about, about – uh, about a half hour ago they left, I think."

"And you're just calling me now?"

"We, uh, we had to get up..."

"They could've gone to the cops, Ken." Bill is speaking through his teeth, struggling not to raise his voice despite now being outside. "They could have reached a cop we're not friendly with, you understand? You should've called me immediately so I could deal with this. You can still use your phone on the fucking ground."

Bill's mind races. He needs to reach out to his friends in local law, give them a heads-up. David Mackenzie, for a start. Pass what they know on to the state troopers they have onside. And John Davison, the detective – he'll be able to get the word around, too.

And, most importantly, Bill needs to get on the road.

"I'm taking over," Bill says. "I should never have left this in your hands. You're a failure, Ken. I was an idiot to trust you with something so important. I expected you to keep her fucking indoors, and you failed at *that*, for Christ's sake."

"Bill, I'm –"

"Save it. I don't wanna hear it. I'm getting on the move right now."

"You're gonna need a lot of guys," Ken says. "Shit, take everyone."

"I don't need your advice, Ken." He hangs up, bristling. He looks back through the windows of the diner. Can see Danny eating. She's not looking back at him. He goes inside to retrieve his coffee. Danny glances up as he reappears.

"Everything all right?" she says.

"Just a work thing," he says. As far as Danny is concerned, he's Laurence's chauffeur. "I need to pick up some friends of Mr. Morgan's. They've arrived...unexpectedly."

Danny nods. She checks the time. "I guess I'd better be quick, then," she says. "Seeing as how you won't be around to vouch for me if I turn up late."

A joke. She's joking with him. Almost makes him want to blow the whole disaster with Taylor off and see how far he can take this joke.

"Maybe next time," he says, then takes his coffee and leaves.

Outside, he's not thinking of Danny's joke. Outside, he's in business mode. Professional, unlike Ken and the others. In the parking lot, on the way to his car, he's already back on his phone, making calls. As he pulls open his door, he realizes he forgot to say goodbye. That doesn't matter. Right now, Danny is no longer at the fore of his mind.

Taylor Hendricks is.

9

Tom trades his truck. It gets him a beat-up old Ford. The Ford isn't worth the truck, and the guy trading knows it. He's eager to get Tom off the lot before he can realize what a bad deal he's making. "Tell you what, man," the guy says, handing Tom the keys. "There's a Springsteen CD in the glove box – I'll leave it in, just for you."

"Uh-huh," Tom says. He knows the trade-off is a bad one, but he doesn't care. So long as the Ford runs, that's all that counts. "What album?"

"Uh..." The guy frowns.

"Doesn't matter," Tom says, taking the keys. "I've heard them all anyway."

He gets in the Ford, taking nothing from his truck but his backpack. The album turns out to be *Darkness on the Edge of Town*. One of Tom's favorites.

Taylor is waiting around the corner from the lot, out of view. She looks the Ford over with a raised eyebrow as Tom pulls up beside her. "This is a piece of shit," she says, getting in.

Tom starts driving. "We need a different ride," he says.

"The state trooper looked to be friendly with your stepfather and his buddies. Chances are they're gonna reach back out to him to help them find us, and he knows the truck. *They* know the truck. So we drive around in something they *don't* know. Something they won't suspect."

"You sound like you've done this before," Taylor says.

Tom grins. "I've been round the block a few times already." Down the road from the lot, he starts to slow the car, pulls to the side.

"What are you doing?" Taylor says, looking around.

Tom stops, pulls on the handbrake. He turns to Taylor. "I'm ready for the truth now," he says.

Taylor looks away from him. Straight ahead, then down into her lap. She scratches the back of her neck, then clasps her hands.

"I've traded my truck for this car so we can, hopefully, go the rest of the way uninhibited," Tom says. "So why don't you tell me where we're *really* going?"

Taylor pulls on her fingers. She scratches at a piece of loose skin on the side of her thumb with a fingernail until it bleeds.

"Does Sam exist?" Tom says. His voice is soft.

"She exists," Taylor says. "But she lives back in Belleville, and we haven't been friends since grade school. She was my last friend. She stuck around the longest. She tried to hold on. She was the first person I could think of..."

"I'm not dropping you in the next town we come to if that's not where you're really going, Taylor," Tom says. "I'm not going to abandon you in the middle of nowhere and leave you to go the rest of the way yourself. So why don't you tell me where you're trying to get to, and we'll go there together."

Tom waits. He knows she needs to think about this. Knows she will not answer immediately. Hesitation is part of who she is. She needs to consider everything. Needs to search for the lies, for the double cross.

She closes her eyes, and she takes a deep breath. One hand is wrapped around the bloodied thumb, squeezing it. "I was...I *am*, going to Oregon."

"What's in Oregon?"

"Portland."

"I'm aware of that. What's in Portland?"

"My brother and his wife. They're the only...the only family I have left."

"They know you're coming?"

She shakes her head. "No, but they won't turn me away. I know they won't."

"I assume he's an older brother?"

She nods. "Eleven years."

"That's quite a difference. What's his name?"

"Josh. His wife's called Tilly. I remember, when I was younger, the first time I met her, I liked her so much because her name was so similar to mine." She falls silent suddenly, the way she did earlier when she realized she was sharing too much.

"So. Oregon, huh?" Tom says.

Taylor nods.

"And once we get to Oregon, to Portland, you know the way to their house?"

"Yeah."

Tom nods. "What's the relationship between your brother and your stepfather like?"

"Josh hates him."

"Then it sounds like you're going to the right place." Tom still hasn't started driving yet. "You've told me where we're really going. Now I'd like for you to tell me why Ken and his buddies are after you. Why you've run away in the first place."

"It's not just going to be Ken," she says. "There's a lot more of them. The Ogre –" She stops herself.

"Ogre?"

Taylor shakes her head. "There's more of them, all right? Like you were saying, it was probably smart to switch vehicles."

"Why are you running away, Taylor?"

She takes a deep breath. She resumes scratching the side of her thumb. The cut there gets bigger. The blood smears. Tom doesn't try to stop her.

He can see the signs. He's seen them all along. She's a victim of abuse. He isn't sure he wants to know what kind.

But he grits his teeth, because he *needs* to know that what he's thinking is true. He *needs* to know that after he drops her in Oregon, with her brother and her sister-in-law, that when he comes back to Washington, to Belleville, when he tracks Ken down, that what he does next is justified. That he's not going off a false assumption.

"Does he hurt you, Taylor?"

"I don't want to talk about it."

"Taylor –"

"I said I don't want to talk about it!"

"I understand. But if you can let me know – you don't have to say it, but if you let me know – then I can make it so he won't ever hurt you again."

She wheels on him. For the first time, he sees tears in her eyes. "*Yes*," she says, baring her teeth. "He *hurts* me. He lets his friends *fuck* me – is that what you want to hear? Why – *why* did you *need* to fucking know that? Why did you make me say it? What can you possibly do about it?"

Tom was right.

A broken arm is not enough.

Something more severe needs to be done.

"I'm going to take you to Oregon," Tom says, getting ready

to start the car moving again. From where they are to where they're going, Tom estimates that it's about eight hours. They'll get there late. "And then I'm going to come back, and I'm going to find Ken and all his friends, and I'm going to kill them."

10

It's been silent in the car since Tom told her what he's going to do to Ken. It's not a stunned silence. Taylor isn't horrified by what he said. In fact, she liked it. It's something she's dreamed of herself, on more than one occasion. Something she's tried to work out the logistics of. She's thought about poisoning his food, but she doesn't prepare it for him. He makes his own meals, as if he anticipates what she might try. Every time she tried to escape, and every time she was brought back to him, she told herself, *Don't overthink it.* Just cut his throat in his sleep.

Except she was locked in her room each night. Ken clearly worried about what she might be thinking. What she might have been planning to do to him. Of course, locking her in her room all day, every day, apart from when she was...*elsewhere*...and forgetting to check the locks on her windows every night meant he was missing the work she was putting in on escaping. It was easy to think up ways to get out. She had nothing else to do. Since her mother had died and Ken had taken her out of school, claiming she wasn't handling the death well (which was true), and that he was going to homeschool her (which was a lie), she'd spent all the time she should have been studying with thinking up ways to get out. She had to mix it up, though. Escape by the window one time, it'll have to be the door the next. Because use the window once, that's when he *does* check it. Use the door the next time, that's when he puts an extra lock on, like a dead-bolt on the outside.

So then, the thoughts of murder turned not so much to *You should've cut his throat in his sleep*, to *Just cut his fucking throat already*.

Except she couldn't.

Despite everything, despite all she's been through and all they've put her through, everything Ken has done, she can't bring herself to do *that*. The times she got close, the times she picked up a knife, her hands began to shake. Sweat ran down her face and her spine. She choked – literally, as well as figuratively.

She looks down at her hands. There is dried blood smeared on her right thumb. She wipes spit on the tip of her finger, uses it to rub it away. She turns to Tom. Watches him drive. He looks straight ahead. He's thinking. Probably thinking about what she's told him.

"Why are you helping me?"

Tom doesn't turn away from the road. "Why shouldn't I?"

"You're putting your life at risk, and you don't know me."

He grunts, grinning. "Isn't the first time. Seems to be becoming a habit for me."

"What, you just drive around looking for people to help out?"

"I don't set out *looking* for these people," Tom says. "Just works out that way."

"Uh-huh," Taylor says. "Maybe damsel types like us are just drawn to you."

Tom looks at her. Perhaps he picks up on the sarcasm in her tone. "You think you're a damsel in distress?"

"Do *you*?"

"No. I just think you're a person in a jam, and you need help. There's nothing wrong with needing help. We all do sometimes."

"When was the last time *you* needed help?"

Tom thinks. "I needed help when I was in Alaska. And I needed a *lot* of help when I was down in Mexico. No, wait – we'd come from Mexico. It was Arizona when I needed the help. Almost died." He chuckles like there's something funny about this.

"You almost died?"

He grunts. "Got stabbed. I got lucky. It didn't hit anything important."

"Who did that?"

"Some asshole. I'd known him a long time. Never liked him. Guess I always knew one day it would come down to either me or him."

Taylor blinks, taking this all in. "Jesus," she says. "How'd you know him?"

"He was my commander back when I..." He hesitates, then glances at her briefly and smiles. "Back when I used to do some government work."

Taylor frowns. *Government work?* "What kind of government work?"

"The kind I can't talk about," Tom says. "Sorry."

"Wow, that...that sounds intense. What kind of...what kind of stuff was it? I mean, without giving details..."

He takes a deep breath through his nose. He's not as quick to answer this as he has been her other questions. "The kind of stuff that makes me feel like I have a lot to make up for in my life," he finally says. "The kind of stuff that, when I come across a person who needs help, I'll give it to them. I feel like there's some stuff in my past that I need to set right. Maybe it's nothing, but it's on my conscience."

This all sounds heavy to Taylor. Tom has been open with her. He's answered everything she's asked, and she wonders if she should change the subject. "Did you do anything *before* you did government work?"

He grins again. "See, that's another facet of my life that weighs on my conscience a little."

"Oh?"

"I was in the Army."

Taylor swallows. "Y-yeah?"

"Yup."

She doesn't want to hear anything more about the Army. She doesn't want to ask anything about it. She's met someone who was in the Army – well, more than the Army, she thinks. She's not sure. Military, at least. She doesn't like that person. She doesn't like them at all.

"So, uh, Alaska, Mexico, Arizona, and now Washington, huh?" Taylor says. "You sure get around."

"I like to travel. I don't tend to stay in any one place for too long."

"Like how you said New Mexico's where you're from, but it's not your home."

Tom smiles. "That's right."

"So you just travel around?"

"And sometimes look for work," Tom says.

"That's your life?"

"Pretty much. In a nutshell, I guess."

"Kerouac with fistfights."

Tom looks at her. "Jack Kerouac?" He laughs. "I've never thought of myself that way. I certainly don't drink as much as the Beats did."

"You read him?"

"Sure I have. You?"

"Only *On the Road*. That's what it made me think of when you said you travelled a lot, and you listed all the places you've been."

"You like to read?"

"I don't get to do much else when I'm locked in my room."

"You have a favorite?"

"Favorite what?"

"Writer, book?"

Taylor thinks about this. "Not really. Nothing or no one I'd point at and call my absolute all-time favorite. You?"

It's Tom's turn to think. "I always enjoyed the classics. I like Russian classics. You read Dostoevsky?"

"No," Taylor says.

"*Crime and Punishment* – you should check it out. We come across a bookshop, I'll get you a copy."

"It change your life? That's what they say about a great book, isn't it – that it'll change your life?"

Tom raises his eyebrows. "Maybe," he says. "Never thought about it. Great book, though."

Taylor looks around. There are other cars, but they're on a minor road, surrounded by trees on either side.

Tom seems to read her mind. "There's probably a faster route to get us to Oregon," he says. "But I feel better sticking to the back roads. Out of the way. Where it's quiet."

Taylor nods. "Sure," she says.

They drive on. "There's a CD inside the glove compartment," Tom says. "Put it in the player, will you?"

Taylor does as he asks. She takes the CD case from the compartment and looks it over. "*Darkness on the Edge of Town*," she says, reading the title. "Sounds ominous."

Tom smiles. "Stick it in."

Taylor does so. The music starts. Tom turns it up.

"I've never heard Bruce Springsteen," Taylor says.

"Oh, yeah? Then you're in for a treat. This is one of his best."

"I'll decide that for myself," Taylor says. She settles back, notices how, as the opening song kicks in, Tom starts tapping his fingers on the steering wheel, keeping the beat. He nods his head a little.

She watches him out of the corner of her eye. Again, she talked to him more than she meant to. She wonders if he's tricking her into it somehow, getting her to converse, to open up – CIA mind games, something like that.

She's staying careful, though. She hasn't told him everything. She can't. He's come through for her so far. He even came *back* for her, rescued her from the clutches of Ken and his buddies. It's in her nature now to hold back, though. To keep things to herself. Self-preservation. She has to stay guarded. She has to keep her distance. Sure, she can talk about books. She can talk about *his* past, *his* history. They can even talk about music. But she can't tell him *everything*. Trusting too much is one way to failure. It's yet another route to disappointment. To recapture. If Tom wants to take her to Oregon and then go back and kill Ken, then so be it. She won't lose any sleep over it.

But for everything else – for every*one* else involved with this – Tom can't help her with them. No one can. It's too much. They're too powerful.

The fact is the only person she can trust is Josh. He's family. Only family she has left. He'll understand. He'll know what to do, even if all they can do is hunker down and hide out. He's the only one who can help her.

11

Danielle Temple has gone by Danny since she was born. It's the name everyone knows her by, including her parents. The only time she uses 'Danielle' is on official documents. Her *name* is Danny. Laurence Morgan, however, has always called her Danielle. From his first meeting with her after she'd been hired as an administrative assistant for the Temple of St. Philomena, his church, he has called her Danielle.

She remembers that meeting, now, sitting at her desk near the entrance to his office, as she signs her name to the most recent round of financial documents she's had to go over before they're sent to the accountant. *Danny Temple.*

He'd called her into his office on her first day, shortly after she'd just arrived and been shown around, while she was desperately trying to memorize where she'd been told everything was, and what her responsibilities were to be.

"Danielle," he'd said, looking up as she entered, holding out a hand for her to take a seat opposite where he sat at his desk. Bill was there with him, standing by his chair, leaning against the wall with his arms folded. Bill was smiling at her. "It's a pleasure to finally meet you."

Danny took the proffered seat, feeling both of their eyes upon her all the while. She'd already been aware of what Laurence looked like, of course. Mid-fifties, but looking so much younger – mid- to late-thirties, in fact. A man who clearly maintained a thorough skincare regime. A mouth filled with perfect, white, capped teeth. A tailored designer suit. The complete opposite in appearance of Bill. "It's Danny, sir," she said as respectfully as she could.

Laurence raised an eyebrow. "Excuse me?"

"My name," she said. She smiled, behaved herself, bit her tongue and resisted the urge to snap her response. It was the first day at her new job, after all, and the pastor was her new boss. "It's Danny."

"I see," he said, tenting his fingers. "And what does it read on your birth certificate?"

"It says Danielle," Danny says. "My parents thought it would look more professional, but they've always called me Danny. It's what everyone knows me by."

Laurence Morgan looked at her, his fingers still tented. He was smiling, but it was a while before he said anything else. She could feel the way his eyes ran over her, looking her over, studying her. His expression was impossible to read. "Do you remember your baptism, Ms. Temple?"

She blinked. "No – no, I don't remember it. I was a baby."

Bill caught her attention. He rolled his eyes. Danny wasn't sure why he was actually in the room.

"I've done quite a few baptisms here in the Temple of St. Philomena," he said. His smile never faded, never faltered. "So many, you'd think I'd have lost count – but I haven't. Do you want to know how many?"

"Certainly."

"One hundred and sixty-four. I remember all of them."

He tapped the side of his head. "How could I forget such a special day? It's just as special for me to have been picked to welcome these newborn babes into God's chosen family. Of course, I don't expect the babies themselves to remember – how could they? Most of the time they scream their way through. They don't like getting wet, and they don't like being handled by someone who isn't one of their parents." His smile turned into a grin, into something playful. "But the point I'm trying to make is the name I read out to the Lord is the name presented to me, and usually that name is the one that's on their birth certificate. And I can say with a great deal of certainty that the name that was read out at your baptism would have been the name on your birth certificate. *Danielle*. So if you are known to the Lord as Danielle, then that is how you shall be known to me."

After that, their conversation turned to more casual things – the names of her parents, where they lived and what they did for a living; how long she has lived in town; how she was enjoying her job so far – but Danny made sure to smile and nod throughout his whole patronizing opening. She couldn't help but shake the thought at the back of her mind, and it stuck with her ever since, all three months she's worked here, that no matter how affable and polite the pastor is, no matter how many doors he holds open and the way he's always sure to say *good morning* and to ask about her evening, she can't help but look upon his smiling face, its megawatt teeth, and think, *What a prick*.

Everyone else who works at the church calls her Danny, including Bill.

She looks the financial documents over once more. A part of her is quite sure they're faked. The numbers are high, certainly, but not as high as she'd expect for a megachurch that regularly fills its two thousand, five hundred seats every

Sunday – not to mention the youth meetings it holds through the week and on Saturdays.

She seals the documents, addresses and stamps them, places them in the outbox. She'll be the one to take them to the post office later, but that's not until later. The last drop-off of the day.

She looks toward Laurence's office. The door is closed, but it's empty inside. He isn't here. It's late in the day, and she hasn't seen him arrive. This is strange for Laurence. He's here every day, though Danny is never sure what he does behind his closed door. Answers emails and phone calls, or makes calls. These are all guesses. Today, she has a list of messages for him. She was hired to be an administrative assistant, though her role seems to mostly consist of being Mr. Morgan's secretary. She doesn't mind, not really.

None of the messages she's taken seem particularly important. If he doesn't turn up by the end of the day, she'll have to keep them in a clear place on her desk so she'll remember to hand them to him tomorrow. Providing he *does* come in tomorrow. He's not ill, though. She's sure of that. He would call in, let them know. She can't leave the notes on his desk. He keeps his door locked. The only times she's ever seen the inside of his office, he's been there, sitting behind his desk.

As if summoned by her thoughts, Laurence finally arrives. With how late it is, she wonders why he's bothered to come in at all.

He's dishevelled. She's never seen him look like this before. He's still wearing his designer suit, but his usually-perfectly-styled hair is unkempt. His face is pinched. He avoids looking in her direction. Doesn't give her any kind of greeting. At his office door he pulls out his keys, fumbles one into the lock, then disappears inside.

Danny watched him all the way. She scratches the corner

of her jaw, then looks down at the list of notes she has taken. She waits, gives him a moment to settle, then picks up the list and goes to his door. Knocks, and waits. There's no response. She isn't sure he's heard. She knocks again, harder. Calls through. "Mr. Morgan?"

He clears his throat. "Come on in, Danielle."

She rolls her eyes at the formal name, then plasters on a smile and steps inside. "Hello," she says, holding up the list of messages.

"Uh-huh," he says, staring at his cell phone, brow furrowed.

"There's been a few calls for you today, sir," Danny says.

"Uh-huh," Laurence says again. He isn't listening.

Danny rocks back on her heels, hesitates. "Would you like me to leave them on your desk?"

"*What?*" He looks up, frowning. Danny thinks it's the first time she hasn't seen him all smiles.

Danny holds up the list. "I have messages," she says. "For you."

He looks at her and the list, still frowning. He blinks. The cell phone begins to buzz in his hand. He gives a start, looks down at it. He waves her from his office. "Close the door," he says.

Danny does as he tells her, the list of messages still in her hand. She doesn't go back to her desk. She takes a step to the side of Laurence's door and listens in.

It's a moment before Laurence answers his phone. More than likely he's waiting, giving her a chance to get out of earshot. He needn't worry so much – when he finally does answer, his lowered voice is muffled through the door. Danny looks around, makes sure there's no one else nearby – another administrative assistant or a cleaner or any of the other numerous helpers the church employs whose job titles or descriptions Danny has never been sure of – makes sure there's no one who can catch her attempt at eavesdropping. She leans in closer, her ear almost pressed up against the wood.

She can't understand a word of what is being said, but there is a glimmer of change. His voice is rising. Slowly but surely, his volume increases. The words remain muffled until the end, when he shouts, and Danny hears very clearly what he says. "*Then deal with it!*"

Then there's silence. Laurence is off the phone. The call has ended. Danny can't hear anything else. She hurries back to her desk, positions herself behind it and acts casual just as Laurence throws open the door. Danny pretends to be typing. The sound catches Laurence's attention as he's turning away, about to leave as abruptly as he has arrived. He stops, looks at her. He looks back into his office, as if trying to gauge whether she could have heard the conversation or not. He closes the office door, locks it, then takes a step toward her. He blinks, shakes his head, smiles his usual smile. It comes to him too easily to be genuine. It's a practiced smile. Like a politician's. "Sorry about all that," he says, waving a dismissive hand toward his office. "What was it you were trying to say?"

Danny looks back up at him and returns his smile. She can plaster a fake one onto her face just as well as he can. "Oh, it was nothing important," she says. "Just a list of messages – calls you missed earlier today when you weren't here." She's just as casual as he is, pretending she didn't hear a syllable of the call. Had she been behind her desk, she would not have heard his shout at the end anywhere near as clearly as she did. "They can wait until tomorrow if you're heading back out."

Laurence looks down at the list on her desk. "Nothing important, you said?"

"I wouldn't say so, no. Nothing that can't wait."

He nods. "Fine," he says. "Good. I need to go out. If anyone calls for me the rest of the day, tell them I'm not feeling too well. If they insist, tell them they can reach me at home. If it's truly important, and if they're important enough, they'll have my number."

"Certainly, Mr. Morgan."

He nods again, looks from her desk to his closed office door again, still gauging, then nods once more, smiles, and heads out.

Danny watches him go, still pretending to type so that he has some background noise to exit to, and waits until he rounds the corner at the end of the hall. She grabs the financial reports from her desk so that she has a prop in case anyone sees her, then leaves her desk and follows the pastor at a distance.

He makes his way down the hall almost at a run, past closed doors behind which are storage cupboards and the occasional office.

The route Laurence takes leads him from the belly of his church and into the front. The part the public sees, where they file in for their weekly sermons. In the auditorium, on the ground, there are four sections of plush leather seats, each separated by an aisle. The aisles join together at the end, lead to the entrance/exit and to other doors, which lead to the stairs up into the balcony seats, as well as the bathrooms and the concession stands. The floor and balcony seats all rise cinema style and point toward the raised semicircle where Laurence stands to deliver his sermons from behind his lectern – though his sermons are quite animated, and he doesn't spend much time behind the lectern.

Danny holds back while Laurence makes his way through the auditorium. She stays by the door to the side of the semicircular stage, hides behind the frame, peering out. Laurence stops as he gets halfway up the central aisle leading directly to the exit. He turns back. Danny doesn't see where he looks, though it's likely in her direction. She presses herself up against the wall behind the doorframe, holds her breath, curses herself for following him. She listens to hear if he's spotted her. If he calls her name – *Danielle* – or the sound of his footsteps coming back toward her. She doesn't hear either, not right away, and then she realizes why – because he's walking away. Continuing on the way he was when he first stopped and looked back. He pushes the door open, out into the parking lot.

Danny hesitates. There's nothing to be gained from following him any further. He'll get in his car – his brand-new Lexus – and drive off, and Danny won't have any idea where he's going.

Unless there's someone out in the parking lot, waiting for him?

Danny considers this, then heads up one of the side aisles and circles around toward the door. Again, like when she hid by the side of the semicircle, she keeps herself hidden. Peers out. There's no one in the parking lot waiting for Laurence. He's already in his car, speeding away, the engine roaring. He barely stops and checks as he pulls out at the far end of the parking lot, merging with the traffic. Danny watches him go. It doesn't take him long to disappear.

12

Tom and Taylor have been driving for an hour and a half, with only one stop to fill up the tank. Tom kept his head on a swivel while he pumped the gas, though he was subtle about it. He put his surroundings to good use – parked close to the building and checked the reflections in the glass, as well as the glass of the vehicles around them. He glanced up and down the road, too. No one would raise an eyebrow at him doing this. Everyone does it.

Most of the journey has been in silence. Tom has noticed how Taylor has stopped scratching the loose skin on her thumb and the rest of her fingers. The blood she drew earlier has dried and been wiped away. Instead of picking, her hands are clasped. They're calm. They don't pull and squeeze at each other. Her hood remains up, though, and he can't see her eyes. It's hard to tell whether she's awake or sleeping. From her breathing, as shallow and regular as it is, he thinks she's still conscious.

She proves him right not long after, when she sits forward a little and motions toward the CD player. "It's started again," she says.

"Hmm?" Tom says.

"Springsteen. The album. It's starting up again."

Tom hadn't noticed. As well as the road ahead, he's been watching the road behind. Staying aware of their surroundings at all times. He even watches the trees, just to be sure no one and nothing jumps out at them. The music has only received half of his attention.

"You tired of it?" he says.

"I like it. It's fine," Taylor says. "But I don't want to listen to the album all the way through *again*. I can't remember the last time I listened to *any* album all the way through just *once*, never mind twice."

"What do you do instead?" he says. "Skip from song to song, disc to disc?"

"Who even still listens to discs?" she says, turning to him now and raising her eyebrows, laughing. "Y'know, you almost looked excited when I pulled the CD out of the glovebox. I've never seen anyone react like that to a CD before."

"Then how do *you* listen to music?"

"Well, when I *could*, I used the internet."

"Ken didn't have the internet?"

"He had it. He just changed all the passwords so I couldn't get on."

Tom nods. It makes sense. Eliminate the ways for her to contact the outside world. Cut her off. Don't give her a chance to call for help, to tell anyone what's going on. He reaches out, ejects the disc. "Put it back in its case," he says. "The radio's yours. Although, I should probably brace myself – what kind of stuff do you listen to?"

Taylor puts the album away. "Just whatever," she says, shrugging, changing through the stations, stopping on each one for just a couple of seconds to hear what's playing, get an idea of it, then moving on. "I don't really know what's current anymore." She sighs, leaves it on a station, and Tom gets the impression it's not so much something she wants to listen to, but that she's just given up on searching. "This'll do," she says.

Tom doesn't recognize it. It's very upbeat and sounds like it's been made on a computer. Even the vocals sound like they've been computerized somehow. He doesn't love it, but he doesn't totally hate it, either. "What is it?" he says.

"I dunno," Taylor says. "Other than Springsteen there, what kinda stuff do you listen to?"

"I listen to a lot of things," Tom says. "The Rolling Stones, The Doors, The Kinks, Bob Dylan, Neil Young, The Beatles, pretty much anything that came out of Motown –"

"Those are all *really* old."

"It's what my dad would listen to. It's what's stuck with me the longest. I guess I'm out of the loop, too, though."

"Uh-huh. How old did you say you are again?"

"Thirty-one."

"Yeah?" She leans forward, inspecting his face. "You look older."

Tom raises an eyebrow. "Am I supposed to take that gratefully or be offended?"

Taylor shrugs. "I'm just saying. You listen to anything that's more up to date?"

"I don't really listen to anything with any great regularity."

"Well, what are you aware of? What do you like?"

Tom thinks. "John Grant, Mark Lanegan –"

"I haven't heard of either of those."

"– St. Vincent –"

"*Her* I know. And like. That's a good one. I'll applaud your taste there."

Tom grins. "Thank you. I appreciate it. I'm glad I've finally named someone who reaches your exacting standards."

"What about, like, Lana Del Rey? You like her? Or Janelle Monáe? The Yeah Yeah Yeahs?"

Tom opens his mouth, is about to respond, when something in the side mirror catches his eye. He looks. A Toyota, coming fast up the empty road behind them. He braces himself, but then it eases off. Keeps a safe distance. Doesn't crowd them. Tom holds his speed steady, and so do they. He keeps an eye on them. They don't come closer.

"What's wrong?" Taylor says.

"Nothing," Tom says, turning his attention to the road ahead so as not to spook her. He glances at the mirror intermittently, but there is no difference in the distance between themselves and the Toyota.

Taylor starts to twist in her seat, to look back, but Tom stops her before she can do so.

"Don't turn around."

She freezes, but she does as he says, settling back into her seat.

"Don't make it obvious to anyone that you're looking," Tom says. "Use your mirror, but just glance at it. Don't peer right into it."

"You're freaking me out, Tom," she says.

"Relax," Tom says. "It's fine. It's not coming any closer, but I just want to be sure."

"What're you gonna do?"

"I'm gonna speed up," Tom says. The Ford is old and beat-up, but Tom can feel that it still has some juice left in it. He's tested it subtly, how it handles, how it increases and decreases in speed. "See if they do the same."

Before he can, before he can press his foot down on the pedal, something else in the mirror catches his eye. Coming up from behind the Toyota, travelling faster than it was before, overtaking it, a Chevrolet gaining on them, but remaining in the outside lane.

Taylor has seen it, too. "Are they just trying to overtake?" she says, her voice high, worried.

Tom looks back at the Toyota. It's sped up, too. It's not attempting to race the Chevrolet – it's coming up on their tail. The Chevrolet is coming alongside them. The two cars are going to try to box them in, cop style.

"Hold on," Tom says, then mashes the pedal to the floor.

The Ford takes off with an unexpected kick. Taylor is thrown back in her seat. The Chevrolet is caught by surprise. It has to fall back into the lane behind them, cutting off the Toyota.

There's a long stretch of road ahead of them. Tom knows he won't be able to stay out in front of them, and they know it, too. They have newer, better, faster cars. It doesn't take the Chevrolet long to catch back up to them. By now, though, there are vehicles in the other lane. The Chevrolet and the Toyota can't pull out. They're stuck behind. They sit close, though. The Chevrolet is closest. Tom feels it nudge their bumper. His foot is flat to the floor. The car won't go any faster.

He realizes Taylor is speaking. It isn't to him – it's to herself, over and over, muttering, "*Holy shit, holy shit, holy shit, holy shit* –" while her hands cling to the seatbelt strap across her chest, the back of her head straining against the headrest.

There's an opening in the other lane. The Chevrolet sees it too and takes advantage. It slips into it, and the space behind the Ford is promptly filled by the Toyota. The Toyota bumps them from behind too, but they're rougher than the Chevrolet.

Tom sees the Chevrolet coming up beside them. He tries to see inside, but the windows are blacked out. The Chevrolet jerks to the side, slams into them. Taylor cries out. Tom grits his teeth. The Chevrolet almost bounces them off the road, into the trees. He battles for control, keeps them from smashing headfirst into a tree. Tom gets them back on the road, but the Chevrolet is on them again.

It slams hard into their side. Tom can feel the impact through his door. The Chevrolet doesn't move. Stays on them, sticks to them, veers into them, trying to run them off the road and into the trees. To take them out completely. The Toyota rams them from behind, too. Tom's arms strain to keep control of the steering wheel, to keep them on the road and out of the trees. He can't see Taylor, can't look at her. Needs to focus on the cars – the one they're in, the one to their side, the one behind them, and the ones up ahead.

The Chevrolet sees the oncoming traffic, and the way the car in the lead is flashing its lights, the person inside slamming their fist down on the horn. The Chevrolet falters, and Tom feels it as they part from the Ford. They're hitting the brakes, getting ready to fall back, out of the way of what's coming. Tom jerks the wheel, slams them, knocks them so they're unsteady, so they struggle. The Toyota sees what's happening, and they pull back, too.

There's a lot of traffic coming. The Chevrolet manages to get itself back under control. It falls behind them, slipping in between the Ford and the Toyota. The long stream of traffic coming from the opposite direction means there's no space for them to overtake, to continue their attempts at sideswipes. Tom keeps his foot down. The Chevrolet continues to bump them, riding their tail, making the Ford hard to control. Tom counts cars. There are four left, and then the Chevrolet, or maybe the Toyota this time, is free to pull back out. However, up ahead, there's a bend. A tight one. Tom sees it. There's a chance the two behind may not have spotted it past him. He speeds toward it. The Chevrolet is already pulling out again, trying to get back up alongside them.

"Bend!" Taylor says, pointing. There's panic in her voice,

feeling how fast they're going, how Tom is showing no signs of slowing.

"I see it," he says, both hands wrapped tight around the wheel, his knuckles bone white. He taps the brakes as they reach the bend, but he pulls on the handbrake and spins the wheel at the same time to skid around the bend. Their back end kicks out across the other lane, but he's able to right it before the car approaching head-on in the other lane can reach them. Not understanding what's happening, the other driver is understandably pissed. They blare their horn, flash their lights, and then they're greeted with another shock as the Chevrolet, who clearly hadn't spotted the bend at all, comes skidding across in front of them, onto the grass at the side of the road, then disappears sideways into the trees.

The Toyota skids into the other lane, too, but it manages to right itself and continues its pursuit.

The road here isn't as straight as before. There are a lot of bends. Tom thinks this will play to their advantage. Speed is against them. The most they can hope for is to attempt to outmaneuver the remaining vehicle.

It's already on them, though. It's ramming them from behind, harder now. Trying to drive them from the road. It feels to Tom as though their back wheels are being lifted from the ground every time they get hit. The Ford is taking a beating. It can't take much more. Already the handling feels off to Tom. He can feel that they're losing power. They can't get away, and they can't maneuver, either. The car is dying. It's almost dead.

The Toyota rams them again. Perhaps it's noticed how the Ford is slowing. How it's limping.

"Why aren't we going faster?" Taylor says. She's noticed, too.

Tom doesn't know how many men are in the Toyota. At most, it's five. There's no way to know if they're armed. They haven't attempted to shoot, but he doesn't think they'd take a chance on hurting Taylor.

Tom checks the speed. Despite slowing significantly, they're still going fifty. Still fast enough to do some damage.

"Brace yourself," Tom says.

"I *am* braced!" Taylor says.

"They're about to hit us hard," Tom says. "After they do, be ready to run."

"What – *what?*"

Tom watches the mirror. The Toyota backs up, readying itself to ram them again. Tom keeps his foot down, putting as much distance between them as he can in preparation. It's not much, but it'll have to be enough. The Toyota speeds up again. It's coming. It's getting closer.

Tom slams on the brakes. He pulls on the handbrake, too. The Toyota hits them hard, buries itself in the back of them. Glass shatters. Taylor screams. Tom is thrown forward. His nose bounces off the steering wheel before the airbag has a chance to activate. He feels the bridge of his nose split, blood running down the tip and soaking into the airbag.

The two cars screech to a halt. "Run!" Tom says, tearing himself from the hold of the airbag. "To the trees!"

He hears Taylor throw her door open. Hears her sneakers crunching through broken glass, rushing around to his side. She doesn't go straight for the trees. She stops by his door as he forces it open, tearing the seatbelt off from across his chest. He reaches into the back through the shattered window, grabs his bag. "*Run*," he says, turning to Taylor as he loops his arms through its straps.

Taylor doesn't say anything. She grabs his arm, and she drags him. Tom wipes the blood from his face, and together they break through the trees, running deep into the underbrush. Behind, he hears a car screech to a halt beside the crash. The way it throws open its doors, slams them again, the way the people from inside it rush out, he knows it's not a concerned passerby stopping to make sure everyone is all right. From the sounds he hears, it's more likely to be the Chevrolet. Soon, they'll be back in pursuit.

They'll be on foot this time, though. Despite the aches he feels from the crash, and the taste of blood as it drips down his nose, Tom can't help but smile at the prospect.

On foot, they're his.

13

Bill has sent Kyle to the hospital. Has told him to tell anyone who asks that he had a bad fall while working on a roof. Donald and Gil aren't as badly hurt as Kyle. He's sent them back out on the road.

Despite Ken's whimpering, he has not allowed him to go with Kyle. Instead, he has made a rudimentary field sling for him and has kept him by his side. They return to the gas station where Ken and the others first encountered the man who is helping Taylor.

Ken is silent. He'd be surly if he weren't so afraid of Bill, and Bill knows it. "When we get there," he says, battling to keep his voice from cracking, "can I at least get some painkillers?"

Bill shrugs the shoulder nearest to Ken. "Sure," he says. "If you think you deserve them."Ken chews on his lip. "It's not so much a case of deserve as that I *need* them."

Bill looks at him. Ken promptly looks away.

The gas station comes into view. Cars are pulling in and out, going about their day. There's no evidence there was an earlier confrontation here except for some drops of blood mingling with the gas and oil on the ground, should anyone care to look close enough.

Bill pulls to a stop in front of the door. He motions for Ken to join him inside. As they make their way down the aisle toward the till, Bill notices how Ken looks longingly toward the shelf of painkillers, but he doesn't go to them.

There are a couple of people in the line in front of them, and they have to wait. It doesn't take long for them to pay and leave. Bill steps up to the counter, smiling, his jaw jutting. The young kid behind the counter gives a start at his hideous grin. Then he looks at Ken, and his eyes narrow when he sees the makeshift sling holding his right arm close to his body.

"Hello," Bill says. "Been here long?"

The kid looks confused. "Uh, no, not really." He looks at his screen. "Do you have a pump?"

"We're not here for gas," Bill says. "How long you been here today?"

The kid shrugs, not understanding. "I came on shift about a half hour ago."

"I see," Bill says. "So you weren't present when my companion here and three of his friends had their asses handed to them out front?"

The kid's eyes widen. "Oh, shit, was that you? No, no, man, I wasn't here, but I heard about it." He looks at Ken's sling again. "Shit, I heard the guy broke someone's bones, but I heard it was a leg."

"It was," Bill says. He checks his reflection in the glass counters behind the kid. There's a line beginning to form behind them. "I assume you have security footage here?"

"Oh, yeah, of course – gotta have cameras, man."

"Uh-huh. And is your manager in? Someone in the back, perhaps?"

The kid nods.

"Take me to him."

"Uh, no one's supposed to go back there – security reasons, y'know."

Bill leans in. The kid flinches. "Make an exception," he says.

The kid looks behind him, to the line that by now is stretching back toward the door, and nods his head, says, "Sure," and motions for Bill and Ken to follow him. Bill hears the people behind them groan at being kept waiting. Someone curses – at them or the kid, it's hard to tell who it's directed at.

The kid takes them down a very short corridor and to a door that's marked 'Manager.' He knocks, calls through. "Hey, man, there's some guys here to see you."

A voice calls back, it sounds like it says *What*, then a moment later the door is opened. The manager stands frowning out at them all. He's twenty years older than the kid he has working for him. He's wearing jeans and an untucked shirt, the top few buttons undone. "No one's supposed to come back here," he says.

"That's what he said," Bill says, pushing the manager back into his office and stepping in with him. He gestures to the kid who brought them here, tells him, "You'd best get back out there before they start driving off with free gas."

The kid hurries away. Ken closes the office door and stands by it.

The manager looks between them both, eyes Ken's sling. "What's going on here?" he says. "Who the fuck are you?"

Bill presses a hand on his chest and with little effort pushes him down into the swivel chair by his desk. "Sit down and shut up," Bill says. "We're here to ask some questions, so you'd better listen."

Out of the corner of his eye, Bill surveys the room. He sees video screens in the opposite corner from the manager's desk. Sees the grainy images of the people outside, coming and going, filling their tanks. He sees the video recorders hooked up next to them. He points. "I sure hope they're in working order."

"They're always in working order," the manager says.

"You ever thought about upgrading to digital?"

"Costs too much," the manager says. "And they work just fine as is." He shakes his head, "Damn it, who the fuck are you? I want some answers."

"I'm sure you do," Bill says. "And I'll give you as much as you need to know – such as how the man beside me and three of his buddies were beat up on your premises earlier, and I'm here for the footage."

"The footage?" the manager says. "You a cop? Why didn't you just say that?"

"I'm no one you need to concern yourself with," Bill says. "Unless you continue to waste my time. Show me the footage."

The manager's mouth works. He doesn't say anything for a while, but just as he's about to, Bill decides he's had enough. The man has already wasted too much of his time.

He reaches down, grabs the manager by the front of his shirt, hauls him off his chair and throws him into the corner toward the camera screens. "Get the fucking footage!" he says. He's done being polite. Done being civil. Time is of the utmost importance. Now he wants what he wants. He turns the manager around and holds him by the back of his neck, pushes his face toward a screen. "Have I made myself clear?"

The manager is nodding. "Y-yes!"

Bill shoves him again, then stands close as the manager looks over the screens. Tentatively, he turns to look at Ken. "Where – whereabouts did it happen?"

Ken steps up, looks at the screens, then points with his good hand at which camera is showing where it was. The manager picks up a remote control and starts rewinding. "When'd it happen?"

"I don't remember," Ken says. "Not exactly. It was probably a couple of hours ago now, but I'm not sure."

"Just tell me if you see anything you recognize," the manager says.

When the time finally comes, Ken doesn't need to speak up. They all see it. They all see it happen in reverse. The manager stops the video from rewinding. Bill leans in close. He watches the man work. He's fast and efficient, and he hits *hard*. It's true, what they've all said – he went through them like they were *nothing*.

The only problem is Bill can't see his face. Most of the action occurs with his back to the screen. "I need to see his face," Bill says. "Go to the beginning. When he first arrives."

The manager has been watching the fight, too. Four on one. He looks impressed. So impressed, he almost doesn't hear what Bill has said, but once he realizes, he's quick to do as he's told. He rewinds, watching closely to see when the mystery man first turns up. They see him pull onto the court. He's driving a pickup truck. He gets out to fill it. His back remains to the camera. It's almost like he's doing it on purpose, keeping his face obscured.

"What does he have to hide?" Bill says, muttering it to himself, not expecting an answer.

The man heads inside to pay. Bill looks at the other screens, searches until he finds the one of the interior of the gas station. He spots it, looks at the people inside coming to pay. The line they'd earlier built up has been mostly dealt with now. Someone walks in to join it. Their face is in full view.

"Mark the time," Bill says, pointing to the screen showing the man in the past. "Then find it on this one." He points at the interior of the station.

The manager pauses the screen they were originally studying so closely. He starts rewinding on the inside of the building, matching up the times. All three of them are watching intently. They see the man enter the building. His head is lowered. And then, when he raises it, he's looking back out the window.

"Find me his fucking face, goddammit," Bill says.

The manager, likely still feeling the aftereffects of Bill's grip on the back of his neck, is eager to oblige. He starts rewinding and fast-forwarding and pausing on the footage, desperate to find what Bill wants.

"Oh," he says, and it's a sound of relief. "I've got him."

The screen is paused. The image is a little blurred, but it's clear enough. Bill can see the man's face. Can see enough of him that he'd recognize him if they were to pass on the streets. "This as good as you can get?"

"That's the best I can do," the manager says. "It's as clear as I can get it – I've been pausing and playing it so much it's like I've been going frame by frame."

Bill grunts. "Y'know, if this were digital, this image would be crystal."

The manager nods obsequiously. "I'll keep that in mind."

"I don't give a shit if you upgrade it now," Bill says, pulling his cell phone from his pocket. "It's too late for us." He sets up his camera and snaps a picture of the screen. He checks the image he has taken, makes sure it's as clear as he can get it. It's as good as it is on the screen. He grunts. "Let's go," he says to Ken.

They leave the building. The kid behind the counter sees them leave. He waves. They don't return it.

In the car, Bill pulls his phone back out. He sends the image to David Mackenzie, one of their organization's many friends in the state troopers. The highest ranking. Bill keeps his message brief and to the point.

I need a name.

Ken knows what he's done. Knows why they came here. "How long will that take?" he says.

"Few hours at the least," Bill says. He starts the engine, pulls out of the gas station. "Could take longer if they don't have anything on the guy. He might have to send it to his friends in other agencies. But one way or another, we'll eventually get an answer."

"We should have him by then," Ken says. "We should have both of them."

"He's slipped us so far," Bill says. "Prepare for every eventuality. Know your enemy."

Ken nods. He rubs his arm in the sling, winces as he touches it.

He didn't get painkillers. He's hurting. Bill grins. The pain will serve as a long-term reminder as to what happens to him when he fucks up.

"Call the others," Bill says. "Find out how things are going. Tell them we're on our way."

14

Eight men have followed them into the woods. They've split up.

Tom hid Taylor. He hid her deep in the woods, and then he came back. He left his bag with her. Told her there's a gun inside. Told her that if she needs to use it, then to do so. She looked scared. He told her just waving it around in a person's general direction if they find her should be enough to scare them off. He's laid low, smeared dirt on his face and hid himself among bushes and branches, behind the thick trunks of trees. They're far from the road now. The sound of passing cars is distant and faint.

Tom got a good look at the eight men now that they have vacated the Toyota and the Chevrolet, respectively. They're mean-looking guys. They have muscles, or they're heavyset. None of them are skinny. They look like they can handle themselves. Then again, so did the big guy back at the gas station, and he was handled easily. If these eight are friends of his, chances are they can be dealt with just as effortlessly.

Tom checked them for weapons when they first appeared. It looked as though only one of them was armed. It's likely they haven't expected too much trouble from a fourteen-year-old girl and the guy she's traveling with. Even if they're aware of what he did to the four men at the gas station. They figure he can't do to eight what he did to four.

The armed guy carried a pistol. It took Tom a while to make out what it was. Had to wait until he got closer before he finally saw enough detail. A Taurus G2c. He held it in both hands, straight-armed, pointing it at the ground.

They've split up, searching. Tom stalks them. The armed guy hasn't come his way. Tom is off to his left. He's going down the center. Tom will catch up to him. First, he'll deal with the two unarmed men coming right toward him.

They're not together. They're all separate, covering more ground. Again, if they've heard about what happened at the gas station, they're not concerned for themselves.

Tom stays behind the tree until the first man reaches him. He slides down low and waits for him to pass. Then he creeps up behind, his feet traveling silently across the ground, brushing aside any twigs and branches that may be in front of him before he presses down with his weight. He wraps an arm around the man's neck from behind, keeps things silent. He chokes him out, lowers him to the ground. He moves on to the next guy. Needs to be quick, to move on, to take them out and get back to Taylor. Then they'll get out of the woods, they'll get another vehicle, and they'll continue on to Oregon.

He reaches the next guy, moving from bush to tree to get to him. This guy is more aware. His head is on a swivel. He's checking his surroundings at all times. His fists are balled by his sides.

Tom snaps a branch on purpose to get his attention. Ducking low behind the bush, he hears the man pause. Listens to his hesitation as the man wonders whether he really just heard something, or if it was his imagination – or an animal. He doesn't want to take the chance. They're here to search. To find. Any suspicious noise, he needs to investigate it. Tom hears him come back on himself, toward the bush. This guy's cautious, though. Taking his time. His head likely remains on a swivel while intermittently staring at the bush, trying to see through it, trying to gauge where the sound came from.

He gets close enough that Tom can see him through the foliage. Tom doesn't move. Lies as still as a statue, but he's coiled, ready to explode.

The man shakes the bush a little. If it's an animal, he's trying to scare it out. If it's whom he's looking for, he's trying to do the same. Hoping it's Taylor, hoping she gets spooked and tries to make a run for it, then he can tackle her. When nothing happens, he deliberates. Tom stays calm, despite how long he's taking. Once this guy is dealt with, he can move on to the guy with the gun. After that, he can round them up and get rid of them all in one fell swoop.

The man on the other side of the bush finally makes his move. He starts coming around. Each step is careful, measured, almost the same way Tom moved across the littered ground, but slower. More careful. Not as experienced.

His right leg comes into view around the bush. Tom moves into action. He sweeps it out from under the man and flips him onto his back in one movement, then covers his mouth to keep him quiet. Before he can struggle, Tom slams the point of his elbow across his jaw, puts him out cold. Tom checks he's truly limp, it's not just an act, then he moves on to the gun handler.

The man with the gun is spinning around every tree, checking it's clear, like he thinks he's in a movie. In his mind he's making his way down a corridor, checking behind every corner. The one thing he's *not* doing, though, while he checks behind every object in front of him, is making sure to look behind himself. Just a quick glance back or a look over his shoulder. It's easy enough for Tom to get up behind him, and it's easier yet to take the gun from him. Both hands are wrapped around the gun. Tom grabs him by his dominant wrist – the right – and yanks it to the side. A shot goes off, but this is fine. Tom has anticipated this. It will bring the men still standing running, and he wants them to be near for what happens next.

With the man's wrist under control, Tom throws his elbow back into his chest, driving the wind from his lungs. Tom twists his arm. He drops the gun, though he was barely holding onto it anymore. Tom flips him over his shoulder onto the ground, still holding his wrist, then kicks him across the face. He scoops up the Taurus, then drops to a knee, holds it out in front of himself. He can hear the other men running toward the sound of the gunshot. They soon come into view. They falter when they see Tom stand, pointing the gun at them. They raise their hands.

They're one short.

Four come running. There's the man on the ground at Tom's feet, and the two he's already put down. That's seven. One is missing.

"One of you isn't here," Tom says. The man at his feet is groaning. He tries to push himself up. Tom presses his boot into his throat, pins him to the ground. "Where is he?"

The four men glance at each other. The one Tom is pointing the gun directly at shakes his head. "I – I don't know."

Tom doesn't have the time to waste getting an answer out of them. "Get out of here," he says. "Get back to your cars and stay there, or else I start shooting."

They don't move. Tom aims at their feet, fires. They hop into action.

"You can tell all your buddies," Tom says, "and anyone else you might wanna send after us, that if you all don't back off now, that if you all keep coming, I'm gonna start doing worse than busting heads and breaking bones. That's your only warning."

The men flee. Tom takes his boot from the man's neck, and he scrambles to his feet. He hurries after the others. There's no sign of the two Tom took out – likely still lying flat. Even if they've come back to consciousness, they'll be counting stars.

Tom doesn't wait until the men are clear of the woods. He turns, starts running, back to where he left Taylor. He keeps his eyes peeled on the way for the eighth man. There's no sign of him. He gets to where Taylor should be. His bag is there, but she is not. The bag's open. His Beretta is out. It's on the ground. Knocked from her hand, more than likely. She never got off a shot.

Tom stays calm. He grabs the bag, slings it over his shoulder, studying the ground as he does so. Searching for signs of where they've gone. Looking for a trail.

He spots it. A piece of fabric snagged on a branch, and a scuffed footprint with a snapped twig a pace in front. Heading north. He follows.

15

Taylor doesn't know the man who has grabbed her. She's never seen him before – not that she remembers, anyway. There's always been a lot of men, coming and going. Men who hang around with Bill, like being near him transfers some of his toughness their way. She doesn't remember all their faces. Barely looks at them anymore.

This guy fits the build, though. He's muscular, and his face is stuck in a perpetual frown, and he's not gentle when he handles her.

He was unfazed by the gun, after she'd scrambled through all the phones in Tom's bag to pull it out. She held it two-handed and pointed it at him. "I'll shoot you," she said, and in that moment she'd meant it – or at least she'd believed she'd meant it. "I'll fucking put you down. I'm not going back there."

The man smirked, and he took a step forward, and that was when Taylor realized what the man had understood all along – she wasn't going to shoot. She couldn't. No matter how much she *thought* she could, she couldn't follow through. Taylor had never fired a gun in her life. But, not just that – not just the practical realities of handling one – she couldn't fire it at a *person*, regardless of what kind of man this person may be.

He knocked the gun from her hands, and as he grabbed her by the throat and dragged her away from the hiding place, Taylor finally felt within herself the roughed-up anger that would have allowed her to squeeze the trigger. By then, it was far too late.

Her feet trailed through the dirt and the leaves, the man's hand remaining at her throat. She clawed at his hand, wishing she hadn't bit her fingernails down so much, wishing she were able to dig them in, to break his grip, to hurt him, to make him bleed.

Unable to claw, she balls her fists and starts throwing them back at his face. His grip around her neck is tight, and she's starting to see black spots. Her breath is gasping and barely reaches her lungs. She feels herself connect with his nose, with his mouth. Feels her knuckles bury themselves in his eye.

This stops him momentarily. He curses, grabs at her with the hand that has been holding her arm. He wraps it around her forearm. Taylor drags it to her face, to her mouth, and she bites. Her nails may not be sharp, but her teeth are.

Now she breaks his grip. *Now* she hurts him. *Now* she makes him bleed – she tastes it.

He cries out, lets go of her neck, spins her, backhands her. Taylor throws herself to the ground, though the blow wasn't enough to fell her. She uses its momentum. Starts scurrying back, kicking at his shins as she goes. She screams.

"*Tom!*"

The man grabs her by the ankle and drags her closer to him. He hauls her back to her feet, hits her again, holding her upright this time. Taylor tastes blood, but this time it's hers.

"You little bitch," he says, hissing, shaking his bitten hand.

Taylor battles back. She kicks at him. Stamps at his feet. She struggles in his hands, and he battles to keep hold of her. He does, though. His hands slip between her flailing arms, grab her by the face. One on either side. She feels pressure in her skull. It's like he's trying to crush it. He's snarling, showing his teeth. Taylor tears at his wrists, trying to break his grip. She can't. He's too strong.

Then she hears something. Something loud and getting closer. Pounding the ground, like hoofbeats.

And then the man's grip is broken. Taylor falls. She rubs her temples, raises her eyebrows, stretches the pain away. She looks to see what has happened, where the man has gone.

Tom has tackled him to the ground. Has pinned him there. He's hitting him. Except he's not using his fist. There's something in his hand. Taylor squints to see. It's a gun. He's hitting him in the face, over and over, with a gun.

The man is lying very still. Tom wipes the blood off the gun onto the man's clothes. He stands, tucks it down the back of his jeans. He turns to Taylor, holds his hand out to her. There is blood on the hand. The man on the ground's blood. "Let's go," Tom says.

Taylor takes his hand, and he pulls her up to her feet.

They run.

16

Bill gets a call. He's still driving. He throws the phone at Ken, tells him, "Answer that."

The phone hits Ken's broken arm. He winces, then answers the phone. "Yeah? No, it's Ken. Yeah, he's here. He's driving. What's happened?"

There's a silence while Ken listens, occasionally grunting. "Shit," he says. He turns to Bill. "They got away."

Bill grits his teeth. He holds out his hand for the phone. Ken gives it back to him.

"What happened?" Bill listens as he's told how his men managed to run Taylor and the guy off the road, but they lost them in the woods. "Lost them how?" Bill says. He wants details. "You make contact, or did they disappear?"

The man on the other end hesitates. "We made contact," he says.

"Tell me."

"He beat down four of us, took the only gun we had."

"One gun between eight of you?"

"She's a fourteen-year-old girl, and he's just some guy from a gas station! There were fucking *eight* of us."

"I told you what he did to Ken and the others. They were four. Did you think it would be as simple as just doubling up?"

"Look, we came quick, like you told us to, okay? Only reason we had a gun at all is because Jay already had it on him."

"So he takes the gun off Jay, and then what? He shoot anyone?"

There's another hesitation. "No, he didn't shoot anyone. He used it to nearly cave Gary's head in, though. He's in a bad way."

"He still breathing?"

"Yeah, but he's all cut up and dizzy and stuff, and –"

"Can he stand?"

"Yeah..."

"Then I don't give a shit if he's a little dizzy. Gary can go home to his mom and get a kiss on the forehead after we're done here, and not before."

The man on the other end sighs. He shouldn't. He should know what to expect. Bill expects a lot from them. He won't settle for anything less.

"Push on," Bill says. "Get after them. Run them to ground. They can't get away from you. Tire them out. I'll catch up to you soon."

"Our cars are in a bad way."

Bill is silent.

The man clears his throat. "The Chevy might still...might still be able to go. But the Toyota is all fucked up."

"Get after them," Bill repeats. "I'll be there soon."

"You should send more men, too."

"Don't be ridiculous."

"You haven't seen this guy at work."

Ken has overheard this. He's trying to get Bill's attention, nodding his agreement with the voice on the other end.

"I've seen footage," Bill says.

"It ain't the same."

"I'll think about it," Bill says. "Now, do as I've said. Run them down. Don't let them get away again." Bill hangs up.

Ken wants to say something. It takes him a moment to get going, second-guessing himself. "Laurence would probably feel a lot better if you called some more men in," he says.

"Laurence will feel a lot better when this is all over and done with."

Ken opens his mouth, but he's still hesitating. "I really want to go and get my arm seen to, Bill."

Bill checks their location. "There's a hospital not far from here," he says. "I don't need you with me anymore. I'll drop you there, and you can call someone to come pick you up."

Ken nods. "Thank Christ," he says under his breath, his left hand stroking his broken arm.

A few minutes later, Bill's phone starts ringing again. He rolls his eyes, thinking it's a continuation of the earlier conversation, a new hurdle in the chase of Taylor and her mystery friend, but instead it's David Mackenzie, the ever-helpful state trooper. Bill answers. "I hope you've got something for me."

"I've got something," David says.

"Don't keep me in suspense."

"Name's Tom Rollins, but I've got something here you're gonna really love."

"Oh?" Bill says. In his head he repeats the name, *Tom Rollins*, keeps it in mind. It's easy enough to remember.

"Oh yeah. He's a veteran."

Bill raises an eyebrow. "That so?"

"Yeah. Ex-infantry. And it's real curious, because it looks like no matter who I talk to, there's only so much of his military record we're allowed to see."

"That *is* curious."

"So I figure I stop chasing my tail and leave it in your hands."

"I know exactly who to pass this information on to," Bill says.

"Ken should've just had me arrest this guy when I pulled him over."

"Yeah." Bill grunts. "He should've. Thanks for all your help. See you Sunday?"

"You know I'll be there."

They hang up. Ken is looking at Bill, expectant. "Well?" he says.

"Name's Tom Rollins," Bill says. "And he was in the Army. Maybe even something specialist, by the sounds of it."

"Yeah? Maybe he was a Marine, like you."

"It's a possibility," Bill says, "but I don't think so." Bill starts flicking through his contacts, one hand on the wheel and one eye on the road. They're still twenty minutes away from the hospital and even further from catching up to where the others are. He finds whom he's looking for – Commander Lou Russo. An old friend, and still in the employ of the US Army. He rings, not expecting Lou to answer the first time around. He's a busy man. Bill is pleasantly surprised, however, when Lou picks up on the sixth ring.

"Bill Lindsay," Lou says, "what an unexpected pleasure."

"It's good to hear your voice, Lou."

"And yours. How you keeping?"

"I'm good. Yourself?"

"Ah, you know. I got complaints, but nothing major."

Bill chuckles. "Speaking of complaints, I got an issue I'm hoping you can help me out with."

"It a big one?"

"Minor at the minute, but has a risk of snowballing."

"A snowball in summer, huh?" Lou says. "That's never good. What can I do for you?"

"Tom Rollins," Bill says. "Name sound familiar?"

"Not really. Should it?"

"Guess not. But if you could, I'd like you to get real familiar with his record and get back to me about what it says. A friend in law enforcement tells me he's ex-Army, but then beyond that things get hazy."

"You having trouble with this guy?"

"Not yet," Bill says. "But like I say, things could snowball."

"I'll get to it now. Could take me a while, but I'll be quick as I can."

"That's all I ask. You know how to reach me."

"Sure thing. Talk later."

Bill drives on in silence. It's clear Ken has many questions, but he's keeping them to himself. Bill is thinking. Tom Rollins. Ex-Army. Maybe more. He grinds his lower row of teeth back and forth over his top. He sucks them. He tosses his phone to Ken, not aiming for his injured arm this time. "Call one of our guys out there," he says. "Tell them I'm sending more men. We'll converge on their location. Then call around, get everyone else. And I mean *everyone*, Ken." Bill looks at him.

Ken nods. "Okay," he says. He looks alarmed, fumbling with the phone.

Bill turns back to the road. "And tell them to come armed," he says. "Turns out you were right. This guy sounds like trouble."

17

It's evening when Tom and Taylor get clear of the woods. Taylor is tired and flagging. She's not accustomed to such long marches across rough terrain.

It's been quiet since Tom chased off the men in the woods. If they're still in pursuit, they're holding back. Tom's made sure to keep checking. He's told Taylor to keep walking straight while he's doubled back to search the area. He never saw anyone. Never found any signs that they were being followed.

They walk down the road, following the flickering of a neon light. There's nothing else around. Tom hopes it's a place they can stay. As they get closer, they see that it's a motel.

"Please say we're checking in," Taylor says.

"We are," Tom says, while looking the area over. There's a couple of vending machines down the side of the building – one for drinks, one for snacks – and an icebox next to it. There's only a handful of cars in the parking lot. Getting a room shouldn't be a problem. "I'm John Teller, and you're

Jodie Teller," he says. "Father and daughter. I doubt anyone will ask, but just in case they do."

"Sure," Taylor says.

He looks at Taylor's face as they near the reception door. She has bruising, dried blood, from when the guy in the woods got his hands on her. They're both covered in dirt and dead leaves. "Wait out here," Tom says. "But stay by the door where I can see you. If anyone pulls in and you recognize them, or even if you just get a bad vibe from them, come in and get me."

Taylor nods.

Tom goes inside. At the desk, checking in, he keeps one eye on the glass door, watching Taylor through it. Watching the entrance to the parking lot, too. No one pulls in.

"Quiet night?" Tom says.

The receptionist grunts. "It's always quiet around here." He's barely given Tom a second glance despite his dishevelled appearance. Had Taylor come inside, he likely wouldn't have raised an eyebrow. He doesn't care. He's just here for a paycheck. It doesn't matter to him who checks in, or why, or what they might get up to behind closed doors.

They go along to the room. Tom still has the Taurus tucked down the back of his jeans, concealed under his shirt. He doesn't pull it out while he checks the room over, but he keeps his hand near it. He motions for Taylor to stand in the corner, away from the window. The room's clear. Two single beds. There's a television on top of the dresser at the foot of the beds. It's a long dresser that goes along the length of the wall, with a mirror in the corner opposite the door. There's a bathroom with a shower, toilet, and sink, and the wall next to the bathroom door is occupied by a wardrobe filled with empty metal clothes hangers that can't be removed from the rail. Tom checks for escape routes. There's a window in the bathroom and another next to the mirror in the main room.

They both lead out to the back of the motel, through the trees. The trees head down an embankment, though they're too thick to see what might be at the bottom. Soon, Tom will step outside, check the perimeter, potentially get an idea of who else is staying here. He'll take a closer look down the embankment, too.

"I'm stepping out," he says. Taylor is sitting cross-legged on the bed furthest from the door but closest to the window. She's still wearing her Converse. She has the television remote in her hand, but she hasn't switched it on yet. "If you decide to take a shower or anything, wait until I get back. Lock the door after me and only answer to this knock." He taps a rhythm on the doorframe. "Got that?"

Taylor nods.

"You hear my voice, but not that knock, it means something's gone wrong and you need to run."

Taylor is unblinking.

"I won't be long. Ten minutes, max."

Taylor nods again. She gets off the bed to see him out, to lock the door after him. Tom waits outside the room until he hears her do it, then he takes a casual walk down the length of the rooms. He looks around, checks the area out, but he's cool about it. Never makes it clear what he's doing. Just a guy out for a stroll. Taking the evening air before it gets fully dark.

Tom takes a deep breath and realizes he's carrying a lot of tension in his upper body. His chest and shoulders are bunched up. It's been a long day. Since he first came across Taylor and her stepfather, they haven't stopped moving. This is the first chance they've had to breathe. He doesn't try to relax his muscles, though. He needs to stay on edge. To be alert.

Most of the doors he passes are silent. There's no one in the rooms directly on either side of them, and he has a feeling the receptionist is purposefully spacing everyone out. Probably so he doesn't have to deal with any noise complaints, especially when there are so few people here. In the rooms that *are* occupied, he mostly hears the sounds of the television playing. Through one door, he can hear the sound of a man and woman loudly fucking. A few doors on he hears similar sounds, but this time, it sounds like two men.

At the end of the row he turns to his left, goes down the side of the building and to the back of it. To the embankment. Leaning over, pressing his weight to a tree, he still can't see to the bottom of it. It's too dark down there now. What little daylight remains does not penetrate so deep. He hears running water, though. Faint, but it's there.

He keeps moving. The rooms are raised, and he can't see into them through their windows, though most of them have their curtains closed anyway. If he wanted to climb in, however, it wouldn't be impossible.

The sounds of the fucking are louder on this side, so close to the windows. One of them, the man and the woman, have their window open a crack. Tom sneaks by, not wanting to make any noise and disturb their privacy. He passes his and Taylor's room soon after and finds that she has closed the curtains. He continues on, returns to the main building, to the vending machines. He isn't sure what Taylor likes, so he grabs some of everything. He returns to their room and struggles to make the knock with his hands and arms full, but he manages well enough that Taylor opens the door a crack and peers out. She's got his Beretta in her hand, pointing it at his chest. She lowers it when she sees it's him.

Tom grins. "That's good," he says.

She grunts and lets him into the room, then relocks the door after him. She returns to the spot on the bed she was occupying before he left.

"You hungry?" Tom says.

She nods, and Tom lays the snacks out before her. He sits down on the opposite bed and opens a bottle of water, takes a long drink. Hydrated, he picks up a chocolate bar and starts eating. "You wanna shower?" he says. "I'm back now."

Taylor shakes her head. It's like she's reverted back to the defensive silence she earlier exhibited in the car, but this time, he thinks it's because she's tired. Her day has probably been longer than his.

"I don't think I'm gonna bother either," he says. His reason being, though he doesn't share this with Taylor, that he doesn't want to be caught unaware if someone comes knocking.

Because those men found them on the road. Somehow, they caught up to them and ran them to ground. This in itself wouldn't be such a surprise, except it was a different group of men than the ones Tom had originally had the run-in with at the gas station. And, since then, Tom and Taylor have changed vehicles. He ponders this, then sees how Taylor is still playing with the remote control, pushing it around on the bed, but she hasn't turned the television on.

"You wanna watch something?" he says.

She shakes her head. "I took a look while you were out," she says, speaking now that she has some food and liquid inside her. "There wasn't anything on." She keeps staring at the remote and pushing it around. Her face is obscured by her hood. "Can I ask you something?" she says suddenly, turning to him.

"Sure," Tom says.

"Why do you have so many phones? In your bag."

Tom grins. "It's an old habit. You know what a burner phone is?"

"I think so. Drug dealers use them, don't they?" Her eyes widen momentarily. "Are you a drug dealer? Is that why you stopped working for the government?"

He laughs. "No. Far from it. They're so you can make calls, but they can't be traced back to you. Well, they *can*, but it takes a lot of time and effort, and the phone has usually been disposed of by the time anyone's able to track it down. Most of the phones in there have never been used. They're just in case I need them."

"I noticed a couple of them had names on them," she says.

"That's right," Tom says. "So if I notice I have a missed call on that particular phone, then I know a particular person has been trying to get in touch with me. And the only reason anyone would try to get in touch with me is if it was an emergency."

"Who's Cindy?" she says. "Your girlfriend?"

Tom smiles, thinking of Cindy. He hasn't spoken to her in a long while now, not since Arizona. Since she effectively saved his life. He's kept meaning to reach out, to touch base, but he can either never find the time, or a reason good enough to impose upon her when he has so much already. He alternates about feeling guilty for not reaching out, and telling himself that he doesn't need to waste her time. "Cindy is a friend. Did you go through all my things?"

"No, I was just grabbing the gun, and I dragged that phone out with it by accident. When I was putting it back, I noticed a couple others had tape with stuff written on them, like hers."

Tom wonders if she saw the picture of Alejandra, but she's too polite to mention it. Wonders if she thought Alejandra was Cindy.

He finishes his bottle of water and waits while she eats. She doesn't eat much. She reverts to pushing the control around on the bed. Tom clears his throat. Sits forward with his hands clasped. "I wanna talk," he says. "That all right with you?"

Taylor looks up, frowning. "We've already been talking, haven't we?"

"I mean about serious stuff," Tom says. "I wanna ask you some questions, and I want you to answer me truthfully. No half-truths, no lies by omission – just the full story. Because I'm starting to think you're still holding out on me."

Taylor tries to hold his gaze, but she can't.

"What kind of business is your stepfather involved in, Taylor?" Tom says.

She doesn't answer. She looks down at her hands. The control has been pushed away now. She's gone back to scratching and squeezing at her hands, like she was back in the car.

"The best way for me to be able to help you is if you tell me the truth," Tom says.

Taylor takes a deep breath. Tom hears how it shudders all the way down into her lungs, like she's about to cry. She doesn't, though.

"What's he involved in that he's able to call upon so many men to help him find you?" Tom says. "The eight men back there in the woods were not the same men who had you at the gas station. Not one of them."

She closes her eyes, her jaw set.

"I need to know what I'm up against, Taylor."

Seconds pass in silence, ticking by, feeling longer than they are.

With a sigh, she relents. "Ken came around soon after my dad checked out. That was about six years ago, now. Ken seemed like a good guy at first. At least, I thought so. Josh never did, but Josh is older, and maybe he saw all the things I didn't because I was still too hung up on my dad leaving us, and I missed him so much, and I knew Mom did, too, and I just wanted her to be happy. And if this Ken guy made her happy, then that was all that really mattered, right?"

She pauses, but it's not so Tom can answer the question. He waits while she gathers herself, straightens her thoughts.

"Josh was already seeing Tilly then. It was like Ken moved in, and he moved out. All the way to fucking Oregon. That's where Tilly's from. Her family was still there, and she wanted to be closer to them. They'd met online, she and my brother, and she'd moved to Belleville to be closer to him. She had her own place and everything, but she just got homesick. So, anyway, they moved away, and it was just me and Mom, left alone with Ken. The bad stuff… That didn't start straight away. Ken was careful about it. He's not stupid."

She pauses, starts picking through the snacks and drinks again. She settles on a can of soda. Tom leaves her to it. Waits patiently while she opens the tab and takes a short drink. She holds it in both hands, looks down at it. "Ken was – *is* – a member of a church. A megachurch. It's called the Temple of St. Philomena. You heard of it?"

"No," Tom says.

"We'd heard of it. It's pretty big in Belleville, maybe through the whole state. I'm not sure. We had a different church. We used to go to that one every Sunday, but Ken insisted we join the Temple. Mom and I. He said it would be good for us – for all of us. He said it would be good for *me*, like I was some kind of wild child or something. I wasn't. I'd never done anything wrong. But Mom agreed with him, because she was happy, and she wanted to keep Ken happy. He talked her into it. He made it sound so good, like something so special. So we started going every Sunday. And it was…fine. It was church, you know? It was just this thing that we did, a new part of our routine. I remember talking to Josh on the phone, back when I still had a phone and I was still allowed to make calls. Josh was never much for religion, and I could pretty much hear him roll his eyes down the phone.

"After a while, Ken started to insist that I take part in the extracurricular classes held at the church, too. At first, it was every Sunday afternoon, after sermon. Then it became every Monday, Wednesday, and Friday evening. The classes were big. We were separated into boys and girls. We never saw each other. The girls' classes, sometimes they were overseen by the pastor of the church, and..." She trails off. Takes another drink. Tom notices how her face has twisted. How her lower lip is trembling. She doesn't cry, though. She holds the tears in. "Laurence Morgan. He's the pastor. He runs the Temple of St. Philomena. He...he took a shine to me. And Ken was pleased about that. *Very* pleased. And then, pretty soon after, it became clear why Ken had been so insistent on us joining his church. So insistent on me going to all those extracurricular classes."

Her hands are wrapped around the soda can. They're shaking. She takes another drink, drains it off, and then she squeezes the can. Crushes it. There's a brief flash of her teeth. She's breathing hard through her nose. "So then Ken started taking me along for extra 'lessons,' and he was telling my mom how it was doing me a world of good. And I was made to tell my mom how it was doing me a world of good, and how much I enjoyed all the extra attention. So Mom was all for it. She was happy to hear it. And she'd let Ken take me along, multiple times a week, and he'd leave me alone for hours with Laurence."

Tom grits his teeth. He balls his fists, but he doesn't say anything.

Taylor twists the crushed can. Breaks it. "There were other girls, too. They were about my age. Fourteen, fifteen, something like that. But those girls weren't for Laurence. I was the only one for Laurence. The other girls, they'd get bussed in from this care home. An orphanage, I guess. They'd get brought to the church, and they'd be passed around. To other men of the church, I mean – high-up members, like Ken. I think that whoever runs the home, they must know what's happening, right? They must be in on it. Maybe they're high up in the church, too. Maybe they go to take their pick.

"Anyway, it wasn't at the church. They didn't come to the church for this. It would look too weird if they did. People would get suspicious. So we'd be taken on these little trips, to this place that Laurence owns outside of town. Businessmen, councilmen, men of influence, they'd all be there. For them, it wasn't like with me and Laurence – Laurence wouldn't let anyone else touch me, but for those other girls, those orphan girls, they got passed around, everyone got to take a turn with them. I'm sure some of them had favorites – *have* favorites – but they weren't so precious. And the Ogre would always be there, too. He'd watch over things. Make sure everyone behaved themselves. The other kids, they were all scared of him. I...*I* was scared of him... I still am.

"Some of the men – those big important men who kept the church safe, who kept everything quiet and made sure nothing ever came back on Laurence, that nothing bad ever happened to him – some of them liked boys, too. I never saw any of the boys, though, because it was like the classes. They kept us all separate. I heard about it, though. And sometimes I could hear them crying. I heard so much crying, and other times I could only hear my own."

With a jagged edge of the broken can, she cuts herself across the back of her left hand before Tom can do anything about it. She presses the sharp edge of the metal to her skin and drags it down. A line of bright red blood forms. When the cut is complete, she presses the can back to her hand, about to cut herself again. Tom reaches out. He places a hand softly on her own. She looks up at him, and she's shaking. There are tears in her eyes. Tom takes the can from her and puts it out of reach.

"I've heard enough," Tom says.

Taylor hears him, but she continues. "Ken told me I couldn't tell anyone. He made that very clear. He said that if anyone found out, bad things would happen. I thought he meant that bad things would happen to me, and I almost laughed, because what could they do that was worse, right? But that wasn't what he meant at all. He told me something would happen to my mom. So I kept my mouth shut, and I didn't tell anyone. And it kept happening, and it kept happening, and it went on for years. And Laurence, he liked to talk to me, too. He treated me like I was...like I was his girlfriend. He'd stroke my hair and my face and tell me how he'd marry me one day, and he'd ask me, would I like that? And it didn't matter that I never answered. I never answered because I was too scared that whatever I said would be wrong, or that he'd know I was lying, and then something bad would happen to my mom.

"A couple of years ago, my mom...died. She...she killed herself. Hanged herself. I thought maybe that it was the bad thing happening that Ken had warned about, but if it hadn't been suicide, the police would have investigated, right? Something would have come to light. But nothing did. I thought it was my fault – it was the bad thing Ken had warned me about, but I'd never told anyone. I couldn't understand. She just...she just killed herself. All of a sudden, she was gone.

"Josh and Tilly came back for the funeral, and they wanted to take me to Oregon with them, but Ken wouldn't let them. Said I had school in Belleville, and 'friends,' that my life was here. And plus, as my mom's widower, he was my legal guardian. That had all been put into writing before she died. So I was stuck in Belleville. But it wasn't for school or for my friends because Ken took me out of school. Said he was going to homeschool me, but all he was doing really was isolating me. Keeping me locked up in my room, away from everyone I ever knew. They couldn't threaten me with my mom anymore, so they had to keep me locked up. I didn't spend all that much time with Ken though, not really. He dumped me with Laurence whenever Laurence wasn't at church. With my mom out of the way, there wasn't any reason for all the sneaking around. I was with him nearly every night. He told me that when I turned seventeen, he was going to marry me."

"Is that the legal age in Washington?"

"I guess so." Taylor shrugs. "I didn't look into it. I just assumed, who could stop him, right? No one has so far." She looks at Tom. "He hides it well, but he's insane. He's fucking deranged. He said that after we were married, we'd have sons together. So many sons. He said he knows they'll be boys because he's prayed for it, and because God has listened. Because he's God's chosen one. We'll have seven sons, and they'll all do great things, because *he* is great, because *he* is chosen – because *he* is God's elect." She shakes her head and watches the blood drying on the back of her hand. She scratches the back of her neck. "I've tried to get away a few times before. They've always caught me. Usually it's the Ogre who comes. I guess he was getting bored of it, so he sent Ken this time. I've never gotten this far away." She chews her lip, scratches the back of her neck again. "I won't go back," she says, shaking her head. "I won't let them take me back, not to him. If they ever catch me again, I'll – I'll kill myself. He can't have me anymore. I'd rather die."

The tears have come, now. They're rolling down her cheeks.

"It won't come to that, Taylor," Tom says. Inside, he feels a fire burning. It's hard to speak through his gritted teeth. "I won't let them take you back. That's a promise."

Taylor doesn't respond to what he's said. She scratches

viciously at the back of her neck, fed up with the persistent itch. She pulls her hood further over her face. "I'm tired," she says. "I think I want to sleep now."

"Sure." Tom gets to his feet. "I'm gonna take another look around outside."

Taylor lies down and turns onto her side, her back to him. She's still wearing her sneakers.

Tom turns and leaves the room. He locks the door after himself and slips the key into his pocket. He looks the parking lot over. He's going to sweep the area again, this is true, but he needed to leave the room to catch his breath. To feel the night air. And, most importantly, to hide his anger from Taylor. The story she has told him has set his nerves on edge. He feels sick. His fists are balled, but he can't get them tight enough.

He leans back against the wall and takes deep breaths. Composes himself. Feels the Taurus pressing into his lower back. It's getting dark now, but there is still some blue in the sky. He checks the immediate area over and then starts walking.

18

Laurence calls Ken. It takes a while to get through. Ken sounds tired and pained when he finally answers. "Where are you, Kenneth?" Laurence says. He doesn't have any sympathy for Ken's pain.

"I just got home," Ken says, sighing, sounding like he's just collapsed into a chair. "I've been to the hospital. Has Bill told you? I had to get Gil to come and pick me up, bring me home."

"Come to me."

There's a pause. "Where are you?"

"I'm at home."

"Is it...is it necessary? Can't we just talk over the phone? I'm – I'm very tired, Mr. Morgan. My arm – it's really in pain. I've taken some painkillers, but it doesn't feel like they're doing much."

It's Laurence's turn to pause. It's a heavy, pregnant pause. He draws it out until he can practically *feel* how Ken is squirming. "I want to speak to you face-to-face," Laurence says finally. "The phone will not do, no."

There's a dry clicking sound. Ken, swallowing. "Okay," he

says, sounding dry. "I'll come along now. I'll have to call Gil back, get him to drive me. He shouldn't have gotten too far."

"Good," Laurence says. "Then I'll see you soon." He hangs up.

He's in his living room. It's a large room, two large sofas, a reading chair in the corner, and a widescreen television on the wall that could pass for a small cinema screen. The room is filled with ornate, antique ornaments – vases, bowls, bronze women in poses – and on the walls are various paintings in the Renaissance style of different stages in the life of Jesus Christ. The rest of the house is equally as large and as plushly decorated. It is the biggest house in Belleville. The biggest house for many surrounding counties. This is not the only property that Laurence owns, either, but most people don't know about the compound he keeps on the outskirts of the town, or what goes on there.

He's worked for this house and for everything else he owns. Laurence Morgan came from nothing. He grew up in a backwoods town in the South that no one has ever heard of, and life there was *hard*. A daily grind of menial, backbreaking labor out in either fields or factories. Laurence knew from a young age that it was not the kind of life for him. It wasn't the kind of place he wanted to spend his days, either. Nothing there. Nothing to see or do. Just the endless monotony of the working days, each blending into the last and the next.

Family and peers picked up on his attitude. They called him lazy, work-shy. They saw how cold and aloof he was, how he thought he was better than everyone else, and they pushed him around and gave him a hard time for it. But was that supposed to be Laurence's problem? The truth of the matter was that he simply *was* better than them all. He couldn't be guilty of a simple fact. They were resigned to their humdrum lives, whereas he had greater ambitions.

Laurence got out as soon as he could save up enough for

a bus ticket. The furthest he could get from his one-horse town was Aberdeen, Washington. Enjoying his freedom, Laurence spent a lot of his time in bars. He'd get drunk, and he'd find women to fuck. Talking his way into their pants wasn't difficult. He'd always been able to talk to women. Back where he came from, the one thing people never accused him of being lazy at was chasing tail. And his success rate was high.

However, getting drunk and seducing women didn't pay the bills. Finding a job, however, was not high on Laurence's list of priorities. He didn't *want* to work. Didn't want to break his back for someone else's benefit. And, as unqualified as he was, unskilled labor was all that was available to him.

Then, one Sunday morning a couple of years into his time in Aberdeen, things began to change. He woke up in the bed of a woman he couldn't remember the name of, and she was scrambling to get dressed. "Shit," she was saying over and over again.

Laurence rolled onto his back, rubbed his eyes. "What's the matter?" he said.

"I'm gonna be late for church," she said.

Laurence laughed, not sure if she was joking or not. "Church?" he said. "You wanna go to church after what *we* did last night?"

Still getting dressed, she raised her eyebrows at him. "Sin on Saturday, salvation on Sunday."

Laurence laughed. "I like that," he said. "That's good. Justify anything with that mindset."

"Don't need to justify anything. It's just a fact. God is forgiveness."

"That's good to hear."

"You should come with me," she said, almost fully dressed now. She went to her vanity table, put in some earrings.

Laurence considered the offer. Then he laughed. "No, I'm good."

She sat down on the edge of the bed. "You *should*," she said. "You'll feel good for it, I promise."

Laurence chuckled, shook his head.

"Come on, I'll buy you breakfast after."

Laurence considered *this*. "All right," he said. "Pass my jeans."

That was the day Laurence's life changed.

The woman – he still can't remember her name despite her relative importance – took him to her church. Except, it wasn't the kind of church Laurence was expecting. It wasn't a large stone building with spires and bells. It was more like the churches back where he came from. A small room. More like a rec center. The seats weren't pews. They were plastic chairs. The preacher wasn't in long white robes. He wore black jeans and a denim shirt. He talked to the people. He laughed and joked.

And then, when the collection plate was passed around, the people reached *deep*. The plate was filled. Laurence only had a couple of dollars on him. He felt obliged to hand them over. As he did so, he quickly calculated how much money was on the plate in crumpled bills. There had to be at least a couple of hundred, and it wasn't finished going around the room.

That was more than a week's wages. And, presumably, the preacher only needed to do this every Sunday morning. Maybe Sunday evening, too. Maybe he had a couple of gatherings through the week. Every time, every single time, the collection plate would be passed around, and the people present would dig deep.

Laurence pondered on this. He thought on it, long and hard, unable to concentrate on the rest of the sermon. He looked around the room, at the other people present. None of them looked particularly affluent. They looked just like him – like they spent every day, every week, and every month scrambling for change to pay bills, pay rent, feed themselves. They wore old jeans, checkered shirts stained with food, or oil, sometimes both. Tattered baseball caps. And every available dollar they had, they dropped into the collection plate. Gave to this man, this preacher, who they believed was one of God's representatives on Earth. A man who could redeem them.

Sin on Saturday, salvation on Sunday.

Laurence hung around after it was over, breakfast forgotten. The woman waited by the door, but she was forgotten, too. Laurence approached the preacher as he pulled on his jacket. Everyone else was waiting for him outside, to thank him, to shake his hand. Laurence had no interest in waiting.

"I just wanted to thank you for the sermon, sir," he said, gripping his hand and shaking it hard. "It was...it was *illuminating*."

The preacher smiled at him. "Well, thank you, son." He called Laurence *son*, but at most, he could only have been about five years older.

"I mean that, sir. It's really opened my eyes to a lot of things," Laurence said.

"I don't think I've seen you here before, son," the preacher said.

"First time," Laurence said. "A friend brought me along. I'm glad she did. May I – may I ask you a question?"

"Of course." The preacher was smiling. He was a friendly guy. He thought he'd reached someone, opened their eyes to God, put them on the right path. Thought he'd gained a new member of his flock. Someone new to fill his coffers a little fuller each week. Laurence was more than happy to let him think this if it got him the answers he wanted.

"I was just curious," Laurence said, "since you found your calling from the Lord, is this all you do?"

The preacher cocked his head, not understanding the question.

"I mean, have you been able to devote yourself full time to your cause, or do you have to hold down a day job at the same time?"

"That's an interesting question."

"I'm just curious if you're able to devote yourself as fully to the Lord as I'm sure you want to."

"Well," the preacher said, "when I first started following my calling, I did unfortunately have to remain a slave to the daily wage race. Mostly, it was so I was able to rent the halls where I'd preach, but over time the people found their way to me, and I've become very fortunate. Now I can devote my days to prayer and contemplation, and when Sunday comes, I'm able to share what I've found with the people who come to see me."

Laurence thought on this. Renting a hall? There had to be a way around that when starting out. When money wasn't as readily available. Somewhere free. A street corner, maybe. Even a fucking field, like with the revival tents. But would people come to a field without a tent?

"I hope I'll see you back here next week, son?" the preacher said, ready to leave.

Laurence snapped back to reality. He smiled. "Oh, you can count on it," he said. And he meant it. He'd be there every Sunday. He still had a lot to learn. And when the time came, he'd strike out on his own, because finally, at last, Laurence knew what he was going to do with his life.

He was going to be a preacher. Didn't matter what denomination. Hell, he'd make up his own.

He was going to be a preacher so he wouldn't have to work.

Well, there was *some* work involved, but it was far better than the laboring or slinging-fast-food jobs that awaited him otherwise. He invested in himself. Bought fancy clothes and got good haircuts. Worked on his accent. His Southern charm might work out in the sticks, but here, he'd need to be more refined. And, as it turned out, he could turn his gift of gab to more than just getting into women's pants. He could use it to get everything he wanted.

And he did. Women. Possessions. A church of his own. And more than that – alcohol, drugs. Every deviant taste he had ever dreamed of, it was his for the taking, and people would *give* it to him. People wanted nothing more than to please him.

Except, along the way, something happened. Something special.

He was *chosen*.

God spoke to him. God told him he was special. God told him that, out of all his representatives on Earth, *he* was the one who meant the most to Him. He was the one with a mission and who would accomplish great things.

The truth came to him in a dream at the end of a three-day bender. High on cocaine and acid, drunk on vodka, he passed out. When he came around, lying on the floor with his head propped against the sofa, a girl was leaning over him, offering him something. "What is it?" he said.

"Peyote." She grinned. "Make sure you chew it."

Laurence was in the habit of taking whatever was offered to him. He chewed it and passed back out.

In his sleep, he was visited by a blinding light, and he knew what it was. What it meant. He understood clearly what it said to him in a language no one else could understand. It was God, and God was speaking to him.

Laurence devoted the next couple of weeks to fasting and prayer, in an effort to get back to God. To hear His voice again. To converse with the Lord. He had been chosen. He, Laurence Morgan, despite his doubts, despite his true intent only ever to make money with the least exertion possible, was God's elect.

Fasting and prayer didn't bring God back to him, though. So Laurence turned back to peyote. It did the trick. It opened the pathway needed. God returned. God told him everything he wanted and needed to hear.

Then, many years later, the day came when he first saw Taylor. He'd been through others already, others like her, but none of them were right. She was the one. The one he'd been waiting for. The one sent from God. He'd never seen a girl more beautiful. He saw her sitting behind her desk, watching the tutor at the front of the classroom, and then it was as if God reached down and touched a finger to her forehead. She was all in light. Laurence understood. *She* was the one. The other half of his whole.

Laurence looks around his room. Thinks about the rest of his home. He came from nothing, and now he has everything. He has all of *this*. Thanks to God. It was a long route to get to where he needed to be, and he started out with the wrong intentions. But he wasn't the first to do so. Even the saints and the apostles were misguided before God came to them. St. Paul springs to mind. Matthew, the tax collector.

Right now, what Laurence wants – what he wants *back* – more than anything is Taylor Hendricks. The chosen one. His other half.

His doorbell rings. Laurence checks the time. He's been lost in his memories for longer than he realized.

His staff have gone home for the evening, and Laurence is alone. He has to answer the door himself. He checks the security camera pointing at the front door before he answers. It's Ken and Gil. Ken's arm is in a sling. Laurence answers, motions him inside. "Wait in the car," he tells Gil.

Gil obliges. Doesn't spare Ken a single glance as he turns and goes back to where he has parked his car in the driveway. It's clear he thinks Ken is about to get into trouble, and he doesn't want any part of it.

He's not wrong. Laurence is not happy with Ken.

Ken hovers in the hallway, not sure where to go.

"Dining room," Laurence says, pointing.

The table in the dining room is long. It seats twelve. Laurence takes a seat at the head of it and motions for Ken to take the chair on his left. Ken does so. He sits very meekly, his knees pressed together. Laurence reclines, regards Ken from his leaned-back position. "So," he begins. He lets the word hang in the air. Ken cannot look at him. With his left hand, he strokes his broken arm. "What do you have to say for yourself?"

Ken stops stroking his arm. He looks at the ground.

"There aren't any answers down there," Laurence says. "Look at me."

Ken does so reluctantly. "I'm sorry," he says, his voice very small, close to breaking.

"Sorry isn't good enough, Kenneth." Laurence sits forward. "She's at my place for almost two weeks, and there are no issues. The first night she is returned to you, she escapes." Laurence stares. Ken shifts uncomfortably. "Have you grown lax, Kenneth?"

"I don't know what happened," Ken says. "I don't know how she was able to get out..."

"You don't?"

"I mean –"

"You haven't searched her room to find out how this happened?" Laurence knows he has. Laurence knows exactly how she got out, just as Ken does.

"She got out the window," Ken says, defeated. "She'd been working at the lock. I...I don't know how I missed it."

"Carelessness," Laurence says. "*That's* how you missed it. You should have been checking her room every morning and evening. There should have been *no* chance she could have escaped. I pay you enough money, Kenneth. I paid off your mortgage, didn't I? What else do you need to spend your money on? I certainly pay you enough to up your security if need be. You *know* how much she means to me, Kenneth. You know how important she is to me. To all of us. To the future of the Temple of St. Philomena. Together we'll begin a dynasty of seven sons who will keep the Temple alive, who will ensure its future and its prominence. None of this happens without her."

"I understand," Ken says, head lowered. "I'm sorry. I'm *so* sorry..." It sounds like he's crying.

Laurence grunts. "Look at me, Kenneth."

Ken does. He wipes his face.

"This will never happen again, will it?"

Ken shakes his head. "No. I promise. I won't ever be so careless again."

"Good," Laurence says. "I believe you, Kenneth. That's why I needed you here. You can say anything on the phone. I needed to look into your eyes and see the truth for myself."

Ken nods. He understands.

Laurence sits back, waves his hand. "Now that admonishments and apologies are out of the way, we can turn our attention to more constructive things. Bill is out there now, Bill and all his men, and I have no doubt that they will bring Taylor back to me. *But*, just as Bill always says, we have to be prepared for every outcome, don't we? Taylor and her new friend have managed to avoid recapture so far today. We need to think – if they're to slip through our net again, where could they be going? Where would Taylor go, Kenneth?"

"I've thought about this," Ken says. His face is bright now. He sees an opportunity to shine. "She'd go to Josh's. Her brother. I'm sure of it. It's the only place she *could* go. She doesn't have anyone else."

"It wouldn't be good if she were to reach him."

Ken shakes his head in agreement.

Laurence taps a perfectly manicured fingernail against his chin. "You need to call him, Kenneth. You need to talk to him."

"He doesn't like me," Ken says. "He won't listen."

"Then you need to *make* him listen. Do you understand? You have to call him, and you have to show concern, panic, make it clear to him that you are worried about his sister. That she just hasn't been herself lately. That you're concerned she's going to hurt herself. You have to tell him she's run away from home, and you're scared for her. You fear she's having a breakdown. She's been telling stories lately – such stories – and not a word of it is true. Do you understand? If she reaches her brother, we need him to tell us she is there. We need him to keep her there for us."

Ken bites his lip. He doesn't look so sure.

"I sense doubts, Kenneth."

"It's just – like I said, he hates me. He won't believe me."

"Then you're going to have to *make* him believe you, Kenneth. You said earlier you were sorry for what you did, correct? This is how you make it up to me."

"Bill will get them before they get anywhere near Oregon," Ken says. "I'm sure of it."

"And so am I," Laurence says. "But I'm sure that even Bill himself would agree that calling ahead is the best course of action. Preparation is half the battle. I'm sure I've heard him say that before, haven't you?"

Ken nods. "Okay," he says, relenting. "But it's late right now. I should wait until morning to call him."

"Very well," Laurence says. "That sounds agreeable. Come

the morning, we'll know if Bill has captured them. But if he hasn't, I'll find that to be cause for concern."

Ken nods.

Laurence stands, and Ken does the same. Laurence reaches out, places both hands upon his shoulders. He squeezes. "Don't let me down again, Kenneth."

"I won't," Ken says, with all the conviction he has.

Laurence pats him on the cheek. "Off you go, then," he says. "Rest that arm. It looks sore."

19

It's late when Bill hears back from Commander Lou Russo. "Speak to me," Bill says, answering the call. Bill doesn't have much patience for preamble. He's been in his car for hours now, and his body is tightening up. He's sore. He's been pulled to the side of the road for a half hour, though, but he's yet to have gotten out of the vehicle.

"I'll tell you what I've got," Lou says, "but I'm not sure how much of it you haven't already heard."

Lou fills him in on Tom Rollins's backstory. It ends abruptly, with some heroics in Afghanistan.

Bill waits. Nothing follows. "And then what?" he says, expectant.

"And then his file gets *heavily* redacted."

"And that's everything?"

"Everything I could find officially. I asked around, called some people I know. There's some hints he's done work for the CIA, but nothing concrete. You know how that sounds, right?"

"Special Forces," Bill says, intrigued. "Black ops, more than likely."

"Uh-huh," Lou says. "That's what I thought, too. He goes off grid for a few years, and then, whenever he seems to have popped up since then, the information has either been redacted again, or the details are too fuzzy to make sense of."

"That's interesting," Bill says.

"Yeah, it is, but I get the feeling it doesn't help you out all that much."

"It helps me enough," Bill says. "I know he's dangerous, well trained, and I need to be careful."

"Sounds that way," Lou says.

"I'll be sure to keep it in mind. Thanks for the help, Lou."

"Any time. Sorry it took a while. Whatever it is he's done to upset you, whatever part of your business it is that he's got himself involved in, be careful, Bill."

"Always am. I'll be in touch soon, Lou. Been good talking to you. It's been too long."

Bill hangs up, thinking over what Lou has told him. He smirks to himself. He looks forward to seeing what Tom Rollins can do in person.

He turns his head, looks over the road from where he is parked and across the parking lot bathed in the neon sign of the motel. He looks to the room where he knows Tom and Taylor are right now. They can't escape him. His men are ready to move in. In a few minutes, he'll be getting into position, too.

Soon, very soon, he'll have them both.

20

Taylor has been drifting in and out of sleep, but now she's awake. It's still dark. She's not sure what time it is, but she thinks it's late. She stays on her side, turned toward the wall. She tries to close her eyes, she tries to sleep, but sleep doesn't want to come. Her mind races. Remembering what she told Tom. She told him the truth. She told him everything. She never thought she'd share that with anyone. Not even Josh. Not even Tilly. Not more than they needed to know, anyway.

She chews on the skin around the edges of her thumbnail. She can taste blood. She probes the thin cut on the back of her left hand. Traces the line of it. She picks at it. Smears blood across the back of her hand.

"You awake?"

She freezes. It's Tom's voice. She thought he was asleep. After he came back from his sweep, while she pretended to be sleeping, he turned off the lights and lay down on the bed. He hasn't moved since. Not that she's been awake the whole time to know for sure, though. She stops moving now. Pretends to be asleep again. She doesn't answer him.

"If you're awake," Tom says, "and wonder where I'm going, I'm just doing another sweep."

Taylor doesn't respond. Doesn't turn to him. She can't. She can't face him. Not after all that she's told him. She knows he'll look at her different now. Think different of her. See her as what she is – broken. Defiled. Worthless.

So she pretends to be asleep.

Tom leaves the room. He locks the door. When he's gone, Taylor rolls onto her back. She sighs, presses her hands into her eyes.

She believes Tom. Believes him when he says he'll get her to Portland, to her brother, and that he won't let them take her back to Laurence, or Ken. But that doesn't change how he'll see her. What he'll think. It'll be better when they get back on the road. They can travel in silence. Taylor can hide her face behind her hood. He can drop her off, and that'll be it. It'll be over. Tom will have done what he's said he will, and he can go on his way, guilt-free, and forget all about her.

Taylor doesn't think she'll get back to sleep tonight, or this morning – whatever time it is. There's too much racing through her head. Having told her story, what has happened to her and what they did to her, saying it out loud has brought it all back. In the past, she tried not to think about it. To pretend like it hadn't happened, even when she was in the middle of it. But now it's vocalized. It's out in the open. Another person knows. Her life story has been certified. There's no coming back from it now, and every conscious thought takes her back to Laurence. Lying beside her. Behind her. On top of her.

She scratches roughly at the back of her neck. The itch is always in the same spot. She can't shake it. She squeezes it, sure it must be a pimple. Nothing comes out. If it *is* a pimple, it isn't fully formed yet. And still it persists. She's starting to think it's a bug bite. When she gets to Josh's, she might have to get it checked out.

She hears movement outside the room. Right on the other side of the door. It must be Tom, back so soon. There mustn't be much to see out there. It's late, after all. And the motel is on a back road, out of the way. Likely situated on what used to be a highly used road before a highway was put in nearby, bypassing everything in this area.

Something scrapes in the lock. It keeps scraping. It doesn't sound like a key. It doesn't slide into place, find its grooves, and smoothly turn. It's searching.

Someone is trying to pick the lock.

For a moment, Taylor lies frozen. Out of the corner of her eye, she stares at the door, expecting it to be thrown open, for a multitude of dark, shadowy figures to come bursting into the room, to swoop upon her, scoop her up, take her away from this place. To take her back. Back to Belleville. To *him*.

Taylor manages to snap herself back to reality. She moves. Rolls to her left, off the bed, and lands on the floor with a thud she hopes isn't as loud as it sounds in her ears. She scurries under the bed and presses herself as flat as she can. It's dark in the room, but as soon as whoever it is gets inside, they'll turn on the lights. She won't be hidden for long.

She can see under the other bed, Tom's bed, straight to the door. She stares at it, breathing hard, feeling her heartbeat rise, waiting for it to open. Whatever is in the lock is still scraping, still searching for purchase. Taylor tries to calm herself. To steady her breathing before they enter. She gulps down air. She wonders where Tom is. Wonders how he didn't see these people on his sweep.

The door opens. Taylor clamps her mouth shut. She holds her breath. The sound of her heart, the rushing of her blood, is pounding in her ears. She lies as still as she can. Two sets of legs enter the room. Two men. They don't talk.

Don't whisper. They stand within the doorframe, and she can imagine them looking the room over, getting their bearings. They stay in the dark for now. They're probably looking at both of the beds, wondering why they're empty.

One of them chuckles. Taylor's heart skips a beat. She wonders if some part of herself is visible. If they've spotted the tip of a sneaker poking out from under the bedframe. Surely not – surely they aren't close enough.

The light is turned on. Taylor winces against it. Braces herself. Soon they'll have her. A meaty hand will grab her by the ankle, drag her out from under the bed. It won't be gentle. In fact, it will revel in hurting her. It will hope she bangs the back of her head against the frame on her way out.

A third pair of legs appears in the doorway, behind the two men. They move fast and silent, and Taylor almost missed them coming. She hears a loud crack, and then one of the men crumples, hits the ground on his side. Taylor can see his face. She doesn't recognize him. His eyes are closed, grimacing. He reaches weakly to the back of his head, blood pouring from a wound there.

The other man is muffled, his legs start kicking, but not for long. He goes limp. He's dropped, too, and Taylor doesn't recognize his face, either.

She looks at the third pair of legs, though. The jeans and the boots, and these she recognizes.

Tom.

She drags herself out from under the bed. As she pushes herself up, the window behind and above her is smashed. The closed curtains catch the breaking glass. It tinkles harmlessly on the carpet directly below. Arms start pushing through the curtain. Someone is climbing in from the outside.

Tom has seen it, too. He runs to the window, kicks the figure forming in the curtains back outside. He turns to her, reaches out his hand. Taylor takes it. He hauls her to her feet, then wraps an arm around her waist and lifts her up. "There's more coming," he says. He tears open the curtain and hauls them both up into the frame. The man he kicked back through it is lying on the ground, holding his back. There's another man directly below the window, still standing where he boosted the other guy up. Tom stomps down into the center of the still standing man's face, crushes his nose, then pulls his leg back and kicks him in the side of the head, knocks him down.

There's noise at the door behind them, coming into the motel. Taylor looks. More men are coming into the room. Four of them. Before she has a chance to turn back around, Tom has leapt from the window with her in tow. They land on the fallen man he kicked in the face. The man cries out at the impact. Taylor hears something crunch. Tom lets go of her.

"Down the embankment," he says. "Through the trees, into the dark." Tom's head snaps to the side then, down to the end of the row of motel rooms.

Before Taylor can look to see what has caught his attention, the man who was kicked out the window is struggling back to his feet. Tom grabs him, spins with him. Taylor hears small explosions. Blood bursts out of the back of the man Tom has grabbed, whom he's shielding them both with. Taylor looks to the end of the row. It's the Ogre. He sees her.

He's smiling at her.

Tom drops the corpse, pulls a handgun from the back of his jeans. He returns fire. The Ogre ducks back behind the corner. Tom grabs Taylor, and they start running. Down the embankment, through the trees, into the darkness, like he said. Taylor can't see anything. They're moving so fast she almost stumbles. It happens more than once. Tom keeps her upright. He guides the way, and she does her best to stay close. She notices he has his backpack on. She wonders when he slung it on his back. If he maybe left the motel room with it when she was pretending to be asleep. She wonders if he left prepared – if he knew the men were coming. That they were moving in. He wanted to get the drop on them. He did seem to return to the room very abruptly, just as she needed him.

They reach the bottom of the hill and skid to a stop. Taylor can hear water running. She blinks hard, trying to get her eyes to adjust to the dark. She finally sees the ravine.

Tom looks back up the hill. "They're coming," he says.

Taylor can't see anyone, but she can hear them.

"Into the water," Tom says. "It's moving fast. Try to stay close. Keep hold of me."

He looks at her, waits for her to respond. "Okay," Taylor says. She reaches out to him.

Tom takes her hand, laces his fingers through hers, then wraps an arm around her, and they dive into the water.

21

The water is fast-flowing. It doesn't take long to drag them away from the spot where they first jumped in.

Tom keeps hold of Taylor, holds tight, holds her close. He pushes her to the surface, out of the water, while he holds his breath. His lungs are burning.

They hit a bend, are thrown into the bank. Tom hits the back of his head against the dirt. His grip loosens. He feels Taylor slipping away, scrambles for her hand, for her body. She's out of his reach.

Tom breaks the surface, gasps for breath. He shouts Taylor's name.

"*Tom!*" Her response is faint.

He spots her, the current carrying her away. She battles to stay out of the water, but even as she called his name, he heard how she gurgled it.

Tom swims in her direction. He's a strong swimmer, and the current helps him move faster. The way Taylor flails against the water, struggling to keep her head above it, to breathe, manages to slow her down. They hit another bend, though, and it drags her under. Tom sees it happen. He grits his teeth and dives under the water, kicks his legs as hard as he can. Spots her through the murk. He pushes himself, gets close, gets so his fingertips are brushing her arm.

Then he has her. He's holding her and dragging her back to the surface. He wraps an arm around her from behind and holds her close, then swims to the side, to the bank, against the current. By the time he reaches it, everything hurts. His heart is hammering, and his lungs are straining. He reaches, struggles to find a purchase. There's nothing to grip. They continue to slide down, dragged by the water, until there's a bush, a root, and he grabs it.

His limbs are tired, and he can't lift them both out. It takes all his strength to keep hold of the root, to hold them into place. He sees how it's starting to tear out of the ground. There's a risk it's going to break, to tear loose in his hand, and he'll have to start all over again.

With a deep breath, he hauls Taylor onto the bank. She doesn't scramble away. She's not moving. This worries Tom. It panics him into some newfound reserves of strength. He drags himself out of the water, clawing at the wet dirt. He gets onto the ground, but he can't stop, can't catch his breath. He scurries straight to Taylor on hands and knees, rolls her onto her back.

She's not breathing.

Tom commences CPR. Thankfully, it doesn't take long. She rolls onto her side, coughing, then vomiting the water out of her lungs. She falls back and gasps, running a hand up her face and brushing the wet hair out of her eyes.

Tom drops onto his haunches, composes himself. He looks back the way they've come, the way they were carried. They're far from the motel now. He looks around. There's no longer a hill. Just trees, woodland, as far as he can see. No sign of a road. The men are no doubt back on their trail, but he doubts they'll have thrown themselves in the water after them. They'll either have continued down the embankment on foot, or they'll have returned to their vehicles. It's hard to tell where the nearest road is. If they have driven, they'll have to continue some of the way on foot.

"We need to keep moving," Tom says.

Taylor is coughing. She's still gasping for breath. She tries to push herself up, but she's weak. Her clothes are soaked through. She squelches when she moves. The water is dripping off her.

Tom gets to his feet. He offers his hand, and she takes it. He pulls her up, but she can't keep her balance. She coughs again. It's hard for her to take a full breath. She bends over, hands on her knees, wheezing. She vomits again, and this time it's bile, filled with the partially dissolved remnants of the candy she earlier ate.

Tom wants to keep moving. He doesn't think they're far enough away to be comfortable, but it's evident that Taylor is unable. She needs to rest. She needs a chance for her clothes to dry, too, or else she's at risk of hypothermia.

"Can you walk?" he says.

Taylor tries to answer, but she can barely talk.

"I'm gonna carry you," he says. "We'll rest for a while, but I want to get us away from here, away from the water. If they catch us up, this is where they'll look for us."

Taylor nods. He scoops her up in his arms and carries her through the wood, looking for a suitable place to take shelter. He spots a high mound of earth, a fallen tree behind it. It will provide adequate cover, and it's far enough away from the water. He goes to it, sets Taylor down. She's breathing better now. Not coughing anymore. Not sounding like she's constantly about to either throw up or pass out.

"Rest," Tom says. "I'm going to start a fire. We'll warm up, dry our clothes, and then we'll move on."

Taylor nods, propping herself up with her back against the mound of earth. Slowly, she lets herself slide to the ground. She takes deep breaths, filling her lungs.

Tom gathers firewood and moss. He searches through his bag, rummaging in its lower depths until he finds a lighter. He always tries to keep one handy. He can't remember where he picked this one up. Texas? Arizona? Maybe Mexico? It doesn't matter. He holds the flame to the moss until it takes. It's a small flame. Gently, he blows on it. The fire catches. It spreads. While it grows, he checks the rest of the contents of his bag. It has survived the wet. He bought it for its all-purpose capabilities, but this is the first time it has been submerged in water. He pulls out his Beretta. The Taurus was lost in the water. He tucks the Beretta into his waistband, in the Taurus's place. Keeps it close, should anyone find them.

The fire is burning well. He gathers up more wood to keep it going, then finds some stones they can lay their clothes on. He pulls a spare shirt out of his bag and hands it to Taylor. "Take your clothes off and put this on," he says. "It's big, and it'll probably fit you like a dress, but at least it's dry."

He turns his back to her and removes his own clothes, lays them down by the fire. When Taylor has undressed and put on his shirt, she does the same.

"Not too close," Tom says. "We don't want to burn them."

He puts his boots and her sneakers close to it, too.

"I'm gonna do a sweep," he says, not relishing the idea of walking through the woods barefoot. "Just to be sure we're safe here."

Taylor nods and returns to the mound.

Tom sets off, taking care where he steps. Avoiding protruding branches that could burst through the sole of his foot.

He makes it a quick sweep. He doesn't want to leave Taylor alone for long, especially not so soon after he's just had to resuscitate her. The area is clear. Save for a few small animals and birds in the tops of the trees, nothing makes a sound. He thinks about setting a trap, trying to catch something for them to eat, but his adrenaline is still high, and he isn't hungry. He imagines it's the same for Taylor. Besides that, he doesn't plan on hanging around here long enough to need to eat.

On his way back to their makeshift camp, he thinks on how the men keep finding them. They haven't left a trail, he's sure of it. Tom is always careful. Always covers his tracks, regardless of whether he thinks someone is trying to find him or not. But, despite changing vehicles, travelling on foot through woodland and changing up their routes to ensure they're not heading in a straight line, the men keep managing to find them.

Tom's brow is creased as he rounds the mound back into the camp. Taylor is still awake when he returns. She gives a start at the sight of him. "I didn't hear you," she says.

"Sorry," Tom says, imagining how the sight of an armed half-naked man appearing out of the woods must have momentarily made her feel. He goes to the fire and checks their clothes. The fronts are starting to dry. He turns them over to get the backs, then adds some more wood to the fire. "How you holding up?" he says, speaking to her over his shoulder. "You breathing all right? Any dizziness, headaches?"

"I'm fine," Taylor says. Then she scratches the back of her neck.

Tom stops, stares at the gesture. Remembers all the times he's seen her do it – in the car, on foot, in the motel room. All the times he's just shrugged it off as a bug bite. He turns to her. "How long have you had that itch, Taylor?" he says. "It seems persistent."

"Mm," she grunts, scratching again. "It *is* persistent."

"How long?"

She looks up at him, confused. "I'm – I'm not sure. I think a bug might've bit me."

"That's what I thought, too," Tom says. "From one of your nights sleeping in the woods, right? But how long have you actually had the itch? Does it predate the woods?"

Taylor has to think about this. "I – I don't know. I can't remember, I, I think –"

"I need to check the back of your neck." He doesn't move straight to her when he says this. He waits for her response.

Taylor looks at him. She probes the itchy area. "Okay," she says.

The light isn't good. He beckons her closer to him, nearer the fire and the glow it is casting. She sits cross-legged in front of him, and Tom angles his body so the light can get to it best. If it *is* just a tick or some other kind of bug, he'll have to try to get it out. Something he should have done back at the motel, but she was tired, and he didn't want to disturb her. She's been through so much already, but Tom curses himself for allowing this to deter him. As soon as he looks, though, he sees no sign of a bug having burrowed into her flesh. Instead, he finds a small scar. It's tiny, almost imperceptible. He leans in close to see it properly. There's dirt in it, which he has to brush aside. A small white scar, with the curve of a smile.

Tom inspects the area, probing with his fingers. Pinching the flesh, searching. If Taylor is in discomfort, she doesn't make a sound. Doesn't tell him to stop.

Then Tom finds something. It's small, but it's there. It's hard, and it's round, and it's embedded under her skin. He takes a sharp breath and takes his hands away.

Taylor turns. "What?" she says. "What is it? What'd you find? Has something bit me?"

"They've chipped you," Tom says. "That's how they keep finding us – keep finding *you*. They've put a chip in your skin."

22

It's late when Danny checks in with her real job.

She knows her editor, Michael O'Hare, won't be at the office. He's a family man. He'll be at home. She checks the time. He might even be in bed at this hour. He doesn't keep the same dedicated hours that she does. Having a wife and two children might have something to do with that, but Danny isn't burdened by a family life. Regardless of the time, she calls him.

It rings for a while. He doesn't answer. Danny calls again. This time, Michael answers. He doesn't sound happy about it.

"What's up, Danny?" His voice is groggy. He yawns. "You know what time it is?"

"It's late, yeah, I know. But I figured I'd check in."

Michael yawns again. "Oh, yeah? You got something worth checking in *with*?"

"Well, *no*, not really. But I know how you get, Michael. I know you start to worry when I'm out in the field."

"I wouldn't call doing administrative work being 'out in the field,' exactly. Where are you now? Home?"

"No, not yet. I'm in the parking lot of the Temple."

"Yeah? They have you working so late?"

"I hung back," Danny says. "In the vain hope I'd manage to find something. And y'know, I had some paperwork to catch up on."

"Mm. Seems most of your searches in that place are proving to be in vain, Danny. I'm starting to suspect you just like having the two paychecks."

"Something will come up, Michael. I know it will. I just have to be patient."

Michael sighs. "Danny, you're the only one who believes in this story."

"That doesn't mean it's a lost cause. That doesn't mean there *isn't* a story."

"Or else it's an entirely quixotic endeavor."

"*Quixotic* – I see someone's been checking their word-a-day."

"I'm an editor, Danny. It's my job. It's also my job to know when staff are tilting at windmills."

"And you think that's what I'm doing?"

"I can almost guarantee it at this point. It's not the first time I've seen it. You have any idea how many stories I've had to kill in the field?"

Danny doesn't want to think about it. She looks up at the megachurch, at the sheer size of it. It reminds her of her high school – except her high school building was probably smaller.

Danny is good at her job. She's done it since she left college at twenty-two. She's thirty-four now. She's investigated working conditions, voter fraud, tax evasion, drugs – she's *always* got her story, no matter what it took. She's travelled throughout Washington State, wherever the investigations have taken her, but she's always called Belleville home. And, for as long as it's been there, she's always been aware of the Temple of St. Philomena.

There's no one in Belleville who isn't. It's too big to ignore.

Until she started on this story, she'd never been inside the Temple. She had her own church. Sacred Heart, run by Father Peter Dudley. She's known Father Dudley all her life. He baptized her. He gave her First Communion. Danny never had any reason to go to the Temple.

There were others in her church who'd been, though. Out of curiosity more than anything else. They always brought back the same story. *I didn't like it,* they'd say. They preferred their own more modest church. *There was just something... something* different *about it all.* That was as much information as anyone could give. A general vibe about the place. Or, as one person described it, *It's more like a cult than a church.*

One Sunday, Father Dudley caught Danny at the door. "Would you mind holding back, please, Danny?" he said. "Just until everyone else has gone. I won't take up too much of your time."

Danny went back inside the church, took a seat on a rear pew. Ten minutes passed before Father Dudley was through saying goodbye to his parishioners. He sat down beside her. Danny expected him to start talking straight away, but he didn't. There was a pause. A long one. She had to turn to him. He looked straight ahead. To the altar. To the cross. Thinking. Deliberating. She could see the way his jaw worked while he wrestled with whatever was weighing on him.

"Father?" Danny prompted.

He blinked, then turned to her and smiled. "How's work, Danny?"

Danny blinked. "It's...it's fine," she said.

"Working on any stories at the minute?"

"Not right now," she said. "But I'm afraid that if I were, I wouldn't be able to talk about it."

"No, of course, of course." The priest ran his hands down

his thighs, smoothing out his trouser legs. "I always enjoyed that story you wrote, the one about the poor drug addicts."

Danny had to think. She'd written more than one.

"Especially the part about the young girl who had her baby taken away from her," he said. "It broke my heart, that one. I still pray for that poor girl every night. And her child, too."

"Cassie," Danny said, knowing the story he was talking about. It was a couple of years old. "She's doing better now. She's been in rehab. Last I heard, she'd been clean six months. She gets supervised visits with Polly."

Father Dudley smiled. "That's good. My prayers were listened to."

"Seems that way."

Father Dudley nodded. "You're good at what you do, aren't you, Danny?"

"I like to think so. People I work for think so, too. Least, they keep me on the payroll."

"I wonder, have you ever..." He hesitated. His jaw silently worked. "Have you ever thought maybe there's a story at the Temple of St. Philomena?"

Danny wasn't sure how to respond. Whatever she'd thought the priest was going to say, this wasn't it. "I suppose it's crossed my mind that maybe there's some tax evasion going on," she said finally. "Or maybe some money laundering. It's a big church. *Really* big."

Father Dudley fell silent again. It was a loaded, heavy silence. He stared at the back of the pew before him, looking almost pained. "There's...there's a family I'd like you to look in on. They go by the name of Wilkins. Maybe...maybe there's a story there. Maybe there isn't." He opened his mouth like he was about to say more, but he didn't. Stopped himself. He turned to her, smiled sadly, then nodded his goodbye before he stood and left.

Danny took the bait. She was never able to resist. The Wilkins family. She assumed they were in Belleville. She looked into them. It didn't take her long to find them.

Terry Wilkins, his wife June, and their daughter. Scarlet. Scarlet is fifteen now. Three years ago, when she was twelve, she was a regular visitor to the Temple of St. Philomena. So were her parents. Scarlet attended all the after-school groups held at the church. She was there most nights.

And then, all of a sudden, she wasn't. They weren't members of the church anymore. They weren't kicked out – they stopped attending. It raised some eyebrows among the other members, but then they were forgotten.

Until they brought a lawsuit against the church.

Looking into the lawsuit was difficult. No one wanted to talk to Danny about it. No one wanted to talk about the Wilkinses. Eventually, she greased the palm of one of her contacts in law enforcement, persuaded him to take a look at the file and tell her what it said.

The contents were grim. The Wilkins were claiming pastor Laurence Morgan had sexually assaulted their daughter, Scarlet.

But then, a few months later, the Wilkinses recanted all their claims.

At almost the same time, Scarlet Wilkins was taken out of school. The family isolated themselves. They stopped talking to their friends. They never went out.

Danny tried getting in touch with the Wilkinses. They wouldn't return her calls. The silence was deafening. Danny went directly to the home. June answered the door. Danny managed to charm her way into the house. She'd built her whole career on the back of how charming she could be.

She told June she'd been in contact with other families who had attempted to bring a lawsuit against the church. It was a lie, but Danny didn't let herself feel too guilty about it.

She wanted their story. She wanted to know what had happened, why they had made their accusations, and why they had recanted.

June was hesitant. And then Terry walked into the room. "What's going on here?" he said. Danny would never forget the look on his face as June told her husband who Danny was, and why she was there.

He looked terrified.

And then he looked angry. "No," he said. "We have nothing to say. Now please leave our home." He kept glancing over his shoulder, toward the stairs.

Danny tried to charm him, too. Terry wasn't as susceptible as his wife. His fear was still palpable. He was growing antsy, desperate for her to leave.

And then Scarlet came down the stairs. Danny saw the defeated expression that replaced Terry's fear.

Danny got a good look at their daughter. The first thing she noticed was just how anorexic-thin Scarlet was. How her hair was cut short like she'd hacked it off herself. Scarlet, in turn, took a good look at Danny. She was confused, but she looked as fearful as her father. As fearful as her mother, too.

The sleeves of Scarlet's shirt were short. Danny saw her forearms, her wrists. She saw the vicious-looking scars that were crisscrossed there, bright pink against her pale flesh. Scarlet saw where she was looking. She hid her arms behind her back.

Danny had been around enough victims – of violence, of sexual violence, of abuse, or drug abuse – to know that Scarlet was a victim.

Danny was ushered out of the house soon after. She didn't protest. The family were clearly scared. Something had spooked them. Spooked them so bad it caused them to drop the charges they were trying to press, and effectively go into hiding from their own lives.

Something to do with the church.

Something to do with Pastor Laurence Morgan.

"Sometimes they're not windmills," Danny says to Michael.

"What's that?"

"Sometimes they're not windmills," she says. "Sometimes they *are* monsters."

He grunts.

A few months after her meeting with the Wilkins family, she got the administrative job in an effort to peek behind the curtain. She hasn't been able to get the family out of her mind since.

"Listen, what I was trying to say before – give me another month here. Okay? Just a month."

"That's not very long. You've already been there a while, and you haven't got anything. What makes you think a month is gonna change that? You got a sniff of something?"

"No, I don't," Danny says, figuring it's best to be honest while she's laying her cards out on the table. "I don't have anything, but I feel like you're gonna give me a deadline that's a lot shorter, so I'm getting in ahead of you."

He grunts again, and this time it sounds like a laugh. "I was gonna say two weeks."

"One month," Danny says. "And if I don't have anything by then, I'll break down his fucking office door and see if I can't find something incriminating that way."

"You know I don't condone that, Danny..."

"I don't expect you to. Pretend you didn't hear it. But either I leave here on my last day having found something, or I prove to myself once and for all that this whole thing has been a bust. Just a colossal waste of my fucking time."

"All right," Michael says. "Fine. You can have a month. From today. I'll be counting down. Oh, and next time you call me, try to make it a more sociable hour, huh? This time of night you run the risk of waking the kids, and if you do that, there's no telling how long it takes to set them back down."

"I'll keep that in mind," Danny says, though she knows she won't.

She ends the call and stares at the church. At its entrance, and its walls. At the dark secrets she is certain it holds within.

She takes a deep breath. She thinks of the Wilkins family. Thinks of them all locked away in their home, too scared to leave it. Jumping at shadows. She thinks of Scarlet and the scars on her wrists.

There is a story here. That much is certain. There is a truth waiting to be found. A truth larger than what happened to the Wilkins family. More than Scarlet. In one month, she'll know what it is.

Part of her is terrified by the prospect.

She starts the engine of her car and pulls out of the lot. Puts the church behind her. Puts distance between herself and it, except it never leaves her. Not really. It's a part of her now. It has become a part of her life. The story will stick with her until she knows what the full details of the story *are*. And even then, it may never leave her.

23

It's dawn. Early morning sunlight is beginning to stream through the trees.

Back at the motel, Tom took catnaps. Fifteen-minute intervals of sleep, so he was able to stay alert, but remain rested at the same time. At their makeshift camp in the woods, he hasn't slept a wink. Not since discovering Taylor is microchipped. Since knowing the men looking for them could find them at any time. They already know where they are. Tom's kept the fire burning. No point letting it die. If they're coming for them, a fire wouldn't help them get here any faster. They already know the way.

He's kept the Beretta close at hand.

Taylor is still sleeping. She's curled on her side, her back to the mound of earth behind her. A few hours ago she started to tremble, the heat from the fire not reaching her. Tom took the last spare shirt from his backpack and draped it over her as a poor blanket. He covered her bare legs. She stopped trembling, at least.

Tom checks their clothes. They're dry now. The fire is dying out, and he doesn't attempt to rebuild it. They'll be moving soon. They need to get back to some form of civilization. Need to get their hands on another vehicle.

Need to deal with the microchip.

While pulling on his clothes, Tom hears a noise. He quickly finishes getting dressed and then goes to the corner of the mound, peers around it. Turns his head to the direction of the sound. He hears voices and movement.

They're here. They're coming.

Tom wakes Taylor. They don't have long while the men pick their way through the woods. He passes her clothes to her and keeps watch, gun out. He can't see them yet, but they're getting closer.

"I'm ready," Taylor says.

Tom nods, grabs his bag, slings it onto his back. "Stay close to me," he says.

He ducks low, and she follows, and they leave their camp. Tom hears how the men are alerted to their movement. How they change direction. They have a tracker. There's no doubting it now.

He holds Taylor's wrist, guides her between the bushes and the trees, points out potential trip hazards. There's nowhere for them to hide – there's no point. They need to keep moving. Need to get out ahead of the men before they can catch up.

They're on the move for twenty minutes. The men have fallen silent, likely attempting to creep up on their moving target. They're not running, though. Not giving chase. Letting them tire themselves out. They don't know Tom has become aware of the chip, and they don't want to give themselves away.

The sound of a road up ahead. Tom can see it through an opening in the trees. "Get to the road," he says. He can't see any vehicles, but he can hear them approaching. "Wave something down. I'll wait here – if they catch up to us, I'll deal with them."

Taylor nods, turns, runs to the road. Tom takes cover behind a tree and ducks low, gun raised, watching, waiting. There's no sign of them. No sound. Behind him, though, he hears something coming to a stop. Something loud.

Taylor calls his name. Tom looks toward her. She's managed to wave down a long-haul truck. It sits idling by the side of the road. Tom looks back through the woods. He can see the men now. He thinks they might have seen Taylor or heard her call – may have seen the truck she's waiting beside – because they've started running. Tom fires a couple of shots in their direction. They haven't seen him behind the tree. They drop to the ground, startled, and scramble for cover. Tom turns, bolts for the truck, putting the gun away as he goes. The truck is far enough away and loud enough that the driver will not have heard the gunshots. He won't be alarmed when Tom appears.

He helps Taylor up into the cab, then climbs in himself, looking toward the trees. The men are cautiously approaching the treeline. Tom slams the door shut. He turns to the driver, who eyes the two of them with an eyebrow raised.

"Don't let us keep you," Tom says. "Let's go."

The trucker pulls back onto the road. "This your dad?" he says to Taylor.

She nods. "Yup."

The driver looks between them. "I see the resemblance," he says. To Tom, he says, "Why're the two of you hitchhiking? You ain't got a car?"

"Broke down," Tom says, looking in the mirror. The men haven't emerged from the woods. They've probably doubled back on themselves, gone back to their vehicles. The truck rounds a corner, and he can't see where they came out anymore. "Had no choice."

"You walked through the woods?" the driver says.

"We broke down late," Tom says. "We needed to find somewhere to stay the night, and the woods were the most covered place."

"Shame you didn't break down a couple of miles back," the driver says. "There's a motel back that way."

"Yeah," Tom says. "That's a real shame." He and Taylor exchange glances. "How far until the next town?"

The driver thinks about it. "Ain't too far. Maybe about a half hour. That where you wanna go?"

"Guess that depends," Tom says. "What kinda town is it? The kind that has a garage, a drugstore, a supermarket?"

"If it's the one I'm thinking of, yeah, it's got all those things."

"Then yeah," Tom says. "That's where we'll get out."

24

When Josh's alarm sounds, he's quick to turn it off so it doesn't disturb Tilly. He checks she's still sleeping, then creeps down the hall to the bathroom. Into the shower. He washes and shaves, but when he gets back to the bedroom, Tilly is already out of bed. He grins to himself and gathers up his uniform. He works for the power company. He checks the time. He's got an hour before he starts, and only a twenty-minute drive to get there.

When he heads downstairs, he can smell pancakes. He finds Tilly in the kitchen, frying. She's in her dressing gown, her hair piled up in a loose bun atop her head. Josh comes up behind her, wraps his arms around her. She gives a start.

"Jesus!" she says. "Don't scare me like that. I'm cooking!"

Josh laughs. "I thought you'd heard me coming," he says, and kisses her on the side of her neck.

She chuckles, then shrugs him off, says, "Let me finish up here. I'm almost done. Take a seat. Pour yourself some coffee."

"Don't mind if I do," Josh says, grabbing himself a mug. "You didn't have to do this," he says, turning back to her.

"Do what?" Tilly says.

"Make breakfast. You're supposed to be off work. I thought you would've wanted to sleep in. I tried to be quiet."

"Yeah, well, I woke up, figured there was no point in just lying around."

"You didn't have to make me breakfast."

"Well, it's for me, too. And what would you make for yourself otherwise?"

Josh holds out his mug. "You're looking at it," he says.

"Then I'm glad I came down." Tilly drops the pancakes onto a plate, then places the plate on the table. "Come on, sit down."

Josh takes a seat and pours syrup over his pancakes. As he passes the syrup to Tilly, the phone starts to ring. They look at each other. "It's early," Josh says. "That's never a good sign when the phone's ringing this early in the day."

"Mm." Tilly grunts her agreement.

"Especially when it's the landline," Josh says.

"Who even has our landline number?" Tilly says.

"Not many," Josh says, standing from the table and going to where the phone is on the wall. "Hello?"

"Josh, it's me – don't hang up."

Josh almost does. "*Ken*," he says, sneering.

Tilly sits up.

"Yes, it's me – but just listen, please, okay? I'm not looking for trouble."

Josh presses the phone hard into the side of his head, mashing it against his ear. He breathes hard through his nose. He thinks of his mother.

Tilly can see the look on his face. She watches him, concerned.

"What do you want, Ken? I don't want to speak to you any longer than I have to."

"It's about Taylor."

Josh feels his heart rate quicken. "What about her?"

"She's –" Ken takes a deep breath. "Listen to me, okay? Just hear me out. Taylor has run away, and I can't find her."

Josh's brows narrow. "She's run away? Why's she run away, Ken?"

"I – I don't know. I just went to wake her for school yesterday morning, and she was gone."

"She's been gone a full day, and you're calling me now?"

"I've tried to find her, Josh. I've tried looking for her, but she isn't in any of the places she usually hangs out."

"Yeah? And where *are* those places, Ken? Come on, Ken, name them for me."

Ken stumbles over his words.

"I thought you were just looking for her in all those places yesterday, Ken. Why are you struggling now?"

"Listen, listen, I did find one place she's been –"

"Uh-huh. This oughtta be good."

"I saw some security footage from a gas station, and in it, she's getting in a car with some guy. Older than her – early thirties, maybe. I didn't recognize him, anyway. But I saw the footage, and it got me worried. I got – I got some bad vibes from what I saw, you know what I mean? I got some bad vibes from *him*. I mean, why's a fully grown man giving a ride to a fourteen-year-old girl anyway?"

"I dunno, Ken. Maybe she looked cold and hungry and alone, and maybe he was being a nice guy."

Ken hesitates, stumbles over his words again, then manages to blurt out, "You didn't see the footage, Josh. I saw it, and I'm telling you I didn't get a good feeling. I'm worried about her. Real worried."

"You called the cops? Reported her missing?"

"Yeah, of course I have, but I had to wait twenty-four hours. You know how these things are. Calling the cops was the first thing I did this morning, right before I called you."

Tilly is watching him still. She looks concerned, one hand over her mouth. She listens intently.

Josh balls the fist not holding the phone, thinking about his sister. About where she could be. If she's run away from Ken, the only place she could come is here, to him and Tilly. Ken knows this. That's why he's calling. "What do you want, Ken? Why are you calling to tell me? I could've taken Taylor in, she could've come here and lived with me and Tilly, but you blocked that. Even the fucking court ruled in your favor despite the fact Taylor explicitly stated she wanted to come live with me and Tilly. All because Mom named you the legal guardian in her will. Why she did that, I'll never understand, but here we are. So why're you calling me now?"

Ken takes a deep breath. "Because I need your help." It's clear this isn't easy for him to say. "Because we both know she's going to head to you. When she gets there, she's probably still going to be with the guy from the gas station. I don't like it, Josh. If and when she gets there, I need you to call me, let me know she's arrived. Let me know she's okay, and then I can come and pick her up. But don't let her know you've called me – she might try to run again, and who knows what that guy might try. Be careful around him, Josh."

Josh snorts.

Ken is shaken by the noise. "What – what's that supposed to mean?"

"It means you're full of shit, Ken, and I know it." Josh squeezes the phone, wishing it were Ken's neck. He's still pressing it hard into his head, angry, and worried about his sister. "Why did she run away, Ken? Why's she run away from you, huh?"

"I – I –"

"Save your excuses, you piece of shit. I've never liked you, asshole, and you know it – and you know I've never trusted you, either. I sure as shit don't trust anything you're saying right now. In fact, you've just got me wondering why Taylor has run away from you and she hasn't called me yet. Come to think of it, why she hasn't called me at all in, like, a year."

"Josh, you don't understand –"

"You might've charmed our mom, but your snake oil doesn't work on me, asshole, so save your breath. If Taylor turns up here, you'll never know about it."

"I'm her legal guardian –"

"Yeah, and you can shove the piece of paper that says so up your ass. Don't call here again." Josh slams the phone down. He breathes hard. His hands are shaking.

"What's happened?" Tilly says.

Josh takes a shuddering breath. "I need to call work," he says. "I can't go in today." He shakes his head.

"Josh, *what's happened*? Speak to me – you're worrying me. Is Taylor all right?"

Josh turns to the table. He takes a seat, pushes the plate of syrup and pancakes aside, his appetite gone. He tries to calm himself enough to tell her what Ken said, but it's hard. When he finally gets to the end, he finishes with, "So I need to be here. If she gets here today, I need to be here for her."

Tilly reaches across the table, her own breakfast forgotten, too. She takes his hands, strokes his knuckles.

"I bet that asshole doesn't let her have a phone. There's probably no way for her to get in touch with me."

"Maybe you should go to work," Tilly says. Josh looks at her, but she continues, "It could help take your mind off things. I'm here all day – if she turns up, I'm here for her. And I'll call you at work, let you know she's arrived. You could come straight back once you know. There's nothing to say she's going to reach us today. We don't know where she is."

Josh considers this.

"Should we call the police?" Tilly says.

Josh shakes his head bitterly. "No point. First of all, Ken

already has. Secondly, even if they find her, they'll just take her back to him. He said it himself, he's her legal guardian. At least if she gets here ahead of them and him, we could maybe try to hide her for a while, deny that we've seen her, while we try to straighten things out legally." He sighs at the prospect of having to go through the courts again, in the vain hope of gaining custody of his own sister from a man who shares no blood with her. He knows the ruling would likely go in Ken's favor again. "It's all we can try."

"We could try to go through an Oregon courtroom this time," Tilly says. "If she makes it to us. They might lean more in our favor, just on account of her already being here. Maybe the fact she's had to travel so far all by herself would send some kind of message, too."

Josh grunts. "It's sending some kinda message to me..."

"What do you mean?"

"Why's she doing it, that's what I mean. Like you said, it's a long way to come all by herself. She doesn't drive. She doesn't have any money. She's gotta hitchhike and rely on the kindness of potentially dangerous strangers. Doesn't that scream to you that something must be wrong in Washington?"

"Well, she never wanted to stay with Ken in the first place."

"Mm." Josh clenches his jaw, scratches his arm. "I think you're right," he says finally, checking the time. "I should go to work. Waiting around here isn't gonna help anything."

Tilly nods, strokes his hands again. "If she turns up – *when* she turns up – the first thing I'll do is call you."

Josh gets to his feet, feeling suddenly deflated. He was in a good mood when he woke. Was in a better mood when he saw the pancakes. Now, he's worried, and it's already eating away at him. He knows he's going to be on edge today. "If I haven't heard anything, I'll call at lunchtime," he says. "Just to check in."

Tilly stands too, walks him to the door. She leans up, kisses his cheek, then embraces him. "I'm sure she'll be fine, Josh," she says into his chest. "She's a tough kid. She'll be here before we know it."

Josh strokes her back, but he's distracted. "Yeah," he says absently. "You're right. I'm sure you're right."

25

The trucker drops Tom and Taylor in the next town, as requested. Tom misses the name of the town. It doesn't matter. He doesn't intend on being here long.

He looks around, gets his bearings. It's a quiet-looking place. The main stretch of road only has a few cars parked either side of it. A couple go by, people heading out of town, either to work or just passing through. There's a diner. He can see life in there. The two waitresses inside are hurrying around, the breakfast rush just beginning. Down at the end of the block, on the corner, he spots a building with a neon 'Hotel' sign hanging off its side. Tom spots a drugstore over the road from where they stand. He goes to it, Taylor in tow. Inside, he purchases a box of the biggest Band-Aids he can find, some tweezers, painkillers, a lighter, and antiseptic solution. Then they go directly to the hotel, check in to a room.

The room has two single beds, like back at the motel, but they won't do any sleeping here. There's a table in the corner, with a mirror propped on it, and a chair beneath. He goes to the window, takes a look, checks the road. They're four floors up, and it's a good vantage point. The road is clear. Nothing approaching that raises alarm. The town is bigger than it appears at first glance. It stretches out behind the row of buildings directly opposite. There's a car dealership on the other side of the road. He can make out a few prices in the windows, and they look cheap. That's good. He can't afford, and doesn't need, anything expensive.

"Wash the back of your neck," Tom says. "Right where it itches. Use soap. Get it as clean as you can."

Taylor nods and swallows. She knows what he's going to do.

"And swallow a couple of these." He hands her the painkillers.

While she's in the bathroom, Tom spreads the items he bought in the drugstore out on one of the beds and pulls the chair up next to it. He takes his KA-BAR from his bag and sterilizes it with the lighter and some of the solution. Taylor returns before he's finished. She stands in the bathroom doorway and watches what he's doing, her eyes trained on the knife.

"It's big," she says.

"It certainly isn't a scalpel," Tom says. "But it's the best we've got. Don't worry – I'm going to be careful. Take a seat."

Taylor does. He hands her a pillow. "I'm not going to lie and say this won't hurt," he says. "Because it will. The painkillers are only going to dull it so much, but we have to make do with what's available to us. If it gets too bad, bite into the pillow. I know it'll be hard, but try not to make too much noise."

Taylor nods, holding the pillow to herself while sitting in the chair. She suddenly looks very small and very young. Tom feels an ache in his chest. He grits his teeth and replaces it with fire, with anger. Once he gets her to Oregon, it's a feeling he can return to Belleville and deal with head-on.

Tom stands behind her at the chair. She lowers her head, tilts it to the side for him to better see. He presses the tip of the knife to the little white scar. He struggles to keep his hands steady, not wanting to do this. He doesn't want to hurt her.

There's no alternative.

"Brace yourself," Tom says. He pushes the blade in. Taylor shoves the pillow into her mouth and bites down on it. He feels how her shoulders tremble, but she holds herself as steady as she can.

He takes the knife out and grabs the tweezers, tears them from their packaging. He holds the cut open as wide as feels comfortable with two fingers, then puts the tweezers in, searching for the microchip. Taylor whimpers. She makes a noise into the pillow, screaming into it, but then Tom feels something solid. The chip. He doesn't hurry. He stays calm. Is careful in what he does. He doesn't want to lose it. Doesn't want to force it deeper. He gets each prong of the tweezer around it, and then he increases the pressure. Grips it. He lifts it from the skin. He has it. It's out.

He drops it on the bed and pours the rest of the antiseptic solution over and into the wound. "That's it," he says. "It's over. I got it."

Taylor lowers the pillow. "Jesus Christ," she says.

The cut is small and doesn't require any stitches. Tom dries the area. The wound is clean. He dresses it with one of the big square Band-Aids.

"There, we're done," Tom says. "You did good. I've seen grown men scream over less."

Taylor stands from the chair. She sniffs hard and wipes her face. Her eyes are watery, but she hasn't been crying. "Let me see it," she says.

Tom holds the chip up.

"It's tiny," she says. "I don't know when they could've put it in."

"They ever drug you?"

"Maybe. I think so, but I don't know for sure. There were times I'd pass out and wake up alone in bed, but I figured I was just...y'know...all used up. Exhausted." She stares at the chip, unable to take her eyes from it, hardly believing that it was inside her for who knows how long.

"It's probably gonna keep itching for a while," Tom says. "While it heals. Try not to scratch it."

Taylor nods. "What're you gonna do with it?"

Tom places the chip on the table in the corner of the room. With the handle of his KA-BAR, he smashes it, then brushes the remnants into a wastebasket. "They'll panic," he says, "when they realize it isn't working anymore. Let's go."

26

Bill drives his Subaru, but he does not ride alone. Vehicles filled with men at his command follow close behind. An unmarked convoy in mismatched vehicles. More immediately, a man named Henry sits beside him. Henry's job is to navigate. He has the tracker.

"They've been stopped a little while now," Henry says. "In the next town. They're probably trying to hide out again."

Bill chuckles. Sitting ducks. They'll go in more carefully this time. Bill will lead the way, handle Tom himself. Leaving it up to the bumbling idiots with him is not an option. Tom is too well-trained, too dangerous. All they're good for now is fodder. Pawns to wear down the main prize.

Henry makes a choked noise suddenly. Bill glances at him. His eyes are wide, staring at the tracker.

"What's the matter with you?" Bill says.

"*Shit*," Henry says. "It's – the tracker – it's, it's gone off!"

Bill frowns. "The fuck do you mean?"

"Exactly what it sounds like – it's not tracking anymore!"

Bill grabs the tracker out of his hands, looks at it. It isn't giving a reading. He throws it back into Henry's lap. "They've found it," he says, dumbfounded. "God fucking damn, they've found it."

"Oh, shit," Henry says. "What do we do now?"

Bill looks at the tracker again, then at Henry. "How far are we from the town they're in?"

"Uh." Henry appears nervous at how Bill doesn't look at the road ahead of them. He looks back at the screen. "Not far. Just a few miles."

"Then we go to their last known location." Bill turns back to the road. He puts his foot down. The cars behind are caught off guard. They struggle to keep up.

27

The car dealership opposite the hotel is as Tom hoped it would be. Shitty cars at affordable prices. They won't last long, but they'll last as long as Tom and Taylor will need them to. And now, with the chip gone, they won't have to worry about speed so much anymore, either.

Tom has already picked out a car. A nondescript Honda with some rust around the rear passenger wheel arch, and a couple of dents on the driver's side, but nothing else concerning. He's looked at the other vehicles available. The Honda is the fastest vehicle on the lot.

And the most affordable.

"It's a piece of shit," Taylor says.

"Certainly is," Tom says. "But it'll get us to Oregon, and that's all we need from it."

The owner of the dealership has been eyeing them from his office. Tom noticed him earlier through the glass, peering out from behind the aged computer monitor on his desk. He steps outside now, a heavyset man adjusting the belt of his trousers, already with a broad smile on his face. The top of his head is balding, with a few wisps of hair combed across it as some kind of disguise. He sweeps them over and slicks them down into place as he approaches. "Morning, folks," he says once he's close enough.

Tom turns to him, nods, then points at the Honda. "We want this one."

The man raises his eyebrows, taken aback. His grin slips away. He's been expecting some haggling to take place first. "That sure is a mighty fine choice you've made," he says, recovering himself and his grin and seeing an opportunity to upsell. "But have you taken a look at –" He starts spreading his arm in a broad gesture toward the other side of the lot. The more expensive side despite the multitude of dents, scratches, and rust.

"We want this one," Tom says. He looks the man in the eye.

"Sure thing," the owner says, shrugging, figuring a sale is a sale. "If you wanna accompany me to my office, I can grab the keys and the paperwork."

Tom and Taylor follow him to the double-wide that serves as his office. "Wait out here," Tom says to Taylor when they get closer to it. "Keep an eye out. Watch the road. If you see anything, come and get me."

Taylor nods, then steps to the side of the door as Tom and the man go inside. She leans against the side of the unit and rubs the back of her neck where the Band-Aid is.

The man settles down behind his desk, sifting through the reams of paperwork he has there in order to find the appropriate documents. He's not in any kind of rush. He makes small talk while he searches, though doesn't say anything that requires a response. Most of the time he's just laughing at his own jokes. Tom keeps an eye on the window, toward the entrance of the dealership. From where he is, he can't see Taylor where she waits by the door.

There don't appear to be any other salesmen working at the dealership, nor any sign that anyone else who works here could just be on their day off. It seems to be a one-man operation.

"Here we go," the man says, pulling out a file and grabbing a pen. He pulls keys out and places them on the desk between them. Tom can see the Honda symbol on the fob.

Tom reaches into his bag while the man begins the paperwork. He counts out the exact amount of cash for the Honda. He counts what he has left, too. Enough for gas and food. It'll do. After they've been to Oregon, and he's returned to Belleville, things should slow down after that. He'll be able to go back to concentrating on finding some work, making some money. He'll go to one of his safety-deposit boxes with the money left over from his CIA days, kept under a fake name, from back when he was on the run. He'll take just enough to keep him afloat until he's able to find some work.

"*Tom!*"

He turns at the sound of Taylor hissing his name. The man behind the desk hears it, too, looks up. Taylor is leaning toward the office. She motions over to the road, mouths, *They're here!*

"At the hotel?" Tom says.

She nods. "They just pulled up."

Tom turns back to the man. He hasn't gotten far through the paperwork. Tom drops the money on the desk and grabs the keys. "Keep the file," he says, standing. "We don't need it."

"But – but – I need details!" the man says as Tom leaves. "I don't even know your name!"

"Make it up," Tom says.

He and Taylor cross the lot back to the Honda. Taylor is frantic. Tom makes a *cool it* motion with his hand. "Just stay calm," he says. "Walk beside me. Keep the pace. You're out of view."

He looks left out of the corner of his eye, to the hotel. Five cars have pulled up in front of it. The men inside four of the vehicles have gotten out, are running into the building. The last place they know the tracker was.

There are two men in the fifth vehicle, the one that hasn't emptied. It's a Subaru. The bigger of the two, the driver, gets out of the car now, looking around, his brow hooded as his eyes search the local area. His jaw juts out. Tom recognizes him from the motel. The man who shot at them. Even at distance, Tom can see his bottom row of teeth digging into his top lip.

Taylor sees him, too. She takes a sharp intake of breath. "The Ogre," she says, and there are tears in her voice.

The Ogre looks right at them. His grimace turns into a smile. He dives back into his car, back behind the wheel.

They're at the Honda. Tom unlocks it. "Get in," he says.

Taylor dives through the open driver's door and scrambles to the passenger side. Tom follows her in, starts the engine.

"They're coming!" Taylor says.

Tom puts the car in reverse as the Ogre's Subaru slams into the side of them, pushing them across the lot. Tom spins the wheel, staying in reverse. He puts his foot down, twisting the vehicle, and gets out from in front of them. He catches a glimpse of the Ogre. He's laughing. His passenger, however, is hanging on, terrified.

Tom keeps the car in reverse, putting distance between them. When they slipped out from in front, the Ogre lurched forward. He's scrabbling for control now. Tom slams the Honda into gear and charges across the distance he has opened, rams them back, knocking the passenger away from his door. He mustn't be wearing his seatbelt – he's thrown across the Ogre. With them distracted, and the Ogre blinded, Tom rams them again, pushing them sideways now. He forces them into a row of the other cars. The Ogre pushes the passenger off him with force, just in time for Tom to ram them again.

"Get the gun!" Tom says. Taylor dives into the bag at her feet, searching for the Beretta while Tom rams them. She holds it out to him.

Tom winds the window down. Before he leans out, he looks back toward the hotel. The men who ran inside haven't come back out yet. He turns back to the Ogre, gun raised. He sees how the owner of the car dealership has come running out of his office at the sight of the destruction, his arms raised, but when he sees the gun, he throws himself flat to the ground and covers his head.

Tom aims for the Ogre, fires. The Ogre throws himself down. The first bullet doesn't break through the glass, but the second does. It buries itself in the headrest. Tom lowers the gun, aims for the wheels. He blows out the two front tires, then ducks back inside the car. He throws it in reverse, disentangles it from the Ogre's vehicle, then spins the wheel and the tires, burning rubber on their way out of the lot. The men from the hotel are only now returning to their vehicles, their search fruitless. He sees how they're looking for the Ogre – the man in charge. Tom puts them in the rearview, leaving them behind as he speeds out of town.

28

When Laurence arrives at the church, the atmosphere changes. It darkens, becomes heavy and oppressive. Danny hasn't seen him like this before. He's stormed into the building like there's a dark cloud hanging over him. His brow is deeply furrowed, hooding his eyes. He doesn't say good morning. Doesn't so much as spare Danny a single glance on the way to his office door.

With keys in hand, he turns to her finally. "No phone calls," he says, his face as dark as the mood he has dragged in with him. "And no visitors. I don't want to see anyone unless I tell you specifically I'm expecting them. Is that understood, Danielle?"

"Yes, Mr. Morgan," Danny says. "Of course." She hesitates, then asks, "Is something wrong?"

He doesn't answer. He turns back to his door, unlocks it, steps inside his office.

Danny stares at the closed door. She's never seen the pastor like this before. Of course, she hasn't been here very long, and she wonders if this kind of thing is a regular occurrence. She makes a mental note of the date, in case it becomes important later. She'll write it down tonight, when she's at home. When the time comes to write her story, will this be a turning point? Is this the beginning of something?

Maybe not. Perhaps, as she's briefly thought, this isn't an uncommon occurrence. She'll have to try to ask around, get some ideas from the people who have worked here a lot longer than she has. See if they regularly have to weather the storms of his mood swings. If nothing else, it could serve as background, show just what kind of character the pastor really has. Nothing is wasted. She needs to pay attention to every little detail.

Every day, when Laurence Morgan has arrived at the church, as he's passed by her desk and wished her a good morning or commented upon the weather, Danny has thought about Scarlet Wilkins. Every second she is in the church, she thinks of Scarlet Wilkins.

She hides these memories, though. Shields them from herself. Compartmentalizes them. She's good at her job. Good at disguising how she feels. So whether she believes Laurence may have assaulted Scarlet, whether she believes there may be something worse at hand, whether she thinks he's a monster or not, she never lets it show. Laurence would never know she thought anything at all.

The phone on her desk rings. It's an internal call. It's coming directly from Laurence. "Yes, Mr. Morgan?"

"Kenneth Arnett is coming to see me," he says. "He should be here soon. Do you know what he looks like?"

"I'm sure I'll recognize him when I see him."

"Mm," Laurence says. "He's here often enough. His arm's currently in a sling. You won't miss him. I'll see *him*, and no one else."

"Sure thing, Mr. Morgan –" He's hung up before she's finished talking.

Danny puts the phone back down, intrigued. Something is going on, she's sure of it. Something has happened.

Before Ken Arnett arrives, one of the other administrators comes in, a folder under one arm. Tracy Connelly. She goes to knock on Laurence's door. Danny almost misses her. She calls her name, manages to stop her in time. Shakes her head to let her know that's not a good idea. Tracy looks confused. She approaches Danny's desk. "What's wrong?" she says. "What's happened?"

Tracy Connelly has worked here seven years. She showed Danny how to do her job. "Mr. Morgan isn't very happy," Danny says.

"Oh?" The lady is surprised. "How come?"

"I don't know," Danny says. "But he's in a bad mood. He made it very clear he doesn't want to be disturbed."

The frown hasn't left Tracy's face since Danny stopped her from knocking on the office door. "How peculiar."

Danny sees her chance. "Does this kind of thing...happen often?" she says. "I mean, Mr. Morgan has always seemed so – so *chipper* to me. Always smiling. This is the first time I've ever seen him in anything other than a good mood."

Tracy looks toward Laurence's door with concern. "That's how he *always* is," she says, turning back to Danny. "He's always so happy. Always in such a good mood, so pleased to see everyone. There's only one time I can think of when he was in a bad mood, and that was so long ago now. A few years back." She shakes her head. "An awful business, but it was all resolved in the end."

Danny cocks her head, intrigued. "What business was that?"

Tracy is looking to the side, into the past, distracted. She turns back to Danny. "Hmm? Oh. It was that awful Wilkins family, making such terrible, unfounded accusations." She shakes her head vehemently. "It still makes me so mad just thinking about them – how they wormed their way into our church, all the while with deceit in their hearts."

The Wilkinses. Danny keeps her face neutral. It's easy to do. This isn't the first time she's been on a story and a person has said something to her, and she's had to pretend like she doesn't know what they're talking about. She practices this facial expression in the mirror sometimes. "What deceit was that?" she says. "What did they do?"

"I won't go into it," Tracy says. "It doesn't bear repeating. But they came here looking for their pieces of silver. They saw a good man like the pastor, in a building like *this*, and they sought to take advantage of that. But the pastor has worked *hard* for all of this, and he puts his money back into the church, back into the community. All that he does for children – it can't be overstated. And that's why it just makes me so *mad* when I think of the Wilkins family..." She has to take a moment to compose herself. "Anyway, I certainly hope nothing like that has come up again." She takes the folder she's carrying out from under her arm. "Could you please give this to Mr. Morgan for me? When he's ready for it – it's nothing important, just the new work roster for the next couple of months. He always likes to take a look at it."

"Sure," Danny says, taking the folder from her, thinking about what she has said. She saw the Wilkins family in person. She went to their house. She saw no deceit in their faces or their manners. Only fear. "I'll get it to him as soon as he's up to seeing it."

Tracy smiles, then turns and walks back the way she came, sparing a longing look at Laurence's closed door as she passes.

As she leaves, a man with his right arm in a sling appears from around the corner. Danny recognizes him, but as if to cast out any doubts, the woman passing nods at him and says, "Morning, Ken."

He nods back at her, then strokes his broken arm through the sling. Danny can't help but notice how pale he is. Like he's in a lot of pain, or else like he's about to be sick. Or maybe as if he's nervous about something.

"Mr. Arnett?" Danny says.

"Uh, yes," he says, stopping. "Hello."

"Mr. Morgan's expecting you."

Ken nods. He hesitates at the door, stares at the handle.

"You can go right in," Danny says.

Ken gives a start. "Okay," he says, not looking up. "Sure." He sighs, then takes a deep breath and holds it in his lungs. He knocks twice, then pulls down the door handle and steps inside.

Danny watches him go. The door closes behind him. There's silence.

From her desk, Danny can never hear anything that happens in Laurence's office. She never knows if he's on the phone. If ever there's anyone in there with him, she can't hear what they're saying to each other.

She can, however, if she's right outside the door.

Danny looks down the corridor, makes sure no one is coming. She slips out of her shoes, then slowly stands behind her desk, listening for anyone approaching. After warning her co-worker of Laurence's sour mood, she imagines word will spread and people will know to avoid this area. To avoid him.

She creeps to the closed office door in her stockinged feet and turns her ear to it, listens.

The voices within are muffled, but she can make them out. "He didn't buy it. He won't help." Ken's voice.

Danny wonders who *he* is. She wishes she'd got to the door sooner, heard them say whoever they're talking about.

Laurence doesn't say anything for a long time. When he finally speaks, his voice is low. Danny can't make him out, but she's nervous on Ken's behalf. She can sense the menace in the pastor's tone. When Ken responds, his voice has lowered, too, and she doesn't hear what he says, though it sounds monosyllabic and brief.

From this point on, Danny can't hear what they say. She gets her ear as close to the door as she can without touching it. She wants to press it right up against the wood, but she resists. To do so might move it, make noise, alert them to her being here. She's getting frustrated, wishing she knew what they were talking about.

Then she hears the scraping of chairs. They stand. Danny quickly turns on her heel and returns to her desk. She gets back into her chair and is acting casual when the office door opens. Ken comes out first. She slips her feet back into her shoes. Laurence is right behind him. Danny looks up, smiling and expectant.

Laurence turns to her. His expression hasn't improved any since he arrived. If anything, it's gotten darker. Whatever news Ken has brought him has not been good. "I'm going out," he says. He's talking in a hurry. He wants to get going, but needs to impart some instructions before he leaves. "I don't think I'll be back today. Hold my messages – and if anyone asks, tell them I'm not well and you don't know when I'll return. I don't want a day full of calls from people waiting on me when I get back."

"Yes, Mr. Morgan."

He turns and leaves, and Ken keeps up.

Danny watches them go. She thinks about following again, like she did yesterday, but it would likely reveal as little to her now as it did then.

Lowering her face back to her desk, to her work, she realizes something. Snaps her attention back to the closed office door. She runs through her memory of the last couple of minutes, remembering the brief interaction she had with

Laurence after he came out of his office. She plays it back, making sure.

He didn't lock the door.

He's never left the door unlocked before. Not even when venturing down the corridor to the bathroom. In his rush, he's forgotten.

Danny bites her lip. This could be her only opportunity to get inside without him present. First, she needs to make sure. To be sure that she's right, and that he forgot to lock it – and to be sure that he's really gone, and that he isn't going to remember and hurry back, walk in on her while she's going through his desk.

She hurries to the corner. Doesn't bother kicking off her shoes this time. She looks down the corridor where Laurence and Ken went. There's no sign of them. They're gone. She hurries back to the office door. She takes a deep breath, much as Laurence did earlier when he first arrived, and she tries the handle.

She was right. It isn't locked.

She steps inside, but doesn't close the door completely behind herself. She leaves it open a crack. This isn't her first time in here, but it's her first time in here without Laurence present.

The ostentatious, varnished wood desk is directly in front of her, with the plush leather chair behind it. It's pressed up against the wall where he's thrown it back in his rush. There are two wooden chairs on the opposite side, but they're both in their usual place. Despite being one-armed, Ken has not wanted to leave a mess on his way out.

There's a filing cabinet in the left corner. Danny's left. She goes straight to it. There are three drawers, unlocked. She doesn't linger on them. They're filled with financial and staff records, but she doesn't need to study them. They don't hold any keys to what she wants to know, even if one of her earliest suspicions of the Temple, that it's laundering money, was a story she was expecting to uncover. Most of these files, especially the ones in the top drawer, have passed her desk. She has looked over them herself. She knows they're airtight. If there *is* money laundering happening (and she has no doubt that there is), whoever Laurence's crooked accountant is, he does a good job.

Danny makes sure to close every drawer after herself, to make sure she hasn't left anything out of place, nothing that could be noticed.

She turns to the desk, and the first thing that catches her eye is a picture resting on top of it. It's in color, but it's on a piece of A4, looks like it's been printed off the computer it lies next to. It's a headshot of a soldier. He's in uniform. He looks to be in his early twenties. Danny hasn't seen him before. She knows that Bill Lindsay has a military background, and maybe this is an old friend of his. Someone he's bringing into the fold, whom he's found a job for. There's a name on the printout, black block writing in a white bar. It says, 'Pvt Tom Rollins.'

Danny leaves the picture of the soldier alone. Whoever he is, whatever the reason for his image being here, he doesn't concern her. She goes to the drawers built into the desk. There are two on the right-hand side – one small, one large – and three on the left. They're all locked. Danny pulls a couple of clips out of her hair and twists them so she can pick the locks. She learned how to pick locks a long time ago. She's self-taught. It's frowned upon by Michael and many others at the paper, but it's helped her get results that were otherwise not forthcoming. The lock on Laurence's door, unfortunately, is not the kind that can be picked. It if were, she would have been in here a long time before now.

She works through all the locks on the drawers before she opens a single one. She sits in the chair and goes through the left side first. The top drawer has an address book and a yellow stress ball with a smiley face on it. The middle drawer is filled with loose pens and a pair of scissors. As she closes each one, she makes sure to relock them. The third drawer, the bottom drawer, gives Danny reason to pause. As she opens it, she hears whatever is inside rolling around. It's a clear glass bottle. At first glance, it looks like it's medicinal. It holds a clear fluid. Danny is careful picking it up, not wanting to leave prints on the glass. She turns it round, reads the label. Potassium cyanide.

Danny stares at the label for a long time, wondering why he has it, why it's in his drawer. She's aware of only one use for it – poison, but she doesn't want to jump to conclusions. She pulls out her phone and searches potassium cyanide. Turns out it's used for fumigation, electroplating, and extracting gold and silver from ores. She sees no current need for any of those things.

She notices something else in the drawer, previously obscured by the bottle. A small plastic bag. She takes it out, checks the contents. Small, green buttons. They look like cacti. Danny knows what it is. She's done enough stories on drug users and sellers to recognize peyote.

She delicately replaces the peyote and the bottle of cyanide and locks the drawer. She moves on, but she can't shake the presence of either of them from her mind. Particularly the cyanide.

On the right, in the top drawer, there are some notepads. Danny takes one out, flicks through it. There are notes and ideas jotted down for potential sermons. She puts it back how she found it.

Then she opens the bottom right drawer. The big drawer. It is filled with photo books. Danny's eyes narrow. The covers are blank. They're black and nondescript. There are three of them, piled on top of each other. She takes out the top one. It is filled with photographs. With Polaroids. Pictures of young girls and occasionally boys, too. They're in classrooms. The classrooms here at the church. There is nothing untoward about these pictures. The children are all fully dressed. In most of the shots, they know their picture is being taken. They smile at the camera. There are some, though, where they seem to have been caught unaware.

Danny flicks through the book. She starts to see some of the same faces reappearing over and over again. She sees them get older. The newer pictures are at the back. They're all still so young. Just kids. Barely into their teens. One girl appears more than all the others. There are more pictures of her alone than the others, too. Closer to the back of the book, the pictures are only of her. At a guess, Danny would say she's fifteen. Maybe fourteen. They are no longer in the classroom. The girl is staring straight into the camera. She is not smiling except for in one, and the smile is forced. It does not touch her eyes. It shows all of her teeth, and she looks more like a cornered animal than someone posing for a portrait.

But despite her strained expression, there's something eye-catching about her. Danny could imagine her being very beautiful if she didn't look so scared. She reminds her of the famous picture of the Afghan girl from the cover of National Geographic. They even look a little alike, except this girl is white. But in her expression, there's the same mixture of pain and exhaustion, but also resilience.

In one, the girl is sleeping. She's not in a classroom. Danny grits her teeth.

Danny hasn't had any call to be around the children who come to the church. They go to a separate part of the building. She doesn't recognize this girl. She puts the photo book to one side, then pulls out the next. She's thinking of Scarlet Wilkins. Wondering if she will make an appearance.

She does. She's halfway through the second book. Danny's heart catches in her throat, and she feels sick.

There are pictures of Scarlet, but her eyes have been scratched out. In every single one. Even the group pictures, with the rest of the class. Someone – and it can only be Laurence – has painstakingly gone through and removed her eyes from every single photograph.

However, despite the damage to her face, Danny can see how she used to be. When she was younger and vibrant and healthy, and there were no scars on her arms. When her hair had not been hacked from her head. When she didn't hate herself. Danny finds a smile, and she sees how warm it was. How happy. How full of life. How similarly beautiful to the other girl there are so many pictures of.

One of the defaced photos near the front of the book is loose in its holder. Had not been put back correctly. It falls to the ground. Danny fails to catch it in the air. She scrabbles for it when it lands. It's facedown. There is writing on the back. Just two words. Her name. Scarlet Wilkins. Danny puts the picture back, then checks the backs of the others. In the early pages, they're all named apart from the classroom pictures. Toward the middle and back, unless they are new faces, they're not named. She goes back to the first book. To the girl there are more pictures of than any other. She checks. She's named. Taylor Hendricks. Danny memorizes it. Tonight, she'll try to find this girl. Find where she lives. See if she can talk to her, find out what she knows about these pictures. Find out *her* story, and if it's similar to Scarlet's.

The thought turns Danny's stomach. Her mouth is dry. She feels sick.

But she has to know the story. Has to know the truth. In the pictures at the back, Taylor is almost crying. In some, she looks like she wants to kill the cameraman.

Danny spreads the two photo books open on the desk.

She pulls out her cell phone and snaps a few pictures, making sure to flick through. She catches Scarlet Wilkins in the images she takes, and her scratched-out eyes.

The phone on Laurence's desk begins to ring, and Danny almost has a heart attack. She hurries to close the books and put them back in their drawer, and to relock it. She goes to the door, to leave the office, but as she reaches it, the answering machine is engaged.

"Laurence, it's me." Danny recognizes the voice. She knows it well. It's Bill Lindsay. "I don't know if you're still at the church or what. I'm gonna try your cell after this, so if you come back to this message and we've already talked, delete it now. Okay – I know you're already pissed about Ken fumbling the brother this morning, but I've got more bad news. They've got away, and the son of a bitch found Taylor's chip. He's destroyed it. We have no idea where they are now. They're in the fucking wind. This Tom, he's more than just a grunt, I'm sure of it. Special Forces, black ops, *something*. But I'm not concerned. I'll deal with him when we catch up to each other. We're gonna try to get ahead of them now. Like we've said all along, she can only go to her brother's, so we're gonna head there. Hopefully we'll cut them off. I'm gonna call your cell now." He hangs up.

Danny hovers in the doorway, curious. Tom? The soldier from the headshot on the desk? Taylor? Taylor Hendricks?

She leaves the office and closes the door and returns to her desk, but she can't sit still. She chews her lip. It's no good – she knows she won't be able to concentrate on church work, and she's not going to try. She pulls out her phone and sends a message to Michael:

I was right. This story has legs. I'm chasing it now.

She gathers up her things and leaves the building without

telling anyone. She doesn't see anyone on her way out, or all the way to her car.

Tom and Taylor. It has to be the Tom from the picture on the desk. It has to be Taylor Hendricks, the girl there are so many pictures of. It's too much of a coincidence of names for it to be anyone else. And Bill referred to Tom as 'not just a grunt.' That was military jargon, right? Danny believes so.

She starts driving, a mix of emotions fogging up her brain. She needs to marshal her thoughts, get them in some kind of order. This is the moment she's been waiting for. The breakthrough. It didn't take a month. It just took one more fucking day. That's all it ever takes. One day, and everything changes.

She pauses before she pulls out of the parking lot. Her phone is ringing on the passenger seat. It's Michael. She ignores it. She's on her way to the office. She can talk to him there. But when she arrives, first things first. Bill mentioned a brother. Taylor's brother. She needs to find out who he is, and *where* he is.

29

The car took more damage than they realized. Tom can feel it in the way it handles. The way it intermittently loses power, then gains it all back. Watching the fuel gauge, he sees how it's going down faster than it should. If he were to get out and check the road behind them, he'd surely be able to find spots where fuel has dripped from their tank.

"Why do we keep slowing?" Taylor says. She's noticed, too.

"Because the Ogre back there hit us harder than I thought he did," Tom says. In the brief glimpse he caught of the man, Tom can understand why she refers to him as such. He has a severe underbite, though Tom assumes the man's actions also likely contribute to such an ugly nickname. "Who is he?" Tom says. "What's his role?"

"I don't know exactly," Taylor says. "He works for Laurence."

"Who came up with the 'Ogre'?"

"I'm not sure. I heard a lot of the other kids call him that. At first I thought it was cruel – he can't help his face, right?

But he *is* a fucking Ogre. He's horrible. If anyone misbehaves or speaks out, they're threatened with him. Told they'll get a visit from him. When Laurence or any of the others are talking about him, they don't call him the Ogre, though. They wouldn't dare. No one would ever say it to his face."

"What's his real name?"

"Bill. Bill Lindsay. He was in the military too, like you. Except he was a Marine. I know because he told me."

"You spend a lot of time with him?"

"No, but he'd be at Laurence's house a lot, and sometimes if Laurence needed to go out or do something or whatever, he'd get Bill to babysit me. We didn't talk much. He'd just sit and glare at me. I was fine with not talking. I didn't wanna make conversation with him. I didn't even wanna be there. Course, after I'd tried to escape a couple of times, he *did* find himself conversational all of a sudden."

Tom feels the car's power fading again. The car behind them grows impatient. It honks its horn and then overtakes.

Tom made sure to make a few turns after he'd left Bill and the others behind in the town. He went out of his way to get onto a back road that it seemed not many vehicles were on. So far, it's been a mostly quiet journey. The car that has just overtaken them is one of the only other vehicles they've seen coming from either direction.

"What an asshole," Taylor says, shaking her head at the car as it speeds away. "It's not like he can't see we're struggling here."

"Yeah. What would Bill talk about?"

"What? Oh. He'd just tell me stories about when he was in the Marines. It's not like it was anything I ever wanted to hear. I tried not to listen. The stories were pretty gross."

"Oh yeah? What kind of things was he telling you?"

"Well, he never said where he was, but he'd always refer to the people there as Arabs – though I guess that doesn't really narrow it down. Anyway, he'd tell me about how many Arabs he'd killed with headshots, and how many Arabs he'd killed with knives. He told me about this one guy that he gutted, but he kept him alive, and he pulled his insides out in front of his eyes and showed them to him." Taylor shivers. "And about, like, skinning people alive. He called it *flaying.* I had to look up what that meant."

"He'd torture people?"

"It sounded that way. I don't wanna talk about it anymore. I didn't like it when he'd brag about killing people. I don't wanna have to remember it now."

"That's fine," Tom says. He watches the gauge. It's going down slow, but faster than it should be. It's not going to get them all the way to Oregon. "He'd brag about it?"

"Yeah. I think it was supposed to scare me – like, if you keep running away, this is the kind of thing I could do to you. That's how I always took it. But it sounded to me like he was really proud of what he'd done. I didn't like that."

Tom nods. "I've always found, anyone who brags about what they got up to in the military, that tends to be a red flag."

"For a fucking psychopath," Taylor says, thinking of Bill.

"Could be. All the guys I've met like that, they weren't people I wanted to spend too much of my time around."

"Mm." Taylor looks toward the dashboard. She listens to the car. "This isn't going to get us to Oregon, is it?"

"No," Tom says. "It isn't."

"Bastards."

"Yeah."

"So what're we gonna do?"

Tom checks the time. They're into the early afternoon. "I'm thinking we find somewhere to eat, then maybe a motel, and you can catch up on all that sleep you missed out on last night. Then we'll continue on fresh in the morning, with the knowledge they don't know exactly where we are and where we're going anymore. Do you know your brother's number?"

"Not by heart," she says. "I had it saved in my phone, but I haven't had my phone for a long time. Not since my mom died."

"Then we can't let him know you're coming. That you're almost there."

Taylor nods. "When *will* we get to Oregon? It feels like I've been trying forever."

"We'll get there tomorrow. We'll just have to have found another vehicle by then."

"One you can maybe keep in one piece this time?" There's a gleam in her eye when she says this.

"I'll do my best," Tom says, keeping one eye on the gauge and another on the road signs they pass advertising diners and motels. There's a diner ten miles down the road, and it seems like there's a motel right next to it. They can make it that far. The gas will hold out until then. But come morning, the vehicle will be useless. It will have all dripped out. They'll have to find something else.

30

Danny sits alone at her oft-neglected desk piled high with story drafts and copy she needs to edit. It's getting late, and everyone else has gone home. She's the only one left.

Sure enough, when she got here earlier, Michael made a beeline straight to her. "What's going on?" he said.

"There's something rotten in the Temple," Danny said, throwing herself into her creaky swivel chair. "And I've got a lead."

"Did you just walk out of there?" he said. "Do they know you've left?"

"If this lead follows through, I won't even need to go back to hand in my notice. They'll *all* know my name soon enough."

"What's *happening*, Danny?" Michael said, exasperated.

"Look," Danny said, turning to him, giving him her full attention. "There's a lot I need to do, and I don't know how long it's gonna take me. All you need to know right now is it didn't take a month." She raised her eyebrows. "Beyond that, you'll find out everything else once I hand the story in."

Michael didn't leave right away. He stood by her cubicle and tapped a pen against the top of the partition. "Fine," he said, relenting. "I'm going to trust your judgment, Danny. All I'll say is it had better be worth the wait." He turned to leave, but stopped long enough to call back over his shoulder, "Because it's been a *long* wait."

Danny hasn't looked up from her desk and her computer since. She lost track of the time. She didn't notice when her rarely seen co-workers were leaving, and didn't hear them if they said goodbye.

First thing she was supposed to find out was who Taylor Hendricks's brother is, and where he lives – but she got distracted. She looked into Tom Rollins first. Which led her to the story of him preventing a terrorist attack in Dallas. This caught her off guard. She wasn't expecting such a story. She fell into a hole of reading the background of what happened in Dallas and the aftermath. Shortly after that, any stories about Tom Rollins trailed off. Seems no one knows where he went.

Which makes her wonder what he's been doing in their small town in Washington State. Makes her wonder how he got involved in all of this.

Running up against a dead-end looking into Tom Rollins's background (though she's stored the knowledge of his involvement in the back of her head – a story that brings in a hero from a thwarted terrorist attack is an angle she was *not* expecting), she moves on to finding out about Taylor's brother. This does not take as long. His name is Josh Hendricks, and he lives in Portland, Oregon, with his wife, Tilly. Finding his address is easy, too. She writes it down, then looks it up on Google Maps. Plots her route. It'll take her eight hours to get there. She checks the time. She'll grab something to eat and then head straight there. She'll arrive early in the morning. She has no idea whether Taylor is there already, or if she'll have to wait. Hopefully Taylor got there safe and sound a while ago. Hopefully the Hendricks are more open to conversation than the Wilkins family were. Hopefully, they can answer her questions. Hopefully, they can tell her exactly what is going on behind the scenes at the Temple of St. Philomena. And, if it's as bad as she thinks, hopefully, they can all bring a lawsuit that will stick.

31

Laurence is at home. Ken is with him. They wait. They're expecting visitors.

Laurence has had to make some calls. To tell his higher-ranking parishioners to come to his home immediately. They need to talk. His tone made it clear that this is an important gathering. That any plans they may already have need to be cancelled or postponed. This won't wait.

Ken checks the time. Out of the corner of his eye, he sees how Laurence is pacing the floor. "They shouldn't be long," Ken says.

"They should have been early," Laurence says. "I made them very aware that they needed to get here as soon as possible."

"It's late," Ken says. "Some of them are old. They were probably sleeping already."

"I would have called them in sooner, but I needed to hear from Bill." Laurence purses his lips, shaking his head, remembering what Bill told him. About how they lost Taylor. *Again*. And, worse, how the man she's with – Tom Rollins –

how he seems to have found the chip in her neck, and how he destroyed it.

Laurence has had to think about this news since. To pray on it. To wait for an answer. He left Ken waiting while he retreated to his study. He keeps some peyote in his desk. He took a small amount, then got down on his knees, and prayed hard for some divine intervention.

The answer came, like it always does.

Laurence made the calls.

Now they wait.

Ken goes to a window and looks out, down the driveway. He stands there for a while.

"Do you see anything?" Laurence says.

"There's some headlights coming now," Ken says. "Too dark for me to see who it is."

"Good," Laurence says. "I'll be in the dining room. When they're all here – and only when they're *all* here, Kenneth – bring them in to me."

Laurence leaves and goes to the dining room. He takes a seat at the head of the table. He checks the time, then closes his eyes and waits. He makes a silent prayer. Part of him has always known this day would come. The whispering of God in his ear, a warning, telling him to be prepared. Well, Laurence listens. He has been prepared. He's been prepared for a long time now.

The front door opens and closes multiple times. Ken and the men who enter converse in hushed tones. Finally, when the door to the dining room opens, Laurence checks the time. From the first arrival, fifteen minutes have elapsed. He'd like to know who was late. He'll ask Ken about it later.

"Gentlemen," Laurence says, not standing, "take a seat. We have much to discuss, and I'd rather get straight into it." Ken hovers by the door. Laurence motions agitatedly for him to sit, too.

There are six men, not including himself and Ken. His highest-ranking parishioners. The most powerful members of his church. Laurence looks around the table, into each of their faces. Carl Smith – businessman. Bob Rhodes – councilman. Stanley Allanson – councilman and friend of Bob. He brought Bob along to the church in the first place and introduced him to the delights it has to offer. Clive Buck – mayor of Belleville. David Mackenzie – state trooper. John Davison – head detective for the Belleville police. All six men have made great contributions to the church, both financially and personally. In turn, Laurence has rewarded them, spiritually and physically. The church means the world to them, and they will protect it with their lives.

At least, this is what Laurence expects of them.

"There is something you all need to know," Laurence says. He proceeds to tell them of recent events. Of how Taylor has run away, and how she is being assisted in her escape attempt by a mysterious man named Tom Rollins. "Bill is after them," he says, and this information calms them somewhat. "And I have every confidence that he will track them down and bring Taylor back to me."

There are murmurs of agreement.

"*But* if he *doesn't*, if things go badly, we need to be prepared for what will happen next."

The men look at each other. They turn back to Laurence. Bob Rhodes is the first to speak, as if their gazes have silently nominated him. "What happens next?"

Laurence clasps his hands together and looks at Bob for a long time. He looks each of them in the eye, lingering each time. When he's done, he speaks. "I need you all to keep your phones on you at all times and to be prepared at a moment's notice. If I call you, you are to come running. And I don't mean like tonight – you cannot drag your heels. You are to come to me *immediately*, to the Temple of St. Philomena. We will meet together there, and we will take the next step of our journey together. Time is of the utmost importance. When I call you, you must come."

Clive Buck shifts in his seat. He clears his throat. "And what, exactly, does the next step of our journey entail?"

Laurence smiles. "Why, we ascend, of course."

"Uh-huh," Clive says, scratching his cheek. "I, uh, I think I'm gonna need a bit more information than that."

"And I am fully prepared to give it to you – to all of you – but I keep getting interrupted." He smiles at Clive, then at Bob.

"Uh, sorry," Clive says.

"When I call you, you must come to the Temple. And when you come, bring your chosen ones."

"If we're not already with them, how are we supposed to get them?" David Mackenzie says.

"Take them if need be," Laurence says. "Use force if you absolutely have to. It won't matter if you need to expose yourself. Get them, and bring them. And then we will drink together, and then we will ascend."

"Drink? Drink what?" Clive says.

"The blood of Christ. Blessed by God Himself. Something that will bring us closer to Him. It will take us directly to Him, bathed in a heavenly glow. Just us and our brides and our holy thoughts, on a direct journey to the kingdom that awaits us."

They realize what he's talking about. Clive shifts in his seat again, and this time Stanley does the same. Carl Smith swallows. Some of the color has drained from his face.

"But this is only if Bill doesn't bring Taylor back," John Davison says. "Right?"

Laurence nods. "That's correct."

"So you won't have her if he's not successful."

"Sometimes, to get close to God, we need to make sacrifices. With or without Taylor, I have more than earned my heavenly reward."

John nods at this, understanding, satisfied.

"I don't –" Clive says, shaking his head, grinding his jaw, balling a fist atop the table. "I don't think – I mean, how can we be sure..." He trails off, unable to think straight. He shakes his head again. "This feels extreme. There has to be another way, something else..."

"Clive is right," Stanley says. "This just seems too much. When I first joined the Temple, when *any* of us first joined, we weren't told there'd be anything like this. You just promised us – you promised us we could have a good time. That it would be discreet; no one would ever know. You made promises. You lured us in with these girls, and now – no –" He trails off, gasping. He composes himself. When he continues, his voice is small. "There has to be something else we can do rather than just killing ourselves –"

"Uh-uh-uh," Laurence says, shaking a finger. "That's not what we're doing, Stanley. Suicide is a sin, correct? Indeed. We are embracing our immortality. God has spoken to me. He has told me the path we need to take."

Clive and Stanley both still look doubtful.

Laurence looks around the table, studying each of the six faces. John's is firm. He understands. He knows what needs to be done. As do David and Bob. Carl remains pale, is clearly as unsure as Clive and Stanley, though he's not vocalizing his feelings.

Laurence knows what he needs to do. He needs to regain control. To put things in order. "Gentlemen, you need to understand," he says. "That if Taylor talks, your lives on this plane will no longer be worth living. There are those who don't understand the purity of our love and our guidance from the Lord."

They consider this. Deep down, they know he's right.

Laurence is not finished. He has another push left to give. "And Bill will be on hand," he says. "I'm sure he would hate to have to find any of you if you were not to come when I call."

If the threats of the police and negative public opinion cannot sway them, the promise of a visit from Bill will make things very clear to them.

Clive and Stanley have nothing left to say. They lower their heads, avoid eye contact.

"That will be all, gentlemen," Laurence says, dismissing them. "Keep your phones close. When the time comes, I don't want to have to call any of you twice."

32

Taylor showered and got a full night's sleep in the motel room. Tom slept intermittently and made sure to regularly sweep the grounds. The chip being found and removed was no reason to become careless. Carelessness could get them caught.

"How do you feel?" he asks when Taylor wakes.

"Good," she says, stretching and yawning. "I feel really good. What time is it?"

"It's still early." Outside, the morning sun is shining. It pours through a crack in the curtains. "Once you're dressed, we'll get moving."

"We're close to Oregon now," Taylor says, rolling out of bed and gathering up her clothes. She pauses. "Do you think they could still find us?"

"They'll still be looking. I've got no doubt about that. We need to be prepared in case they *do* find us."

Taylor finishes getting dressed. Tom gathers up his things. Checks through his bag. He pulls out his Santa Muerte pendant, holds it in the palm of his hand. Looks at it. He looks back at Taylor, then back at the pendant. He stares at

Santa Muerte for a long time. He deliberates. Pulls the picture of Alejandra out of his bag. She smiles at him. She'd understand.

"Taylor." He stands, turns to her.

"Yeah?" She looks up at him. She's smiling. She's hopeful. They're nearly in Oregon. She's nearly at her brother's home, where she'll be safe. This is nearly all over for her. For the first time, she looks happy to Tom. She's clean and well rested. She brushes a strand of hair behind her ear, and she looks her age. Any other fourteen-year-old. She doesn't look tired and beaten and haunted. She looks just as she always should have.

"I've got something for you," Tom says. He holds out his hand.

Taylor frowns. She doesn't understand. She steps closer, inspects what he's holding out to her. "A necklace?"

"It's Santa Muerte," he says. "Do you know who she is?"

Taylor shakes her head. "I've seen the image before, but that's all."

"She brings protection," Tom says. "She's brought it to me for a long time now. I want you to have her."

Taylor's eyes go wide. She's touched by the gesture. "I can't take that," she says. "I appreciate it, and it's a beautiful necklace, but she's yours. I can't take her from you. You've already..." She looks at him. "You've already done so much for me."

Tom holds the pendant out, doesn't lower his arm. "When I was in the Army, someone gave this to me because she didn't want me to get hurt. She knew that where I was going, she couldn't come with me. She gave me this so Santa Muerte would watch over me. So Santa Muerte would visit me where she couldn't. And now, all these years later, I'm still alive. I'm not saying it was a piece of jewellery that kept me breathing. She represents something. She represents the person who wanted to keep me safe. And now I want to give her to you, to keep you safe, for the times I'm not around."

"What about the person who gave it to you?" Taylor says. "She won't be upset you've given it away?"

Tom smiles. "No, she won't. She'll understand. She'd want you to have it."

Taylor stares at the pendant. Tentatively, she reaches out and touches it with the tips of her fingers. She picks it up and looks at it closely. She turns it over in her hands, then looks back up at Tom. "Should I put it on?"

Tom nods.

Taylor slips it over her head. The pendant rests against her chest, at the top of her sternum, where her collarbone meets in the center. She keeps a hand pressed against it. "How's it look?" she says.

"It suits you," Tom says. "Make sure you take care of her. She'll do the same for you."

Taylor nods. "I will. I promise. Thank you."

Tom picks up his bag. It feels lighter without the pendant inside, though he knows this is all in his mind. "Let's go," he says. "Oregon awaits."

33

They took a car from the motel's parking lot. Tom jimmied the lock and hotwired the ignition. Using his KA-BAR, he swapped the plates with the vehicle next to it.

They've been driving a few hours. They're in Oregon now. They crossed the border a little while back. Taylor saw the sign. "Holy shit, we made it," she said, laughing giddily, hardly able to believe it. She played with the Santa Muerte pendant, twisting it between her fingers and thumb. Tom noticed how she does this now instead of pulling on her fingers and scratching her hands. If he'd realized it could distract her from harming herself, he would have given it to her sooner.

Of course, parting with something so important to himself, so sacred, wasn't easy to do. But it felt right. Taylor needs Santa Muerte more than he does.

Tom has followed the signs to Portland. When they reach it, Taylor starts giving directions once she recognizes some landmarks. "I know the way from here," she says. "It's been a long time, but I've never forgotten it. All the while I was by myself, when I was hoping someone would pick me up and give me a ride, I thought about this route over and over in my head, so I'd know where to tell them to go. Even before I'd got away, I'd think about it. I memorized it."

"That's good," Tom says. It's his first time in Portland. "Because I don't have any idea where I'm going right now."

Taylor laughs. "We're not far. We're almost there." The smile hasn't left her face since they entered the state.

She guides Tom into a suburban neighborhood. There are wood-pillared porches and manicured lawns and, in some instances, white picket fences. There are children's bicycles propped down the sides of buildings. A couple of skateboards. There are signs of the chaos of children playing, but everything is in order. Everything is kept neat. Today is a school day. A workday. Most of the driveways are empty, the people inside at their nine-to-fives. The road is mostly quiet.

This place looks good. It looks safe. It is a home. It is warm and inviting. A place for children to grow up safely, without concerns for the monsters of the world, safe from their grasp.

"There it is," Taylor says, pointing, trying not to bounce in her seat.

Tom sees the house. Josh and Tilly Hendricks's home. It looks the same as the others. It stands proud and inviting. A safe refuge. There is a car in this driveway. "Is that your brother's?" Tom says.

"I think it's Tilly's," she says. "She must be home. Josh is probably at work. He works for the power company."

Tom pulls to a stop in front of the house. His eyes are searching the street, the road, the few cars that are parked on it. None of them look familiar. None of them look like the ones that have been chasing them. They're all empty, too.

Taylor unstraps her seatbelt. Tom holds out a hand to

stop her bolting from the car. "Take your time," he says. "Don't run off. Stay close to me."

"But we're *here* –" she starts to say, but then she stops herself. She understands. She nods her head once, solemnly. "Okay," she says.

Tom gets out of the car first, then heads round and opens the passenger door for her. He continues to look, to search for signs of anything out of place. He looks into the windows of the other homes. He looks into the windows of Josh and Tilly's home. Upstairs, the curtains are closed despite it being nearly midday. The front window is elevated and hard to see into from where they are. They go to the porch, and they knock.

There's no answer. Taylor looks at him. "She could be sleeping," Tom says. "The curtains are drawn upstairs." For all he knows, Tilly could work nights.

"Should we try the handle?" Taylor says.

Tom tries it. It's locked. He knocks again, glances back toward the road, looks up and down it. It's quiet. Everything is still. The people at home don't hear anything going on outside. They can't hear the knocking. They go about their chores, or they watch daytime television or read a book. Eat a late breakfast, maybe. Or perhaps they're still sleeping. As Tilly might be.

"We'll try the back," Tom says. They go down the side of the house. There are no bicycles propped here. No skateboards or scooters, either.

Tom stretches his arm across Taylor's chest as they reach the corner, to stop her. She doesn't make a sound as she walks into his arm. She halts. He feels her body tense. She's ready to react at his say-so. Ready to turn and race back to the car.

Tom is looking at the back door. It's closed, but he spots signs of damage. Splintered wood in the frame. A boot print near the handle that someone has poorly attempted to wipe away. The splinters, too, someone has attempted to disguise. To pick them out. They didn't get them all. The back door has been kicked in, then slotted back into place.

Tom pulls out his Beretta. Taylor sees. She swallows. "Stay here," he says. "You hear anything wrong, you run. I'll catch up."

He sees her nod out of the corner of his eye. He steps forward, peers around the corner of the kitchen window. There's nothing to see inside. The blind here has been pulled down. He can't see in, but anyone inside can't see out, either. He goes to the back door and tries the handle. It's been left ajar, as if letting in an early-morning breeze. A gentle push opens it the rest of the way. Tom steps inside, gun raised. The kitchen is clear. He steps lightly, moving through to the living room, not making a sound.

There are signs of a struggle. Someone has attempted to put things back into place, but they don't look quite right. The sofa and the footrest at odd angles. A scratch in the wall, chipping the paint, and a picture frame knocked off-center. It's a picture of a couple. Tom assumes them to be Josh and Tilly. They look young. Tom wonders if it's an old picture. If it's from before Josh moved out of the family home, came down to Portland.

There's no one in the room, but to his right is a door leading down to a basement, and another next to it, presumably for a closet. The basement makes him nervous. Someone could be there, hiding, waiting to spring out. Tom remembers the last time he was dragged into a basement. He doesn't want to repeat that experience. He edges toward the door, footsteps still silent, gun raised. He needs to make sure it's clear.

There are steps on the stairs, descending. Tom wheels to the sound, gun raised. He doesn't think it's Tilly, just waking, bleary-eyed and yawning. The steps are too heavy for a woman. Whoever it is, they're wearing boots, too.

The steps stop before they can come into view. Tom hears a voice. It's coarse and hard-edged and used to being listened to. "I assume you've got a gun pointing my direction right now," it says. "That right, Tom?"

They know who he is. Doesn't make a difference. Tom stands his ground.

"I'm coming down," the voice says. "I'd suggest you lower your weapon."

Tom doesn't. He keeps it aimed right where it is, then turns his head and shouts, "Taylor, *run*!"

The voice up the stairs barks, "Get her! Get him!"

The door to the basement slams open, and a row of men rush out. One of them bolts straight for the back door – after Taylor – but the rest of them are coming Tom's way. He lowers the gun, but before he can loose a single round, he's tackled around the waist and driven back across the floor, to the wall. He strikes back with his knees and slams the handle of the gun into the back of the man wrapped around him, but then other men are grabbing his arms and pinning them, holding him in place. They take the gun from him. They're about to start hitting when the voice from the stairs speaks up. "Don't harm him," it says.

Bill Lindsay steps into view. He's smiling, a hideous grin, his jaw jutting out so far it contorts his whole face. Tom can understand why Taylor refers to him as the Ogre.

Tom quickly counts the other men, the ones who emerged from the basement. Seven of them have swarmed him. Eight, including the one who's gone after Taylor. Nine, including Bill Lindsay.

Tom wonders if they have others holding back, in reserve. They might be with the vehicles, hiding them, ready to pull them to the front of the house when they're summoned.

Bill steps close. He's carrying a gun. It's a Beretta, too. Same as Tom's. Army issue. "I hear you're a military man," Bill says, looking him over, appraising him. "Makes sense. I'd have caught you a long time before now if you didn't have training. But I *have* caught you."

"Uh-huh," Tom says. "I hear you're a sadistic asshole."

Bill laughs. "I'm flattered," he says, "to hear that Taylor talks of me." He raises his gun then and brings it down across the top of Tom's head. The handle impacts with Tom's skull, but on its way down, the barrel catches him across the brow. Warm blood starts running down his face. Tom is already dizzy when Bill hits him again. The edges of his vision darken, and the blood gets in his eyes. Tom battles to remain conscious. The men on either side of him are propping him up. Through the blood, he sees the eighth man return. He has Taylor.

34

Danny has stopped once on her way to Oregon, for a food, fuel, and bathroom break. Other than that, she's driven through the night and the morning. Her eyelids feel like sandpaper, and her lower back is aching. The coffee she bought when she stopped at the gas station, which she has sipped from intermittently for the caffeine, is freezing cold beside her. She finds this out the hard way as she takes a drink and almost gags, has to spit it out the window.

The use of Maps leads her straight to the suburb where Josh and Tilly Hendricks live. She knocks the app off, then crawls along the road, counting door numbers, searching for the one she needs.

Then, out of the corner of her eye, she sees a young girl burst from alongside a house and keep running. Danny slams on the brakes, startled and panicking, thinking she's closer than she is, that she's about to run out in front of her, but instead the girl veers left and flees across lawns, and then Danny sees why she's running. A man follows behind her. He's fast, and he's gaining.

Danny sits frozen, not understanding, watching it play out in slow motion as the man tackles the girl to the ground, wrestles with her for a bit before he's able to get the upper hand and subdue her. Then Danny counts up the door numbers and realizes the girl has just run from the house she's searching for. The home of Josh and Tilly Hendricks. Except she looks too young to be Tilly.

Taylor.

Danny can't get a good look at her face. As the man hauls her up, she continues to thrash. He carries her back the way they came. Toward Danny. Danny doesn't know what to do. She turns off her engine and ducks low behind her wheel before the man has a chance to see her.

Head bowed, she breathes low. It's the only sound she can hear. Eventually, she risks raising her head to look over the dash. The man and the girl – Taylor? Was it Taylor? – are gone now. Presumably back into the house.

Danny thinks about what to do. If she should try to get closer to the house. If she should call the police. She kicks herself for not reacting sooner, for not reacting *better*. She should have driven straight on toward the chase. She should have confronted the man. She may not have been able to fight him, to stop him from what he was doing, but she could have stalled him, caused a scene, drawn the attention of people inside their homes.

It's too late now. Too late for *that*. Now she needs to decide what her next move will be. How she can *actually* help.

Before she can reach a decision, three black minivans pull up in front of the house. Danny stays low. A group emerges from the house, coming along the side, from the back. The same way the girl ran from. The girl is with them now. Two men hold her, one on either side. They drag her despite how she struggles. They bundle her into the back of one of the cars.

Among the other men behind them, there is a man being carried. His head hangs low, and Danny thinks he is bleeding. She can see it dripping from the top of his head. He's not unconscious, though. He raises his head enough that she recognizes him from the picture she saw on Laurence Morgan's desk. He's older now, but it's him. Tom Rollins. Tom and Taylor. She's found them.

But she's not the only one.

Then, last out, strolling leisurely, is Bill Lindsay.

"*Shit!*" Danny ducks lower, praying he doesn't see her. That he doesn't notice her car. She's not sure he'd recognize it. She remembers the last time she saw him, at the diner, when she'd gone somewhere she didn't ordinarily go in an effort to get some work done. That was only a couple of days ago now. Remembers how he took a phone call and left abruptly. That must have been to do with Tom and Taylor.

Cautiously, she peers back over the wheel. Bill appears to be overseeing things. Tom is put in the back of a separate car. The men handling them spread themselves out among the three vehicles. Bill gets into the back of the vehicle with Taylor. The small convoy drives away. Danny presses herself into the passenger seat to stay out of view of them. She sits back up once they've passed, and watches their retreat in her side mirror. Her heart is pounding. She holds her breath and wraps her hands around her steering wheel. She needs to call the cops. Tell them what she's seen. She watches the mirror. The convoy is getting further away. The cops wouldn't get here in time. She kicks herself, realizing she didn't take any notice of the license plates. Three nondescript black minivans. It all happened so fast. By the time the cops could get here, it would be too late. They could be long gone.

"Okay," she says, starting the engine. "Okay. *Fuck*."

She spins the car around in the middle of the road, and she follows them.

35

Taylor readied herself to scream as she was dragged to the car. Bill had come up behind her, though. She didn't hear him. He'd worked out what she was about to do. Likely heard her deep intake of breath. He clamped a meaty hand on the back of her neck and spoke into her ear. "Do you know how easy I could snap this?" he said.

It stopped her from screaming, but now, trapped in the back of a minivan with him on one side and one of his men on the other, she wishes she had. Damn the consequences, and what he might have done, because she's trapped again. A captive. *Their* captive. And they're taking her back to *him*.

"You've given us the runaround for longer than I would've ever thought you could," Bill says. Neither of the men on either side of her makes accommodations for their bulk, so Taylor is crushed, her shoulders bunched up toward her ears and her hands clasped between her thighs. "But it's over now, and it'll never happen again. I'm going to make sure of that personally."

"Fuck you," Taylor says, but it's not as defiant as she hoped it would sound. The air is crushed from her lungs between the two of them, and all she managed was a wheeze. "Where's Tom?"

Bill chuckles.

"Where's my brother? Where's Tilly?"

"Don't worry about them," Bill says. "You'll see them both soon enough."

"You have them?"

"I said don't worry about it," Bill says. He's grinning, his jaw jutting, and he looks very pleased with himself. He reaches over and places a hand atop her head, turns it so he can inspect the back of her neck, the bandage there. He lets go of her, says, "And you'll be getting another one of them. Don't think just cos you found it the first time, that you're home free. You're gonna be chipped, and you're gonna be watched twenty-four-fucking-seven. You think it was bad before? You've got no fucking idea, sweetheart."

Taylor doesn't respond. She doesn't want to think about it.

"Y'know, out of all the kids we've chipped, you're the only one we've ever had to actually fucking track down. The only one we've ever had to make use of it for." He speaks over the top of her head now, to the man on the other side of her. "Just goes to show it's worthwhile, though, right? Just like I said it would be."

"That's what you said," the man agrees.

Taylor closes her eyes. The blood is pounding in her ears. She stares through the front seats, out the window to the road ahead. It stretches before her, but she knows where it leads. To Washington. To Belleville. To Laurence.

She feels outside of her body. She disassociates. She closes her eyes and pretends she's somewhere else. Anywhere else. Not between these two men. She's in the passenger seat.

She's nodding off. Tom is driving. He's taking her to her brother. Taking her to safety. Everything is fine. Everything is going to be all right.

36

"You remember me?"

Tom is dizzy, but he has remained conscious. He blinks the blood out of his eyes and looks to his right, to the man talking to him. He's thickset, and there is bruising around his neck. Tom remembers him just fine from back at the gas station. Remembers how he got the bruises, too. "Not a clue," Tom says. "You expect me to remember every random asshole I come across on the day-to-day?"

The man glowers. "It's *Donald*, motherfucker," he says, spitting. "And I'm gonna make sure you remember it."

"Uh-huh." Tom yawns. Donald is to his right, and there's another man on Tom's left. Guy in the passenger seat, and another driving. The two either side are trying to box him in. Tom stretches out.

His wrists are bound behind his back. He's sitting on his hands. The bindings feel like plastic cable ties. "Where's Taylor?" he says.

"Don't matter," Donald says. "I didn't come here for her. I came for *you*. Got the call and I came running."

"I'm flattered," Tom says. "Or maybe a little creeped out,

I'm not sure yet." Tom looks through the windshield. There's a vehicle up ahead that they're keeping pace with. When he was dragged from the house, Tom didn't get a good look at what they were being dragged to, what they were being put in. He has to assume Taylor is in the car up ahead.

He looks around. The driver and the front passenger aren't facing him. The driver is concentrating on the road ahead and following the vehicle in front. The guy to Tom's left is watching, listening to Donald. Donald hasn't taken his eyes off Tom.

"Ain't looking so tough now, are ya?" he says.

"I dunno," Tom says, "we could always take these bindings off and find out just how tough we are. Of course, I've already had a sample of what you're bringing to the table, and it isn't up to much. These three gentlemen, however..." Tom glances around the car again, and he's got all of their attention now. The front passenger looks over his shoulder, an eyebrow raised. The driver is watching him in the mirror.

"Back at the gas station, I wouldn't have guessed you were so talkative," Donald says. "I'm gonna enjoy shutting you up."

"Sure," Tom says. He turns his attention to him fully, smiles at him, holds his eye. He gets his body into position, angling himself so the guy on his left is directly behind him. "Unless I shut you up first."

Before Donald can respond, Tom head-butts him. Then before the guy on Tom's left can react, he throws his head back, embeds it in the center of his face. Both men cry out on impact. He hears and feels bones in their faces crunch. He can see blood pouring down Donald's. No doubt if he were to turn to the other, he'd see more of the same. He doesn't have time to inspect his handiwork. The front passenger is unbuckling himself, twisting. Tom hasn't been strapped in. Their mistake. He's able to move more freely. He presses himself back against Donald and raises a leg, kicks the front passenger across the jaw. He falls into the driver, who cries out. He loses his grip on the steering wheel. The car veers. He grabs it again, but before he can right the vehicle, regain control of it, Tom kicks him in the back of the head.

The car goes to the right, spinning hard. They're heading into the trees that line the road. Tom braces himself. He's thrown into the back of the front passenger's seat on impact. He can't see what they've hit. The front passenger gives a choked cry, crushed by the seat and Tom on top of it.

Donald is gasping. He spits blood and unbuckles himself, grabs the door handle. He falls from the vehicle. Tom rolls out after him, over the top of him. When he stands, he sees that they've hit a tree.

Donald is on his hands and knees, coughing. Tom kicks him in the side of the head. He goes down limp.

Tom turns. No other vehicles have stopped yet. They've no doubt seen the crash, but they were going too fast to stop, or else it isn't safe for them to do so. Or maybe they're just not interested. Tom needs to keep moving. Needs to get back on the road, after them. He's lost track of them, but they'll be going to Belleville. The car he was in is totalled. He can't use it. First, he needs to get himself free of the cable ties.

A car pulls to the side. The passenger window rolls down. Before Tom can make a move, the woman inside calls to him. "*Tom!*"

He blinks, not sure he's heard her right.

She waves him over. "Tom, get in!" She pushes the passenger door open.

Tom looks back down the road, the direction they've taken Taylor. He looks back to the woman calling his name. He doesn't have any other option. He gets in her car.

37

Danny uses her keys to cut Tom free from the plastic ties. He regards her warily, clearly wondering how she knows his name. "Start driving," he says.

Danny does. He wants to ask her questions, she can tell – who she is, how she knows him – but it's apparent they need to get moving. "Where's Taylor?" she says.

"She's up ahead," Tom says. If he's just as surprised she knows about Taylor, he doesn't let it show. "We're gonna try catching up to her, but if we can't, it doesn't matter – I know where they're going."

"I reckon I know where they're going, too." Danny pulls away from the side of the road, merges into the fast-flowing traffic and leaves the crashed car behind.

"All right," Tom says. "Now we're on the road, spill. You know who I am, and you know who Taylor is – what I wanna know is how and why?"

"My name's Danny Temple. I'm an investigative journalist. I was doing a story on the Temple of St. Philomena – Laurence Morgan is an enigmatic figure with a mystery background, and my priest gave me a hint that maybe all's not well within the Temple. So I took Father Dudley's lead, but I'll be honest – I didn't think things were gonna get quite so...*murky*."

"You know what they're doing there?"

"Not entirely," Danny says. "But I have an idea, and that's why I've come looking for Taylor. To ask *her* what's been happening, because no one else will talk to me. The people I *have* approached were scared. Hell, they were fucking *terrified*."

"How do you know who I am?"

"Found your headshot on Laurence's desk. From your Army days. You looked very dashing in your uniform, Tom." She winks.

"He just keeps that lying around?"

"I've been working at the Temple – took a job as an administrative assistant, ended up being his secretary. Yesterday, he forgot to lock his door. First time I'd seen him do that – he obviously had other things on his mind – and now I've got a better idea of what those distractions were. I took advantage of his forgetting, and I came across a *lot* of worrying things once I got inside his desk."

"Dare I ask what?"

"Well, for a start, all the pictures of the kids in photo albums. There were a *lot* of Taylor. Made my skin crawl."

"Had every reason to. It's as bad as you think."

"Shit..." Danny tries not to think about it too much, not right now. "Poor girl. I met another. She must've been through the same thing – her name is Scarlet. I found her picture in the books, too. Does Taylor know how many kids this is...affecting?"

"She mentioned an orphanage in Belleville, or maybe near it," Tom says. "People running it must be in on what Laurence is up to. She doesn't know exact numbers, though. She was Laurence's favorite, so he kept her all to himself. At a guess, I'd say it's gotta be dozens. But, historically, how long's it been going on for? It could be more than that."

Danny grits her teeth, a wave of nausea running through her. "I'm gonna find out," she says. "And I'm gonna make sure they fucking burn for it."

Tom grunts. "Race you."

They watch the road. The cars.

"You find anything else in his desk?" Tom says.

"A bag of peyote," Danny says. "Seems the pastor likes to dabble in hallucinogenics."

"You notice him high before?"

"Can't say I have. Oh, and also, the same drawer he kept the peyote in, there was a bottle of cyanide."

Tom's eyes narrow. "Cyanide?"

Danny nods. "Yup. Had me wondering what the fuck he's doing with that ever since. Anyway, how'd you end up getting involved in all this?"

"I saw a kid in trouble, and I helped out. Didn't think it was gonna lead down a rabbit hole as deep as this one."

"So just a Good Samaritan."

"Guess so. What're you doing in Oregon? If you're investigating the church, I assume you're from Belleville."

"I am." Danny nods. "I came looking for Taylor, like I said. I heard Laurence saying she'd try to get to her brother's, so I found out where he lives, and I came here."

"You know what happened to him? He wasn't home, neither was his wife. Signs of a struggle."

"I turned up as they were bundling you and Taylor in the back of their cars."

"And you've followed us since? That's good timing for me. Maybe not so good for you."

"I was trying to catch up," Danny says. "Then I saw the minivan you were in crash and you fall out of it."

Tom watches the road, checks the vehicles ahead. "I don't see them yet."

"They'll go back to Belleville," Danny says.

"I know they will," Tom says, "but I'd like to stop them before they get there. I made a promise to Taylor that I won't let them take her back. I promised I won't let them hurt her again. I may have failed on the first promise, but I don't intend to on the second."

"Well," Danny says, putting her foot down, "we're still in Oregon – you haven't failed that first promise yet."

38

Bill's phone begins to ring. He shifts so he's able to pull it from his pocket, his bulk pushing Taylor further toward the other man. Bill checks the caller ID. It's Donald. Bill frowns, and instinctively he turns, looks back. Their car isn't behind them anymore.

He feels a sinking in the pit of his stomach, and he answers the call. "Donald," he says.

Donald is panting. He groans. "He got away."

Bill presses the phone hard to the side of his head to muffle Donald's voice. He doesn't want Taylor to hear. "What do you mean?"

"He made us crash," Donald says. "You didn't see it happen?"

"It sound like I saw it?"

"I mean, I guess not..."

"What happened?"

"He started kicking, and we crashed. I don't know where he's gone. Fucker kicked me in the face when I was down, and everything went black. Time I come back around, he's outta here. Must've disappeared into the trees or something."

Bill struggles to lower his voice. "So you're saying you don't know where he is?"

Taylor turns her head a little. She's listening.

"No, he's gone."

"And no one you're with saw anything, either?"

"They were hurting. Most of them were knocked out in the crash."

"You're fucking useless, you know that, Donald?"

Donald doesn't have anything to say to this.

"We've got a long way to go," Bill says, not caring that his voice is rising, not caring if Taylor hears and understands now, "if he catches up and tries to stop us, I'll kill him on the fucking road if I have to." He hangs up, speaks to his men in the car. "You heard enough of that? You understand what's happened? We've gotta assume he's coming. Getting hold of vehicles doesn't seem to have been a problem for him so far. Keep your eyes out the windows and on the mirrors. You know what he looks like. I know it's gonna be hard to see who's driving each vehicle we see, but we're gonna have to try. You spot him, speak up. Only one of you I expect to not have a hundred percent of their attention on lookout is the driver."

The men all grunt their acknowledgment. Bill looks at Taylor. She doesn't look back at him. Her bound hands play with something hidden under the fabric of her shirt, a necklace he didn't realize she was wearing. She's trying not to grin, hopeful at what she has heard.

"If you're lucky," Bill says, "you might get to see your friend one more time, right as I'm putting a bullet between his fucking eyes."

This kills her grin. Her hands stop fidgeting and wrap tight around whatever she is playing with. She squeezes it. She bites her lip. Bill sees a small dot of blood appear.

He grins to himself, then turns and looks out the rear window, into the vehicles coming up behind them.

39

"With Taylor's story, we could bring down Laurence – bring down the church," Danny says. "If she speaks out, all the others will talk, too. I'm sure I could get Scarlet to. All the ones we don't know about, they'll follow her example. They've got to."

"Uh-huh," Tom says. "Right now, my priority is getting Taylor back and then finding out what's happened to her brother. I'm not thinking about your story, I'm afraid, Ms. Temple." None of the cars ahead look familiar. Danny overtakes, finds places where it's safe for her to get around the traffic and get ahead.

"The story could save a lot of future lives," Danny says. "And get justice for many others."

"Sure," Tom says. "That's very noble. But like I said, right now, it's not my priority."

Danny rolls her eyes.

"We need to think ahead," Tom says. "In case we're not able to catch up with them. In case we need to follow them all the way back to Belleville. Where would they take her? The church?"

"I've never seen her there," Danny says. "I've never seen any kids there, but it's a big church. They gather in another part of it – I've seen the classrooms."

"Is it secure enough for Laurence and the others to...to do what they do?"

"I've worked late most nights," Danny says. "I've never seen any gatherings. Nothing like that."

"At his house?" Tom says.

"Would he really risk it at his home? I guess he could..."

"The pictures you said you saw of her. Where were they? The backgrounds, I mean."

"Most of them were in the church, in the classrooms. Some of them – there was one of her sleeping. But it was dark, and even if it was in Laurence's home, I've never been inside. I wouldn't know what his rooms look like."

"Do you know where it is?"

"Yeah," Danny says. "I think everyone in Belleville knows where it is."

Tom starts to ask another question, but he stops. They've reached a quiet stretch of the road, and something up ahead has caught his eye. "That's them," he says. Two vehicles, black minivans similar to the one he was in. The one he remembers seeing through the windshield, following close to the one in front of it. There were three outside Josh's house. Identical. Tom was able to see that much, at least.

"That's them," Danny says, agreeing. She speeds up. Tom doesn't have to tell her. Her engine, however, sounds like it's about to explode. It screams in protest. "What's the plan?" she says. "I can get us closer, but beyond that..."

"Do you know which one Taylor is in?"

"The rear one," Danny says. "They put her in the middle, but obviously there isn't a middle anymore."

"Then get me next to it."

Danny crosses the lanes, accelerating. "Jesus, what are you gonna do?"

Tom doesn't get a chance to answer. Up ahead, he sees Bill leaning out the window. He twists toward them. His gun is in hand. He points it.

"Shit!" Danny says.

Bill fires. He hits the windshield between Tom and Danny. They both duck low. Bill keeps firing. Bullets smash through the glass, tear through their seats. Shards fall down between them, on them. Tom hears the bullets thud into the hood. He sees smoke rising. Danny has lost control of the car. He can't see where they're going. There's a bump, and something scrapes the bottom. For the second time in less than an hour, Tom is in a car crash.

40

Taylor hears the many cracks of Bill's gun. She's too scared to turn, to look, to see what's happening. Even if she weren't, the guy beside her has his arm around her shoulders, holding her in place, presumably in case she should try to push Bill the rest of the way out the window.

Bill slides back in. "Did you get him?" the guy holding her says. He lets go of her now she's crushed between the two of them again.

"I got the car," Bill says. Despite this apparent success, he looks annoyed. "They won't be able to come after us. But I didn't get *them*."

"Them?" the other guy says.

"Someone was driving for him. Couldn't see who it was, but it looked like a woman. Almost missed Rollins in the passenger seat." He slams the flat of his hand against the back of the driver's seat. "Circle back! I wanna make sure I got the son of a bitch."

The driver screeches to a halt and spins the vehicle.

Taylor closes her eyes tight. Her heart is pounding. She wills Tom to be all right. Wills him to have gotten clear of the crashed car, for him not to be there when the Ogre catches up.

She opens her eyes again when she feels the car slow, and Bill curses. "*Shit,*" he says. He hits the back of the driver's seat again. "Should've been faster, goddammit! You let them get away!"

Taylor resists breathing a sigh of relief. She sees the crashed, abandoned car.

"Turn us back around," Bill says. "Let's get out of here."

The driver does as he's told.

"Who was he with?" the guy to Taylor's left asks. "Just someone who stopped to pick him up?"

"I don't know," Bill says. "It looked like she was trying to catch up to us. She was driving *fast.*" Bill twists, looks back down the road as they leave the crash scene behind. He blows air out of his nose. Taylor feels it land hot on her cheek and the side of her neck.

"You'll get him next time," the other guy says.

"Damn right, next time," Bill says, though this appears to be scant consolation to him. He shoves the back of the driver's seat again, gives him a jolt. "We can't stay on this road." He shoves the front passenger next. "Call the guys ahead – let them know what's happened, what we're gonna do."

"What *are* we gonna do?" the other guy in the back says. "When we find a road to turn off, I mean."

"We're gonna put the pedal to the metal, that's one thing we're gonna fucking do," Bill says. "But first, we're gonna change the plates. All we need to do is get out of Oregon. Once we're in Washington, we're fine. We've got enough friends there to cover for us no matter what happens."

Taylor finds herself slowly tuning them out. Her ears fill with static, deafening her to everything else in the car. Their words become muted. She clenches her jaw until it aches. She squeezes the Santa Muerte pendant, hidden beneath her shirt, until it hurts her palm. Until it feels like it could break the flesh.

She tells herself, *Tom isn't dead*. The Ogre said it himself – he didn't kill them. Just crippled their car. Taylor thinks of how many crippled cars the two of them ended up travelling in over the course of the last couple of days. It didn't stop them. They kept going.

They turn off the main road. "Make sure no one follows us," Bill says, these words coming through.

Taylor opens her eyes. The road they're on is practically a dirt track. It bumps and jostles them. The other guy in the back has turned, is looking back. As they round a corner, he speaks. "No one coming," he says.

They wait for the car up ahead to stop. It pulls to the side in some bushes, and a man there gets out and goes to the trunk. The other guy in the back, next to Taylor, does the same. He leaves the door open. He goes to the trunk. They're changing the license plates, like Bill said. So cops won't be able to find them. Won't be able to track them from the statements any eyewitnesses to the shooting and the crash might be able to give.

Taylor stares out the open door. To the darkness through the trees beside where they have stopped.

"You wanna try it?" Bill says. He's watching her. He's read her mind.

Taylor says nothing.

"You think you're fast enough?" he says. "You think you can?"

Taylor stares through the wood. Through the trees and

bushes. Into the darkness there. Her body is tense. She feels herself shaking. Desperate to do it. Desperate to *try*.

Taylor swallows. She closes her eyes. She slumps back into the seat and tells herself she will not cry.

Bill chuckles.

41

Tom and Danny move through the woods. Back at the car, they had to move fast. Tom got out of the crashed vehicle, saw Bill's minivan abruptly turning back, returning to them. Looking to finish the job.

He went to Danny's side of the car. The front was embedded in bushes, but the impact had crumpled the wing, which in turn pinched the driver's door shut. Tom pulled it open. He figured there must have been a hidden tree or a stump in the bushes. Danny was resting on the steering wheel, but she was conscious. There was blood running down the side of her face from her temple, matting strands of her hair together. Tom crouched down, looked into her eyes. "Are you all right?" he said. "Are you hurt? Can you move?"

Danny was groggy, but she nodded. "I just banged my head a little," she said. Her voice was hoarse, but not slurred.

Tom looked into her eyes, checking for signs of concussion. He didn't see any. "They're coming back," he said. "We need to move, now." Tom was very aware that they were unarmed.

Danny held her hand out to him, and he pulled her clear

of the car. Bill's minivan was still distant, but it was gaining. Tom looked into the trees. Through the woods would be their best bet. It would provide cover. If Bill and his men came in after them, it would allow Tom a chance to sneak up on them.

They ran into the trees. He dragged Danny along beside him. "We need to keep moving," he said. He glanced back. He couldn't see the road anymore. Couldn't see if Bill had made it back.

Danny pulled her phone out of her pocket. She started pressing buttons.

"What are you doing?" Tom said.

"Calling the cops."

Tom placed a hand over the phone, stopped her from dialling. "No cops," he said.

She looked at him.

"We can't guarantee they're on our side."

"Oh," Danny said. "Shit." She stopped walking. She looked around. She lifted her phone back up, started tapping at it again.

"What are you doing now?" Tom said.

"Finding out where we are," she said. "I have a signal. Let me get Maps up... Here we go." Her face brightened. She stepped closer to Tom, showed him. "We're in luck. We head two miles that way, there's a box store. We should be able to get help there."

Tom looked ahead through the trees. He thought of Taylor. Two miles. That was nothing.

"Let's go," he said.

They've been walking for ten minutes now. Danny is able to move without his support, but she struggles to keep up. Tom pushes on. He thinks of Taylor.

42

The room is nondescript. It's very bland, with no decoration, no furniture, no windows. Only a door, which is locked, and a single bed in the corner with a thin mattress. And in the center of the ceiling, a single flickering bulb with no shade.

Josh doesn't know where they are. Men came to their house early this morning. Josh was getting ready to leave, to head for work, when the knock came. He was upstairs, with Tilly. She was awake, getting dressed. They both looked at each other, and maybe they were hopeful. Maybe they thought it was Taylor. Josh went downstairs, but he must have taken too long. The people at the front door got impatient. He heard the back door kicked in. He spun to the sound. Before he could say a word, before he could see who it was, he was already being rushed. Then he was struck. The blow landed on his head. He didn't see what he was hit with. It was hard, though, and cold, like steel. It knocked him flat on his ass, and before he could look up, he was kicked in the face, then a bag was pulled over his head.

He heard voices and movement as men ran into the house. He couldn't tell how many. He was turned over onto his side, and his hands were roughly bound together, so tight they could have cut the circulation off. He heard the strangers running upstairs, to his room, to where Tilly was. He heard her cry out, and then that cry was abruptly silenced.

Then he was hauled from the ground. It was hard to tell how many hands were on him, bundling him out of the house. He was thrown into the back of something. The ground was hard. Then someone was thrown in next to him, and he heard her cry out on impact and knew it was Tilly. Doors were slammed shut. They were in the back of a van, he was sure.

A voice nearby spoke up. He didn't recognize it. "Two of you just lie there nice and quiet and we're not gonna have any trouble," it said. Tilly whimpered. The man heard. "Two of you are close enough – hold hands if it makes you feel any better. And make yourselves comfortable. We've got a long drive ahead."

The man wasn't exaggerating – it *was* a long drive. Josh lost track of time. He wanted to turn to Tilly, to speak to her, to comfort her, but every time he moved or made a sound, the man in the back with them nudged him with the toe of his boot hard enough to leave a bruise. Josh settled in and hoped Tilly did the same. He tried to stay awake, but he felt dizzy and sick after the blow to the head, and he nodded off a few times, the smell and taste of blood up his nose and in his mouth. He worried about how severe the blow may have been, and that if he fell asleep, he might not wake up.

The rhythmic movement of the van lulled him, though. He was woken when they dragged him out of the back of the van by his ankles and dumped him on the ground. "Wakey, wakey," a voice said, and someone else laughed, then Josh heard another thud next to him and knew they'd given Tilly the same treatment. It annoyed him, the thought of them handling his wife in such a way and then laughing at her. Laughing at both of them.

He kicked out at unseen targets. "Assholes!" he said, spitting and cursing from the darkness behind his mask. "Fucking assholes!"

They softened him up with their boots to stop him being so frisky, then dragged them both inside a building. Only when they were in a room – this room – were the masks removed and the ties cut.

Josh didn't recognize any of the men he saw while blinking the harsh light out of his eyes. Neither did Tilly. She panicked when she saw the blood on his face, but he told her not to worry. "The mask probably smeared it around," he said, though he had no idea how bad the actual cut itself might be. He looked her over. Bruises on her arms where the men had handled her, and more on her shoulders.

No one has come to see them since. Josh has tried forcing the door open, with no success. He's called through it, demanded answers. No one has returned to them.

He sits on the floor now, his back to the wall, his head in his hands. Tilly is on the bed, her arms wrapped around her knees. They've already exhausted their queries – *who are these people? Why are they doing this? Where are we? What do they want?* – and now there's nothing left for them to do but wait. Wait until the answers are brought to them.

"They've gotta come see us soon, right?" Tilly says.

Josh looks up. He probes the scab on his scalp where he was struck. He's been trying to work out what they hit him with. He's narrowed his ideas down to either a gun or a metal pole. He doesn't think it could've been a baseball bat. Whatever it was it was small, small enough for them to conceal, so he didn't catch a glimpse of it before they used it. "Eventually," Josh says.

Tilly blows air. She stares at the locked door. "I'm getting hungry," she says, "and I'm worried I might start needing to piss soon."

Josh grunts his agreement, then laughs. "They *don't* come and see us soon, they're gonna end up with a very messy room. Or cell. Or whatever the fuck this is supposed to be."

Tilly bites her lip. "When you don't turn up for work," she says, "how long do you think it'll take them before they get worried enough to contact the authorities?"

"Too long, probably," Josh says. "They might call the house, but no answer isn't gonna alarm them. And it'll take a few days before someone gets curious enough to come by the house, anyway. By then, any trail might've gone cold. I guess. I mean, I don't know how these things work. All I know for sure is that no one's gonna be looking for us except maybe Taylor. If she turns up at the house sometime soon." He falls silent then, and they both look at each other.

Tilly is the first to say it. "Do you think this might all have something to do with Taylor?"

Josh frowns. He looks around the room. "You think Ken has done this?" he says.

"He's got a lot of friends," Tilly says.

Josh nods, brow still knotted. "Friends from the church..."

Before he can follow this line of thinking any further, the door is unlocked. It's thrown open. Two men stand in it. One of them has a gun. The other is carrying cable ties. The one with the gun motions toward Josh.

"Get up," he says. "On the bed, next to the woman."

Josh doesn't move. He opens his mouth, but he's not permitted to speak.

"On the fucking bed!" the man roars, stepping forward,

poking the gun into Josh's face. Josh does as he's told. "The two of you, face down! Put your arms behind your backs."

They do, and the other man comes forward. He binds their wrists together. As tight as back at the house. Josh feels his fingers go instantly numb. They're both picked up and turned around, shoved down so they're sitting on the edge of the bed.

"Stay there and behave yourselves," the man with the gun says, waving it between the two of them. "I'm gonna be right outside. I hear any trouble, I'll come straight back in."

He and the other man leave the room, but they don't close the door. Two more men come in as they exit, fill the space they have left. Josh knows one of these men. He recognizes the other, though his presence here confuses him.

Laurence Morgan and Ken Arnett.

It's not without a great deal of satisfaction that Josh sees Ken's arm is in a sling. "What happened to you?" he says, not trying to hide his smirk. The pleasure in seeing Ken hurt outweighs his surprise at seeing the pastor here.

Ken strokes his arm, but he doesn't answer.

Laurence stands before them, looking them over. His hands are clasped behind his back, and he rocks on his heels. He smiles, a pursed smile like he's trying to put a good face on the situation. "I'm sorry about the conditions," he says finally. "My friends out there are worried you may try something...regrettable. Hence the restraints."

"What do you want?" Josh says. "Where the fuck are we?"

"Why are you here?" Tilly says to the pastor. She recognizes him from when she lived in Belleville, and she can't understand his presence, either.

Laurence and Ken exchange glances. Laurence raises an eyebrow. He turns back. "Mr. and Mrs. Hendricks, when was the last time you heard from Taylor?"

Josh stares at them both. He's watching them closely. He

saw how they looked at each other. "It's been a while," he says.

"Mm," Laurence says. "Mrs. Hendricks? Do *you* remember any better?"

Tilly looks at Josh; then she shakes her head.

"Mm." Laurence starts rocking on his heels again.

"Why are you asking about Taylor?" Josh says. "What's it got to do with you? What's any of this got to do with you – damn it, what the fuck are we doing here? What is this fucking place? Why are we in restraints?"

Laurence stops rocking. He takes a deep breath. "Taylor is a member of my flock, Mr. Hendricks," he says. "I, of course, care about her well-being, as I do all the members of my congregation. If I can assist Kenneth here in making sure his daughter is safe, I will see to it that I do all that is in my power to –"

"She's not his fucking daughter," Josh says.

Laurence looks at him. "Perhaps not biologically," he says. "But do you see...what was his name, Kenneth?"

"Walter," Ken says.

Laurence snaps his fingers. "That's it. Do you see *Walter* here right now?"

When Tilly speaks, her voice is very small, but it's enough to silence them all. "What is Taylor running from?"

Josh looks at her. They all look at her. She's staring at the pastor, and her brow is knotted.

Josh understands what Tilly is getting at. It's the look on her face that makes it clear. He turns back to Laurence now, and Ken, and wonders why the thought hasn't occurred to him sooner. "What have you done to my sister?" He speaks through gritted teeth.

Laurence runs his tongue around the inside of his mouth. He moves his hands from behind him to his front, clasps them there. "I apologize for your current predicament, I truly do. I hope to have it resolved for you both as soon as possible."

Josh tries to push himself up, to get to his feet. Laurence clears his throat. The man with the gun pokes his head in from out in the hall. He glares at Josh, points the gun at him.

Josh doesn't settle, but he doesn't go any further, either. He shoots a look at Ken. "What have you let him do? Or are you in on it, too?" He glares at the man with the gun, too. He wants to charge the two men, Ken and Laurence, to throttle them, find out the truth, find out what they've done.

"Don't worry about Taylor," Laurence says, looking at Ken and tilting his head toward the open door. They're getting ready to leave. "She'll be here soon enough, and then you can become reacquainted. But only after you come to see things the right way."

"The right way?"

"Well, we can talk about that later. I'm sure you'll come to understand – both of you. But later. We'll have enough time. We all have enough time. Nothing but time."

Ken has reached the door. He's stopped, looking back at Laurence. He seems concerned. Laurence is rambling.

Laurence shakes his head. Snaps out of it. He smiles at Josh, then at Tilly. "Try to make yourselves comfortable," he says. "Taylor will be here soon. Yes, very soon. We're all looking forward so much to seeing her again." He turns on his heel and leaves the room. The man with the gun watches over them while the guy who bound them comes back and cuts them loose. They both leave. Close the door again. Lock it.

Josh is breathing hard. "Taylor," he says. "What have they...?"

"You didn't know," Tilly says. She reaches out to him, tries to comfort him. "You couldn't know. You tried all that you could – we both did – Ken blocked us. We tried to take her away from here." There are tears in her eyes.

Josh gets to his feet. He paces the floor. He feels like he's going to be sick. He goes to the door. He kicks it, pounds on it with both fists. "You motherfuckers!" He kicks it again. He's screaming.

43

Tom and Danny keep moving. Danny struggles to keep up. She's breathing hard. "Jesus Christ," she says. "I used to jog… I'm really wishing right now I stuck to it…"

"This isn't a run," Tom says, leading the way, pushing through bushes and branches. "It's a fast walk."

"It's a *lot* of fast walking."

"We don't have time to hang around."

Danny understands this. She sighs, hurries to keep up. "It's got to have been two miles by now, right?"

"Nearly," Tom says. "Not far now."

They push through the woods. Danny is thinking about her car trashed at the side of the road. Riddled with bullet holes. It was an old car. She bought it cheap and drove it far longer than the life it had left in it. She's amazed she was able to get it to go so fast, to catch up to the car transporting Taylor. The engine was screaming while she did it. If the bullets hadn't blown it out, before long the acceleration likely would have. Still, she'd been attached to it. It had served as her home on more than one occasion, when she'd been chasing a story way out in the sticks and it had made more sense to just hang around day after day rather than heading back to Belleville.

Tom stops suddenly, and she nearly bumps into the back of him. They're at the edge of the woodland, still among the trees. Danny peers around him. Across the road is the Maps-promised big-box store. The parking lot is full.

"Come on," Tom says, checking the road is clear before he steps out.

"Right," Danny says. "We get inside, we'll call for help. But if we can't call the cops, then who –"

"We're not calling for help," Tom says.

"We're not?" Danny says, hurrying to keep up. "What are you gonna do?"

"I'm gonna get us a fucking car," Tom says.

Danny looks around. "I don't see any for sale. And unless they're keeping any in the back –"

"We're not buying it," Tom says. He hops the wall separating the parking lot from the road, then tries the first door handle he comes to.

Danny blinks. "We can't steal a car!"

"Keep your voice down," Tom says, looking around, making sure no one is near, no one is looking. "We don't have a choice. Cover your eyes." He steps back, raises a leg, and kicks through the driver's side window. The alarm sounds. Tom unlocks it from the inside, then ducks down and reaches under the steering wheel.

Danny watches with wide eyes. The alarm is deafening. She looks the parking lot over. Across it, far from them, people going into and coming out of the store have paused, are looking their way. Closer, some people who have just parked and are getting out are now turning at the noise.

Danny feels rooted to the spot. An animal in headlights.

She shakes her head. Gets loose. This is nothing. She's

chasing a story, she reminds herself. More than that, they're trying to save a teenaged girl. Stealing someone's car is wrong, sure, but right now it's the lesser of two evils. She raises her eyebrows at the people closest to them, mouths *We lost the keys*, then shrugs and rolls her eyes.

The alarm cuts off abruptly, then the engine roars into life in its place. Danny turns, gets into the passenger seat. There are small squares of broken glass on her seat. She brushes them off before she sits.

Tom is driving before she's strapped herself in. The speed throws her from side to side, battling to stay upright. "Holy shit!" she says when things finally level out, when they're out of the parking lot and speeding along a straight road. She hits Tom on the arm. "Give me some fucking warning next time!"

Tom's unblinking eyes are staring straight ahead. His knuckles are white on the steering wheel. His jaw is clenched. He doesn't answer.

44

It's early evening when the car Taylor is in gets back to Belleville. They don't stay in the town. They drive straight through it. She knows where they're taking her. It's not the church or Laurence's home. It's the other place. The compound on the outskirts of town, hidden among the trees. They pass the old gas station, abandoned years before and rusted out now, the windows all smashed, and they take the right turn just beyond it, down the dirt road that takes them to the squat building hidden amongst the woodland.

The compound is for privacy. This is where Taylor used to be taken before Laurence became comfortable with having her in his home. This is where the other kids are still taken, so far as she's aware.

She remembers the first time she was brought here. The first time...*it* happened. It was just her. Not the whole class. She was told it was a reward for how well she'd been doing in her studies. She was told it was an educational trip. Her mother was told that, too. But Ken... Ken knew the truth. He knew what was going to happen.

When Taylor arrived, she found she wasn't the only

person there. There was a small gathering of other girls waiting outside. She didn't know who they were. She had a brief couple of minutes to talk to them before they were taken inside, and they told her they were from the care home on the outskirts of Belleville. How they went to the Temple of St. Philomena for classes sometimes. Taylor had never seen them there. They said they were always told it was a treat for them. That Laurence Morgan was a good man to take care of them like he did. When they were led inside, they found there were men waiting for them. Taylor didn't know the men. None of them did, although she remembers hearing one girl turn to another and whisper, "Isn't that the mayor?"

The men were smiling. They came toward the small gathering of girls, and they started talking to them, but before anyone could approach Taylor, she was taken gently by the arm and led to one side. They still handled her gently back then. They're not like that anymore. Now, every touch leaves bruises.

Taylor was taken away from the group and led into a room. The others were left in the entrance hall, talking to the men. Taylor looked back. She saw the men telling jokes and laughing. She saw them offering drinks that didn't look like soda.

The room was soft and plush. It had a chaise lounge and a king-size bed. There was a mirror on the wall, and a bathroom attached. The room was already occupied. Pastor Laurence Morgan was there, waiting for her. He stood in the center of the room, smiling at her. The man who had brought Taylor left. He closed the door.

"Hello, Taylor," Laurence said.

Taylor doesn't want to remember what happened next. She doesn't need to replay it again. It has replayed itself for her, day after day, night after night, for years now. It has been replaced every so often by new occurrences, new defilements, but this first time always comes back strongest, and with it, the memory of how she felt. The slowly creeping realization of what was happening. Of why she had been brought to the room.

She remembers wondering if she was the only one taken to a separate room. When the time came to leave, she saw that she was not. One girl was sobbing. They were all gathered together in the entrance hall again. The men were nowhere to be seen. That was the first time they were introduced to Bill Lindsay. He came in with his hooded brow and his jutting chin, his hulking frame, and he almost didn't look real.

He explained to them how things were going to be. How they were not to tell anyone of what had happened here – how it was a special gift, just for them, and it wasn't to be shared with others – and he implied what would happen if they were not to heed his warnings. He didn't say anything so overt, but it was plain in a way even they, at their young ages, could understand. If they told anyone, they would be hurt. For the girls from the care home, no one would believe them. They'd be kicked out. They'd have nowhere to go. For Taylor, her mother would be hurt. Bad things would happen to them all.

Taylor was silent on the ride back to the church. She assumed it was the same for the other girls on their way back to the home. Bill's words had done what they needed to.

They would be taken back to the compound every couple of weeks. Sometimes more often if they weren't at school. The other girls were swapped around, but Taylor was always with Laurence.

She remembers the time that a girl broke down. She'd had enough. She started screaming, and she tried to run away. She was caught easily. They dragged her away. When Taylor saw her again, a few hours later, she was calmer. She wasn't crying anymore, though her eyes were red, and her face was blotchy. She looked dazed, though. She couldn't concentrate on anything. Could barely walk. It was like she'd been drugged.

Taylor wondered where they'd taken her, but it didn't take her long to find out. When it became too much for her, and she started acting out, too, she'd be taken away from the others, away from Laurence, and she found out where the bad children went.

They went to the *other* rooms. The ones that weren't so comfortable. That didn't have carpets or bathrooms attached or king-size beds. The beds they *did* have were thin and uncomfortable and poked and prodded at the body with every spring beneath. The rooms that were cold and windowless and locked, and where no one came no matter how hard you banged on the door or cried out. No matter how badly you needed to use the bathroom, and you were left to piss yourself, crying in a corner.

The room Taylor is in now. Bundled into and dumped on the floor in the center, dust wafting up from the hard ground and making her sneeze. The other men leave, but Bill stays in the doorway and watches her a moment longer. He's smiling. He looks around the room. "So many memories in here, huh?"

Taylor knows there is more than one punishment room. Sometimes, there was more than one girl acting out. "They all look the same," she says, staying on the floor.

Bill chuckles. "Sure, but you got sent to them often enough."

She'd thought it would get her out of having to see Laurence. That it would make him leave her alone.

She was wrong.

Bill would come to see her. He didn't need to frighten or threaten. He couldn't anymore. Her mother was already dead, and there was nothing he could threaten her with. He couldn't lay his hands on her because Laurence wouldn't allow it. Instead, he didn't waste his energy or his breath. He'd come with a needle. He'd force her down and sink it into her upper arm, and when Taylor woke again, she'd be in the plush room, and Laurence would be beside her. Either still lying beside her on the bed, or just finished pulling his clothes back on.

She wonders if it was on one of these occasions when they chipped her.

"Try to make yourself comfortable," Bill says, then he leaves, and the door is locked.

Taylor looks to the mattress. So many memories come to her from these rooms. She doesn't want them. Doesn't want any of them.

She presses the Santa Muerte pendant against her chest. She closes her eyes, takes deep breaths. They won't break her. She won't let them break her. She was almost free. She can be free again. Properly, this time. Truly.

She holds back the tears. She waits for what comes next.

45

It's late and it's dark when Tom and Danny get back to Belleville. They stop at an electronics store so Tom can buy a burner phone, his others possibly still in Portland unless Bill has done something with his bag. From there, he gets Danny to direct him straight to Laurence's house. She programs her number into the phone on the way, then calls her own cell so she'll have the number. When they reach the house, Danny has to stop at the end of a long driveway. What they can see of the house is in darkness.

"Leave me here," he says. "You go to the church."

They've already discussed this. Danny will search the church, check if they're there. If she finds anything, she'll call him, and vice versa.

She shimmies across the front without leaving the car, getting behind the steering wheel. "Be careful," she says.

"Always am," Tom says. "Same to you."

"Why would I start now?" she says, then drives away.

Tom heads up to the house. He stays to the side, where the driveway is lined with bushes. Sticks to the darkness. Keeps his eyes peeled. The driveway is long, but not *too* long.

He reaches the house quickly. It remains in darkness. He can't see light from any of the rooms, only at the porch, hanging above the front door.

Tom goes around the house, making sure it's clear. At the back, upstairs, he spots an open window. Just a crack, but enough for him to slide his arm in, get it open all the way, crawl inside. There's a trellis on the wall, greenery creeping up it. Tom climbs up, uses it as a ladder. He has to stretch for the open window, but he gets his arm in. He pulls himself inside, rolls through as he hits the ground. It's a bathroom.

The house is still. Tom moves through it, checking the rooms. He can't hear anyone. There's no one to see. The house is as empty inside as it looked outside.

While he's upstairs, he hears a car pulling up the driveway. Tom steps inside a bedroom near the stairs. It's sparsely furnished. Seems like a spare. He goes to the window, looks down. The car has parked. It's a Lexus. Brand new. Even in the dark, it shines. The person inside has gotten out, but they haven't come in the house. They stand by the porch, waiting. They're on their cell phone.

It's a man. He ends the call, slips the phone into his pocket. Tom doesn't know what Laurence Morgan looks like. Wonders if this is him. He's a tall man, lithe. He wears trousers and a suit. Doesn't look like any of the other heavies who have been sent after Tom and Taylor so far.

Speaking of which, whoever he is, he doesn't have Taylor with him.

Another car begins the journey down the driveway. It parks next to the first car. Tom *does* know who this man is. It's Bill Lindsay. The Ogre. Still no sign of Taylor. The other man turns at his arrival, leads the way inside the house. Bill follows him. Tom thinks this must be Laurence. Lights have come on downstairs. He can hear voices. They don't come toward the stairs. They stay down there, in the foyer, talking. Tom listens in.

"...she's at the compound." The voice is rough. He recognizes it from Josh and Tilly's house. Bill. "Secure. We got her there shortly after you'd left. Where'd you go?"

Compound? Tom is out of the spare room now, getting closer. He presses his back to the wall near the top of the stairs. He doesn't chance a look down. He thinks Bill would notice him. He can hear just fine from where he is. He doesn't need to see them.

"I dropped Kenneth off at the Temple," the other voice – Laurence – says. "He needs to get things ready."

"I thought you'd wait for her to arrive. Thought you'd be excited to see her."

"I was, certainly. But we're on a new path now. A path more important than just getting her back, though I'm glad you have. Follow me."

They leave the foyer, still talking. They don't go far. Just into the next room. Laurence makes himself a drink. Their voices are further away now, but Tom can still make them out.

"What do you mean by a new path?" Bill says. "And what's Ken getting ready?"

"I needed to pray, Bill," Laurence says after he's taken a drink.

Bill is silent for a while. Tom doesn't think he's been offered a drink. "Are you high? You dipped into the peyote at a time like this?"

Laurence laughs. "High only on God's love. The peyote doesn't work on me how it does on other people, Bill. It's a key. It's a conduit through which the Lord is able to communicate with me direct."

Bill ignores this. "You went to pray?"

The silence is Laurence's this time. "She keeps running

from me, Bill," he says. "She keeps running, and this time she almost got away. And her helper, Tom Rollins, is still at large. I needed answers, Bill. I needed help. Guidance. How can I make it so Taylor will not leave me anymore?"

"Where'd you go?"

"I stayed at the church when I dropped Kenneth off. Just for a little while. The Lord always hears me better there, I feel. I'm more open to Him, too. More intuitive."

"Uh-huh," Bill says. "And did you receive an answer?"

"I did," Laurence says. He sounds pleased.

"You wanna share it with me?"

"You'll find out soon enough. The Lord spoke to me, and He showed me the way. I made some calls soon after. Spread the good word."

"Calls to who?"

"Clive, Stanley, the rest – all of our important friends. They know what needs to be done. What I, and the Lord, expect from them. For now, I'm going to shower, and then I'll go back to the compound."

There's a pause, then Bill asks, "Where's Ken now? Still at the Temple?"

Tom doesn't hear the answer. He thinks Laurence is taking another drink when he says it.

"Best place for him," Bill says. "Should we go to the compound together?"

"You go now. I'd feel more comfortable knowing you were there, should Rollins turn up."

Taylor mentioned being taken to somewhere else when she wasn't at the church or Laurence's home. Tom wonders if this is the compound. Danny never mentioned a compound at all. He assumes she doesn't know about it.

There is some further small talk about things that don't mean anything to Tom. Church business. Soon after, Bill leaves. Laurence remains downstairs. Tom doesn't know what he's doing. Having another drink, perhaps. Tom stays pressed against the wall, waiting. He chances a look now that Bill has gone. He sees Laurence's shadow stretched across the wall. He's moving around, putting things away.

Then he leaves the room he's in. Tom hears him cross the foyer. He's coming toward the stairs. He hasn't turned the landing light on. Tom steps back deeper into the shadows. Slips into a doorway. Waits.

Laurence's ascending footsteps reach the top. He pads along the carpeted landing. He sighs. Tom hears him getting closer and closer. He's by the door. He comes into view.

Tom steps out of the doorway. Grabs Laurence by the throat. He pushes him up against the opposite wall, slams him hard. Laurence is taken by surprise, his eyes wide. The back of his head bounces off the wall. Tom squeezes. Laurence gags. His eyes are bulging. His tongue pokes out between his lips. Tom lifts him a little higher. Laurence is on the tips of his toes. He can't breathe.

Tom doesn't want to let go. Wants to keep squeezing until Laurence blacks out, then squeeze until all the breath has left his body, and keep squeezing until his heart stops.

No – no, he wants more than that. Something physical. He wants to tear Laurence's throat out. To hold it bloody in his hand right in front of Laurence's face so he can see it as he slowly dies.

He can't, though. For now, he needs Laurence alive.

Needs him to tell him where the compound is.

Tom doesn't let go, but he eases the pressure. Lets Laurence stand on the flats of his feet. Lets Laurence get enough breath that he's able to talk. "*You* –" Laurence says. Tom remembers what Danny said. There was a picture of him on Laurence's desk. A headshot from his Army days. Laurence knows exactly who he is.

"*Me*," Tom says, pushing his face close. "Where is Taylor?"

46

Danny reaches the church. It's Saturday night and quiet. A stark contrast to how busy it will be in the morning. The parking lot will be filled to overflowing. People will mill around by the entrance and inside the foyer, talking to the other members they know, exchanging the news of the week. All of them eager for their Sunday religion, without even the slightest suspicion of what is happening behind the scenes.

She stares at the building. It feels like she's been gone from it longer than she has. Wonders at what point her coworkers realized she was gone. If they said or did anything about her disappearance.

There are lights on inside, but this doesn't throw her. There always are. They might be security, but that's fine. The security people all know her. Nothing untoward has happened yet. She hasn't written a single line of her story.

She goes to the church. It's locked, but she has her key. Inside, she tries not to make any noise. If they're here, if anyone is here, she doesn't want them to know she's coming.

She goes into the auditorium first, but it's empty. She

listens. Can't hear any sounds – footsteps or distant voices. No sign that anyone is present. She almost wants to leave, to head back to Laurence's house and Tom, believing that is where the action will be. Where their answers will be.

But if there's anything there, Tom will be in touch. Her journalistic instincts tell her to keep looking. Leave no stone unturned. She's always listened to these instincts. Her whole career. They've never steered her wrong.

Of course, her instincts had no idea how bad things here really were.

She goes to the rear of the church, where the classrooms are. They're in darkness. She hovers in the doorway, though, looks out across the room. The desks and the chairs. To the paintings on the walls done by the younger children. Smiling suns and flowers. Smiling children holding hands in a row. Interspersed through it all, copy-and-paste scripture enlarged on a Word document and printed out, stuck to the wall. Psalms. All of them tell of God's love.

She imagines these chairs are full. Full of children. Full of damaged children. All the faces she doesn't know, blank and staring back at her, their eyes hollow, their souls shattered. Front and center, Taylor and Scarlet. Scarlet's wrists are bleeding, dripping from the side of her desk, dripping to the floor. An expanding pool that almost reaches Danny's feet. Scarlet doesn't let it show. She gets paler and paler, glowing in the dark, but she doesn't let it show that she's hurting.

Danny turns away from the room. She goes to her desk. To Laurence's office. She wonders if the door is still unlocked.

It is. It's unlocked, the door is open just a crack, and the light is on.

Danny halts, then presses herself against the wall. There's no sound coming from inside the office, but the loudest noise is her heart beating, right in her ears. She edges closer to the frame. She holds her phone close, ready to call Tom.

She doesn't think there's anyone in the office. She can't hear movement or breathing. Nothing at all. Tentatively, she pushes open the door. She's right. It's empty. She's certain she didn't leave the light on or the door open when she was in yesterday. She wouldn't be so careless.

She steps carefully around the room. There are signs that someone else has been here. The chairs at the desk are out of place. The picture of Tom Rollins is gone. Then she reaches the other side of the desk, and she sees one of the drawers is open. The bottom drawer, on the left side. Danny goes to it. She remembers what was inside. The cyanide. It's gone. The drawer is empty.

"What're you doing here?"

The voice comes from the doorway. Danny gives an involuntary cry. It's Ken Arnett. Taylor's stepfather. His hand not in the sling is holding a coffee. Danny presses a hand to her chest, then fans herself, feigns like nothing is wrong – this is fine, this is normal, he hasn't caught her doing anything untoward.

"Oh, I'm so sorry," she says. "I didn't realize anyone else was here. I just called back in to get something from my desk, and I noticed Mr. Morgan's light was on, but no one seemed to be here."

"So you start rummaging through his desk?" Ken's eyes are narrowed.

"I wasn't rummaging," Danny says. "I was just checking."

"Checking what?"

"That everything is all right. That there hadn't been a break-in."

"No break-in," Ken says. Danny sees how the steam rises from his coffee. It's just been made. She never passed the kitchen on her way here. "Just me."

"I see that now," Danny says. She takes a step to the side, away from the desk. Ken doesn't move. He's still blocking the doorway. Danny forces herself to smile. It's hard to be civil when she knows there's a monster standing before her. Tom has told her everything, everything that Taylor told him. "Where *is* Mr. Morgan?" she says. "Is everything all right?"

"Why wouldn't it be?" Ken says.

"Just he seemed very worked up yesterday. I know me and Tracy and a lot of the other girls were very concerned about him."

"Nothing for you to concern yourself *about*," Ken says. "A bit like how, if you see his office light on, you don't need to concern yourself with *that*, either."

"Yes. Well." Danny takes a step forward, but Ken still doesn't move. "May I leave?"

Ken doesn't look so sure. He continues to regard her warily. "What's your name again?" he says.

"Danny," she says. "You know my name, Mr. Arnett. We've met before."

"You always come into the church after hours on a Saturday night?"

"I don't make a habit of it," Danny says. She can play this game. It's not the first time she's been caught snooping somewhere she shouldn't have. "But I forgot my compact, and I was passing by, so I thought, why not? Ordinarily, I'd have just left it until Monday. Or tomorrow, after service."

Ken still doesn't move. He doesn't say anything for a while, either. "What did you see in the desk?"

"I didn't see anything," Danny says.

Ken looks pained. It's hard to tell if it's from his arm or from her words. "You shouldn't have come in here."

"I'm beginning to wish I hadn't," Danny says. "I thought I was doing the right thing. Next time, I won't bother."

"I don't think I can let you leave, Danny," he says.

"And why's that?"

Ken doesn't answer. He just shakes his head.

They both stand. Neither moves. They stare at each other. Neither backs down. Danny grits her teeth. She figures she has nothing to lose, not after tonight. Not after meeting up with Tom. Not after everything that is sure to come next.

"Where's the cyanide gone, Ken?"

Ken's eyes go wide. "How do you –" he begins, but he doesn't finish. "You've been in the desk," he says. He shakes his head. It doesn't matter. He takes a step forward, toward her. Instinctively, protectively, Danny lashes out. She kicks. Her toe connects with the bottom of Ken's mug. The hot coffee flies back into his face, scalds him. He screams. Danny sees how his face turns bright red. How it blisters almost instantly.

He falls back through the doorway, his mug dropped, his left hand wiping at his face, his eyes. His right hand looks like it wants to help, but it's useless. He can't raise it.

Danny doesn't know what to do next. She wants to run, but she can't. She can't leave Ken here – he found her, he could call, warn the others. Could call Laurence or Bill. Tell them he found her. Tell them she knows about the cyanide.

But what *about* the cyanide? What does it mean? What is it for?

Ken comes roaring back into the room. He charges her, knocks her over the top of Laurence's desk. Papers go flying. The computer is knocked off the edge. It hits the ground with a clatter. Danny hits the ground on the other side, hard. She rolls quickly onto her back and looks up in time to see Ken come around after her. His left hand is opening and closing, itching to grab her.

She kicks at him, but he reaches through, hauls her up and onto the desk. He's trying to grab her neck. Danny, however, has two hands. She bats him aside with both of them, pins his left arm to the desk by his wrist. Ken keeps coming. His mouth snapping, biting at her. Danny lashes out.

She grabs the landline off the desk and hits him in the side of the head with it. This knocks him back. She's able to kick his broken arm. He falls to his knees. She punches him, bursts one of the fresh blisters on his cheek. He falls back. She stamps on his broken arm. He screams. It feels good to do it. Knowing who he is, knowing what he's done, it feels good. She does it again.

She gets down on top of him, pressing a knee into his broken arm, her hands on either side of his face. "*Where are they? Where is the cyanide?*"

Ken doesn't answer. He's grimacing, in pain.

Danny applies more pressure to his arm. She slaps him. "Answer me! What's happening? What's going on?"

Ken shakes his head. He won't answer.

Danny breathes hard. She presses her fingernails to his eyelids. "Damn it, tell me, or I'll take your fucking eyes out!"

Ken whimpers. Danny applies more pressure.

"He's gonna drink it!" Ken cries. "He's gonna drink it, and he's gonna ascend! God spoke to him! God told him what to do!"

Danny takes her fingers from his eyes. She slaps him, to make him look at her. "What are you talking about? What do you mean? He's going to *kill* himself? That's it?"

Ken starts to laugh.

"What's so funny?"

"He's not going alone," Ken says.

Danny's breath catches. "Taylor?"

Ken laughs again. "He's taking me with him. And Carl and Bob and Stan and Clive, David and John."

Danny doesn't know these names. "Who are they?"

"And he's taking our brides, too. We're going with him. We're all going up with him. We're all ascending. We're worthy. We're God's chosen. God told him so."

Danny's heart is pounding. Her mouth is dry. "Where are they? Where is Laurence? Where is *Taylor*?"

Ken laughs. "You can't stop us! It's too late!"

She needs to tell Tom. She looks at Ken. She doesn't know what to do with him. She looks at the office door. "Where's the key?"

He stops laughing finally, frowns. "What key?"

"The key – the key to the office door!"

Ken doesn't understand.

Danny checks his pockets.

"What do you think you're going to find in there?" Ken says. "It's too late to join us. My bride's already selected."

"Shut up," Danny says. She finds what she's looking for in his right pocket. The keys. She finds his phone, too. Takes them both. She gets up. Kicks him in the arm again. She grabs the phone from where she dropped it after hitting him, tears the cable out of the wall, then leaves the office, slams the door shut. Ken is still on the ground as she leaves. It's only as she slots the key into the lock and turns it does he realize what she's doing. He's got to his feet, is banging on it from the other side.

"Open this fucking door! Open the door, you bitch!"

Danny ignores him, moving away from the locked office door. She dumps his cell phone and the landline in the wastebasket down the side of her desk. Her old desk. She won't be returning to it. She hurries away. She needs to call Tom. She doesn't know if she should leave the church – if maybe they're here somewhere, hidden. If Laurence and Taylor are here, with the other men Ken mentioned and the girls, their '*brides*.' They could be in this building, with the cyanide. She could already be late – though she doesn't think it's time yet. Ken said he was going with them. Wherever they are, he'd need to be there.

Danny thinks about the cyanide. She thinks of Jim Jones.

She should have taken it with her, damn the consequences of her snooping being found out. It wouldn't have mattered. She should have taken it, and now she wouldn't feel so worried. So sick. Nothing good can come of a bottle of cyanide.

She pulls out her phone to call Tom, tell him what she's found, tell him they need to find him *fast*.

But she doesn't need to call. She already has a message. It's from Tom.

47

Laurence rubs his throat while he drives. There are red marks there from Tom's fingers. Soon they'll turn to bruises.

Tom conceals his phone down by his side, doesn't let Laurence see what he's doing. He types out a message, sends it to Danny.

I have Laurence. Taylor at compound. Don't think you know where that is, will send updates. Don't call. Don't want him to know about you. Won't be able to communicate soon.

He keeps the phone out after he hits send, presses it against his thigh. Keeps it out of view. He'll send route updates on the way.

"Y'know," Laurence says, "I've heard so much about you now. Heard about how you've hurt so many members of my flock. So many beatings, so many broken bones. Even Bill seems impressed by you, and Bill does not impress easily.

After all those stories I've been told, I thought you'd be taller." Laurence's voice is hoarse from the throttling.

"Tall enough," Tom says.

"It would seem so," Laurence says. "But I have to wonder what exactly your plan is here. What do you think is going to happen when we reach the compound? You are *vastly* outnumbered."

Tom grunts. "Wouldn't be the first time."

"My flock reaches far."

"I'm sure it does."

"You can't stop us."

"We'll see about that."

Laurence sneers. "You're very monosyllabic."

"I don't feel the need to use a big word just to try to make myself sound smart."

Laurence rubs his neck again. He clears his throat. "How *is* Taylor?" he says. "You've seen her more recently than I."

"Keep her name out of your mouth," Tom says.

Laurence chuckles. "I'm sure you think you're her savior, her white knight in shining armour, but what you fail to understand is that she is *mine*. She belongs to *me*. She's a gift. A gift from God."

"Do you ever shut up?" Tom watches the route they're taking. He sends Danny updates, the names of the roads they're on. They've left Belleville, are on the outskirts now.

"When you have a gift, you should use it. My voice is my gift."

"A gift from God, huh?"

"Yes. Just like Taylor."

Tom closes his fist and slams the back of it into Laurence's nose.

Laurence's hands fly up from the steering wheel. He loses control of the car, but Tom grabs the wheel, keeps it steady.

Laurence holds his nose with both hands. "I'm bleeding!"

he screeches. His accent slips. He sounds Southern. "You piece of shit, I'm bleeding!"

"I hope I broke it," Tom says. "Now, drive the car."

Laurence takes the wheel again. Blood drips from his nose. It stains his shirt. He's seething. Clearly isn't used to having someone lay their hands on him, and now Tom has done it twice in one night. Tom intends to lay hands on him a lot more before things are through.

"How far out are we?" Tom says.

Laurence snorts. He winds down the window and spits blood. "It's not far," he says. He's not so talkative anymore.

They're in darkness. There are no streetlights. Trees line the road, lit up by the headlights of Laurence's car. "Give me a time," Tom says.

Laurence checks the clock on the dashboard, calculates the distance remaining. "About ten minutes."

Tom sees a building up ahead, on the left. A gas station. The headlights pick it out. When they get closer, Tom can see that it's been abandoned. It's old and rusted out. The car slows. Laurence takes a right through the trees. The road isn't gentle. Tom holds the phone as still as he's able, sends Danny another message.

There's an abandoned gas station. Take the right after it, through the trees. Dirt road.

Laurence starts chuckling to himself. He wipes blood from his top lip. When Tom doesn't react, he decides to tell him what he's laughing about. "Whatever your grand plan is, I certainly hope it's coming into effect very soon."

Tom says nothing.

"Because you're about to be surrounded."

"I'm counting on it," Tom says.

Laurence frowns. He wasn't expecting this.

They pull off the dirt road. The compound comes into view. It's just one building, a flat roof. No one standing guard there, but plenty on the ground, watching out. Plenty of vehicles, too. Like Laurence said, there's a lot of men waiting here. Tom doesn't think he'll get a chance to count them all.

Laurence is looking at him now, smirking. "*Well?*"

"This is it," Tom says. "You caught me."

Laurence is confused. He gets closer to the compound, then, before the car has stopped completely, he throws the door open and runs toward the building, to the men there. "He's here!" he's shouting, pointing back to his car. "Rollins is here! Get him! *Get him!*"

Tom waits until the car rolls to a halt. He sends Danny one last message.

Stay in the trees. Hide yourself. Don't come down to the compound.

He gets out of the car. Men are running toward him. They're hesitant. They've heard about him. Some of them have seen him in action. Tom notices a couple of them have handguns. He can't make out what they are in the dark. He raises his hands. "You got me," he says.

Laurence doesn't come back until Bill is by his side. He's jabbing his finger in Tom's direction, talking animatedly. Tom only hears the end of it, "– and he hit me!"

Bill grunts. "I can see that," he says. He wades through the other men, stands in front of Tom, folds his arms. "If you'd stayed in the minivan with my men, we could've got you here a lot sooner."

"I like to do things the hard way."

"Get him inside," Laurence says. "Lock him up – and I want him watched! I want men on him at all times! He's up to something..."

"Or we could just kill him right now," Bill says.

Tom is ready. Bill is standing close enough that should he make a move, Tom can get in fast. If he has a weapon, Tom will disarm him. He'll fight his way into the compound. It's not a great plan, but it's a fast one. The journey from Laurence's house to here, while not knowing what exactly he was heading into, meant that Tom didn't have as much time to prepare as he'd have liked. He's come here trusting in himself. In his abilities. In what he can do regardless of how outnumbered he is.

Right now, there are eight men surrounding him, including Bill and Laurence. He wonders how many more are inside.

"Not now," Laurence says, wiping blood from his mouth. His nose hasn't coagulated yet. "Not yet. I want him to see. I want him to know that he's failed." He spits blood in Tom's direction. "I want him to know that he can't touch me! He cannot lay a *finger* on me! He has to *burn* for what he's done! He has to be punished, and his punishment shall be his abject failure!"

Bill rolls his eyes. "All right," he says. "Fine." He motions to two men nearby. "Get him in."

They come forward, taking their time. Tom considers his options. He could make a move now, but then they might lock him out of the compound. He wouldn't be able to get inside while they called in further reinforcements.

"Just grab him, for Christ's sake," Bill says.

Two of the men do. They seem relieved when Tom doesn't do anything.

"And keep him guarded, like I said," Laurence says.

Tom lets them lead him inside, getting a good look as they get close. Soon, he'll be near Taylor. Once he's in, nothing will stop him from getting back to her.

48

Taylor has never seen Laurence look so bad.

However, despite the blood on him, his swollen nose, and the bruising on his throat, Taylor does not stand her ground as she'd hoped she would. His presence makes her blood run cold, the way it always has. Her insides turn to water. He takes a step toward her, and she takes a step back. He keeps coming. Taylor freezes. She feels cold all over. Laurence is smiling.

"My dear," he says, almost upon her now. "It's so good to see you again. You've had me worried sick. Do you realize that?"

Taylor begins to tremble. He's close enough to touch her now. His arms are raised. Reaching out. He cups her face in both hands. Taylor's skin crawls at his touch. He forces her to face him. A trickle of blood runs from his left nostril.

"Forever," he says. "We'll be together forever. Bathed in light. We're chosen, Taylor. I wish you could understand that. If only you would accept your destiny and sit beside me."

Taylor wishes she could speak. Wishes her lower lip

wasn't trembling. Wishes she could tell him to go fuck himself.

"How I've missed you." His voice is a whisper. He comes in close, still holding her face. Sniffs her. Smelling her hair and her neck. He straightens and smiles at her. Takes his hands away, but his right lingers long enough to stroke her cheek. He turns and calls to the Ogre.

Bill enters the room. He's been waiting for the summons.

"Take Taylor to her brother," Laurence says. "I'm sure they'll be pleased to see each other."

Bill grabs Taylor. His touch is far rougher than Laurence's. He takes her down the hall, to another guarded room. The men on watch open it up. Bill throws her inside. Josh and Tilly stand at the sudden intrusion. Taylor throws herself at them. They hold each other.

"Oh, fuck, *Taylor*," Josh says, squeezing her so tight the air explodes from her lungs. "Are you hurt? Have they hurt you?"

Taylor can't speak. She's crying. She's reached her brother, but this isn't how it should be. They should be in Oregon. They should be safe. All of them, safe, finally.

Behind them, Laurence clears his throat. Gets their attention. Bill is beside him. His arms are folded. "Isn't this touching?" Bill says.

"Now, now," Laurence says. "Have a heart, William."

Bill shoots him a glance, raises an eyebrow. Doesn't appreciate being called William.

Laurence ignores him, continues. "A family reunion is always such a heartwarming moment. Take a seat, all of you."

Taylor and Josh hesitate, but Tilly guides them to the thin mattress in the corner. They sit. Josh and Tilly keep Taylor between them. They each have an arm around her shoulders.

Laurence clasps his hands together. "The route of this evening is already set for Taylor and myself. What happens next for *you*, Mr. and Mrs. Hendricks, will be decided in this room."

"What are you talking about?" Josh says. "You're always talking – just get to the fucking point."

Laurence lets his arms drop. He smiles at them, though whenever his nose moves, it makes him wince. "You have tested my faith, I'll admit it, but the Lord always provides. Here you are now, back before me, as you should be. And the Lord has sent me a message – He's shown me the way. He –"

"Who are you talking to?" Josh says. He and Tilly exchange glances. "Are you talking to *us*?"

Laurence is unperturbed. "What becomes of Taylor and me next is beyond you. I give you a choice – you can come with us, peacefully, and see us on our way to our ascension, and you may join us, though I can make no guarantee of your end destination. Or if you will stand against us, you can remain here and be left to the whims of Bill."

Bill smiles his hideous, jutting smile.

"What do you mean by *ascension*?" Tilly says.

Laurence smiles at her. It's a patronizing smile. "It means exactly what it sounds like, my dear."

Tilly still doesn't look like she understands.

"Of course," Laurence goes on, "if things were different, there could be a third option. I could have always offered to buy Taylor from you, a large sum of money to ensure your silence. But I feel that ship has long sailed. There's no coming back from where we are now. And I can see from the belligerent expression on your face, Mr. Hendricks, that I don't think you'd take me up on the offer of financial compensation."

"Damn right I wouldn't," Josh says. "Fuck you. Who the hell do you think you are?"

"Oh, there's no Hell waiting for me, Mr. Hendricks."

Laurence has a gleam in his eye. He spreads his hands. "The choice is yours."

The three are silent. Josh and Tilly look at each other. Taylor squeezes Josh's hand. She doesn't know what Laurence has planned, either. Whatever it is, she doesn't like how it sounds.

"Well," Laurence says, "I think we've waited long enough. Your silence is answer enough. Bill, get Taylor for me."

Josh and Tilly hold tight to her, but Bill shoves them effortlessly aside. He takes Taylor and gives her back to Laurence. Laurence puts an arm around her shoulders and digs his fingers in, pinning her to his side. "I'm not a patient man, Mr. and Mrs. Hendricks, and I feel time is of the essence tonight. Therefore, I'm afraid I've had to make the decision for you."

Josh stands, staring at Bill. He puts himself in front of Tilly.

Laurence laughs. "Good luck," he says, turning with Taylor, guiding her from the room. He pauses in the doorway, looks back over his shoulder. "You don't have to be so careful with these two, Bill. I don't care where their bodies are found. Don't worry about making it look like an accident – or a suicide."

Taylor goes rigid. She's able to turn, to see Josh. He heard what Laurence said. What was implied. He's come to the same realization.

"Mom?" Taylor says.

Josh wheels on Bill. "You son of a bitch –" He lunges for him, but Bill laughs and bats him across the jaw, knocks him to the ground.

"I might do it like that anyway," Bill says. "Just so he gets an idea of what she felt when it was happening to her." He crouches down over Josh, takes a handful of his shirt. "So you can see what she saw." He raises his head, looks at Tilly, smiles, then turns back to Josh. “And maybe I’ll give you another kind of show first, too. She sure is pretty, isn’t she? You really lucked out, man. You’re batting outta your league.”

Taylor tries to get away from Laurence, but he’s holding her tight. She feels her eyes hot with frustration and the revelation of what happened to her mother. She’d known – she’d always known – it couldn’t have been true. That her mother would abandon her like that, that she would kill herself. “*Why?*” Taylor manages to say. “Why did you kill her?”

Laurence looks down at her. “She wasn’t as understanding as Kenneth,” he says. “She couldn’t comprehend what we have. How important we are, you and I. She needed to be silenced before she could ruin everything.”

“You’re insane!” Taylor says. “You’re fucking insane!”

“No,” Laurence says. “I’m chosen. Just like you.”

He falls silent suddenly and turns, peers out the corridor, looks down the length of it. Under his breath, he mutters, “What’s that sound?”

49

Danny reaches the gas station. She stops in the middle of the road by it. She's breathing hard and her heart is pounding, as if she ran here. She checks her phone, but the messages have stopped. She can see the turn into the trees that Tom told her about. She grips the steering wheel tight, wondering what to do. She feels she should go down there, finally see this compound. But Tom told her to stay put. He must have a plan.

She gets out of the car and goes to the turn on foot, the dirt road that stretches away into darkness. She wishes she knew how long it was. She squints, but can't make out any lights. Sighing, she returns to the car. Looks around. Reverses into the gas station, conceals herself down the side of the building. Kills the engine and the lights. Stares across the road, to the turn through the trees. She waits. It's hard to do. She likes to be proactive. She holds her phone in both hands in her lap and wills something to happen.

50

The men guarding Tom have patted him down, taken the phone from his pocket. There are four inside the locked room with him. One of them is looking at Tom's phone. He's tried to enter a passcode a few times, but it seems he's finally locked himself out.

"No luck," he says, putting it in his pocket. They asked Tom for the code, but he smiled at him. They knew they couldn't get him to talk. "No calls or messages on the home screen, anyway."

The four men are armed. Two have bats, one has a knife, and another has a lead pipe. They stare at him, and Tom stares back. The one with the lead pipe smacks it against the palm of his hand. "I thought you were supposed to be, like, ex-Special Forces or something," he says.

"That's what Bill said," one of the bat wielders says, the one with hair. The other is bald.

"Aren't they supposed to be, like, smart?" lead pipe says. "You just drove in here and got yourself caught. Don't seem very smart to me."

"None of you seem particularly smart to me, either," Tom says.

"Uh-huh," the guy with the knife – who also has his phone – says. "Enough talk, yeah? Let's just wait until Bill or Mr. Morgan says what they want us to do next. I heard what this guy done to Kyle and Donald."

"Don't let him spook you," lead pipe says. "He just got lucky with those guys, that's all."

Tom stands in the center of the room, his arms folded. They motioned him toward the bed in the corner – which smells faintly of urine – as if expecting him to sit. He didn't. He hasn't been here long. He's been watching the men. Gauging them. They're like all the others he's run into who work for Laurence, with the exception of Bill. They're not professionals. They've had no training. They get pointed in a direction and let loose with a set of instructions. Just regular guys who think they're tough. Now, with weapons, they think they're extra tough.

The door to the room is locked, but Tom knows where the key is. The guy with the knife, with Tom's phone in his pocket, he has the key, too. He slipped it in, trying to be sneaky. It would make more sense to have locked the door from the outside, but these four likely don't want to be left in here with no option for escape.

Tom clears his throat, gets their attention. "Where's Taylor?" he says.

Three of the men smirk. The bald guy with the baseball bat, who is yet to have said a word, does not. He just glares.

"You'll see her soon," lead pipe says. "Laurence says he's planning on taking you along."

"Along where?"

Lead pipe shrugs. "Wherever they're going. I dunno. But you're going with."

"Not soon enough for me," Tom says. "Where is Taylor now?"

"This guy doesn't fucking get it, does he?" knife says.

"What do you expect?" lead pipe says. He's about to say something else, but Tom cuts him off.

"Do you want to know how I was captured? Why I allowed myself to be captured?"

The men are silent.

"It's because you're amateurs," Tom says. "All of you. And you don't concern me. Now, I'm going to ask one more time. Where is Taylor?"

"Say," lead pipe says, addressing the others, "did Laurence say anything about this guy having to go with them in one piece?"

"Didn't specify," knife says. "But I reckon he'd probably appreciate him being softened up a bit. Take the fight out of him, and the smart out of his mouth."

Without a word, the bald guy comes striding in, swinging his bat. Tom ducks it easily and lands a kidney blow, then grabs one of the man's hands wrapped around the handle of the bat and snaps his thumb. He takes the bat and slams it into the knees of the other bat wielder. That guy goes down face-first, slams his nose into the hard ground.

The guy with the knife charges in next. He swipes, but Tom sidesteps his thrust, takes him by the wrist with his right hand, and with his left punches him in the elbow, bending his arm back the wrong way. The man screams. Tom takes the knife off him. He spins toward lead pipe and slams the blade down into his shoulder, making him drop the pipe. Lead pipe starts screaming. Tom turns. Knifeless is close, holding his limp arm. Tom head-butts him, crushes his nose, drops him, then turns back to lead pipe and kicks him hard in the center of the chest. He hits the door, rocks it in its frame. The back of his head hits hard, and he slumps to the ground.

The bald guy is coming in again, weaponless now. His swings are careless and sloppy. Tom grabs his arm in mid-right-hook and breaks it across his knee. The other guy with the baseball bat is pushing himself up. Tom kicks his arms out from under him, then stomps on the back of his head, crushing his face into the ground. Blood squirts out from under him.

Tom goes back to knifeless. He's down, but he's still conscious. He hauls him to his feet, presses him up against the wall. "I said I won't ask again."

Knifeless doesn't need much encouraging. "She's in one of the rooms at the end of the corridor!" he says. "She might be in with her brother and his wife now – they're in the room at the very end!"

Tom pulls him in close. "That didn't need to be so difficult, did it?" He slams him against the wall so he bangs his head, then drops him and goes through his pockets. He retrieves his phone and finds the key. He sends Danny a message. *We'll be coming soon.*

Tom picks up one of the baseball bats, not knowing what he's going to find when he steps outside; then he unlocks the door.

The sounds of the fight from inside the room, the screams, have brought other men in the compound running. The corridor is full as Tom steps out into it. The way behind him is clear. Ahead, they're blocking his route to Taylor. Tom does a quick head count. Six men. Some of them are unarmed, but he sees weapons in other hands – an axe handle, a plank of wood, a couple more baseball bats. He doesn't see any guns. It's too tight a space for guns.

Tom looks them over, makes eye contact with as many of

them as he can. "One way or another," he says, "I'm getting Taylor. Either get out of my way, or get hurt."

Tom gives them a moment. Makes sure they've all heard what he said.

They don't get out of his way.

51

Taylor didn't see what the cause of the noise was. Saw men – some she recognized, some she didn't – flooding into the corridor.

"Stop him here!" Laurence told them. "Don't let him through! If he gets out of that room, kill him!"

Tom.

Taylor tried to tear herself away from Laurence, but he was holding her too tight. He dragged her down the corridor and outside. She was taken too quick from Josh and Tilly. They were still with Bill. She didn't see them, what situation they were in, as Laurence took her away.

They're outside the compound now. At his car. Laurence realizes Taylor isn't bound, and he has nothing to tie her up with. He doesn't let it stop him. He lifts her into the car with him, sits her on his lap. Adjusts his seat so they'll both fit. "You'll sit with me, Taylor," he says. "Stay close. I've missed you so much. I'll never let you go again."

His arm is around her chest, clamping her to him. Her lungs are compressed. Taylor struggles to breathe. Laurence starts the car and begins driving. Taylor stares at the wheel.

She grabs it, tries to wrench it out of Laurence's hand. She succeeds in making him swerve to the left. Laurence slams on the brakes.

"Damn it!" He moves his arm from across her chest and grabs her by the back of the head. He slams her face into the window beside them. Taylor's forehead hits the glass. She hears the thud on impact. She sees black spots.

"Don't do that!" Laurence says. He turns her and hits her across the face with the back of his hand. "I don't want to have to hurt you, Taylor," he says, baring his teeth. "But I won't hesitate to do it again."

Taylor can taste blood. She stares at Laurence. He doesn't appreciate her glare. He strikes her, then watches to make sure she behaves herself. Taylor keeps her face lowered. Her eyes are closed now. Laurence drives. She can feel how he keeps an eye on her while he goes.

52

Tom is halfway down the corridor. He charges with the bat, holds it sideways to push the front two men back, like a small riot shield. The impact drags them along, causes them to lose their balance. They fall. Tom steps through them, kicks the third man in the gut, then swings the bat at the fourth. The bat connects with the side of his face. Dislocates his jaw. Teeth go flying. Blood sprays across the wall.

The fifth man charges in, swinging an axe handle. Tom ducks it. It connects with the wall to his left, tearing a chunk out of it. Tom swings the bat again, across his midsection. He hears ribs crack. The man bends over it as he goes down, pulls the bat out of Tom's hands.

The sixth man has a machete. He swings it in a downward arc. Tom is able to grab the fallen axe handle, stays low and holds it above his head. The machete embeds itself into the wood. Tom twists it out of the sixth man's hands, then comes up slamming the base of the axe handle into his nose, breaking it. He jabs it into his eye next, then punches him in the throat to put him down.

The first two men, the two he knocked off their feet, are up now. They get behind him. One of them wraps his arms around Tom, holds him. The other is able to land a couple of shots to his stomach. Tom gets his legs up, kicks the puncher away. He drives the other back into the wall, then throws his head back. He feels his nose crunch under the impact from the back of his skull. His arms loosen. Tom has made himself dizzy, but he doesn't have time to recover. He stands as the puncher comes in again. He is already dizzy. He can't afford a shot to the head. He's able to get his left arm up, to block a swing, then grabs the puncher by the throat. He spins, kicks the other man between the legs. He falls to his knees. Tom lifts the puncher by his throat and slams him down hard on his back, then turns on the kneeling man and thrusts the point of his elbow into the side of his face, cracking his cheekbone.

Tom stands. He goes to the man with the cracked ribs, wrapped around the baseball bat and whimpering. Tom presses the bottom of his boot against his side and pushes him over. He picks the bat back up. The man curls into a ball, holding himself. He's got nothing left to give.

Tom hears footsteps behind him. He turns. Three more men have appeared. They eye the fallen bodies of the six other men. Two of them hesitate. The third looks at them, silently prompting them to attack. The two don't move. They look at Tom. He can see how scared they are. They don't want any part of what has just happened to their moaning, broken-boned friends.

"There's *three* of us," the third guy is saying, trying to encourage them. "Come *on*."

"There were *six* of them," one of the hesitant two says.

The third guy is younger. He's bigger. Looks like he used to play football. He's brash. He's confident. Wants to test himself against the man he's heard so much about. He sneers at the two with him. "*Pussies.*" He charges.

His charge is sloppy. He's unarmed. Tom is not. Tom has time to prepare. He swings the bat as the big guy gets close. It makes contact with the big guy's right arm. Connects so hard the bat breaks. The bone breaks, too. It bursts through the skin. The left side of the big guy's body hits the wall. Then he looks down and sees what has happened to his arm. Sees the jagged bone sticking out of it. His eyes go wide. He screams loud enough to make Tom's ears ring. Tom holds him by the side of the head and slams it into the wall to shut him up. The big guy slumps to the ground, lands on his front. His mangled arm rests at a bad angle, the point of his broken bone sticking up.

Tom looks down the length of the corridor, past the seven men lying there. Some have broken bones. Some are concussed. None of them are making any effort to get up. The two at the other end grimace at what he just did to the third who was with them. They look at each other. They turn and they run.

Tom turns back around. He kicks open the door at the end of the corridor. Taylor is not in the room. Neither is Laurence. Instead, he finds Bill. There's a man Tom doesn't know on the ground. His face is swollen and bloodied. There's a woman in the room, too. Bill is looming over her on the bed while she kicks and scratches at him. Bill turns at the door opening.

"Rollins," he says, grinning. He gets hold of the woman by the hair, hurls her across the room. When she lands, she rolls until she hits the wall, then scrambles over to the man. Tom thinks this is Josh and Tilly.

Tom grits his teeth. "Where is Taylor?"

Bill doesn't answer. His smile widens. His chin juts out further.

"Laurence took her!" the woman, Tilly, says. "He's going to kill her!"

Tom blinks. Before he can respond, Bill has pulled a gun. A Beretta. It looks just like Tom's. Army issue. Bill is laughing. "You're already too late!"

Tom stares down the barrel. His body tenses, ready to dive to the side. He's not sure he'll be fast enough. Not sure he can escape the bullet.

Tilly throws herself at Bill's arm. The one holding the gun. She knocks it to the side. It goes off. The bullet hits a wall. Tilly wraps herself around his arm and claws at his wrist. Tom redirects his tensed muscles. Launches himself into the room, toward Bill and Tilly. Bill grabs Tilly by the face with his other hand, tears her off him. Tom reaches them. He takes Tilly's place on Bill's gun arm. He pushes it up. A couple of shots go off. Bits of the ceiling fall around them. Tom slams his elbow into the side of Bill's face. Bill drops the gun. He grabs hold of Tom. Bill is bigger and stronger. He drives him from the room, back out into the corridor.

Tom knows the wall outside is coming up behind him. He braces himself. They make impact. Tom exhales to avoid being winded as he's jarred between the wall and Bill's bulk. He gets a knee up, his arms pinned, and drives it into Bill's ribs. Bill doesn't let go. Tom head-butts him in the temple, keeps doing it until his grip loosens. Tom's arms break free. He hits Bill, but Bill hits him back, a fist beneath his eye. Bill grabs him by the throat and squares up another punch. If it makes contact, Tom's head will be sandwiched between the fist and the wall. A concussion, no doubt. Tom is able to twist his head. Bill's fist hits the wall hard. It's right by Tom's ear. He hears bones in Bill's hand break.

Bill may have broken his hand, but he doesn't break his other hand's grip on Tom's throat. Tom hooks his right arm around Bill's left, the one holding him. He wrenches up, breaks his hold, is able to take a breath.

Bill is relentless. He hits Tom in the side, doubles him up. Bill is strong. He brings both fists down across Tom's back. Tom hits the ground. Bill is above him, breathing hard. "Special Forces ain't the same as being a goddamn Marine," he says. He grabs Tom by the back of the neck. Drags him across the ground. Tom looks up. He's taking him to the big guy with the broken arm, the jagged edge of the bone pointing upward.

Bill starts laughing. He lifts Tom's head in both hands, starts pushing him toward the jutting bone. Tom presses both hands flat against the ground, resists the pressure. Bill is strong. He's putting all his weight into the push. Tom's right eye is an inch away from the bone. Tom can see the marrow oozing out of it. If the man on the ground stirs, tries to move, the bone could go through Tom's skull.

Tom's elbows are bending. He puts all his strength into a push-up, getting himself away from the bone. Gets his legs up so he's on all fours, and lashes out at Bill's knee. Bill's leg flies out behind him, and he loses his grip. He falls. Tom takes his head in both hands, uses his falling momentum, and slams it down onto the broken bone. It bursts up through Bill's jaw. The man on the ground is torn back into consciousness, and he screams like an animal. He tries to pull himself loose from Bill's head.

Tom falls back. Bill is still conscious. He can't speak – the bone has burst up through his protruding jaw, has scraped and chipped through his teeth, is pressing against his top lip and nose. He's trying to get the other man to be still so he can extricate himself. The other man is twisting and screaming, crying, like an animal caught in a trap.

Tom needs to finish Bill off. He uses the wall for support as he stands. From behind him come gunshots. He braces himself, expecting the bullets to hit him, but instead the three rounds go into Bill. He convulses with the impact, and then he's still. The other man screams harder as Bill goes limp, his weight pulling the bone through his torn skin, almost severing his arm completely.

Tom turns. Josh has the gun. His face is swollen, and his right eye is closed. He's covered in blood. Tilly is supporting his weight.

They don't have time for introductions. Tom goes to the other side of Josh, takes his weight. "We need to get your sister," he says. They move outside quickly. They leave the screaming man on the ground. Tom does not have much sympathy for him. He was protecting a pedophile.

He pulls out his phone on the way, calls Danny. "Get down here – *now*!"

53

Tom is driving. Danny sits up front beside him. He's pushing the car for all it's worth.

Behind them are Josh and Tilly. Josh is hurt, but he's alert. He's sitting forward, staring through the front, to the windshield.

Danny has told them what happened at the church – her confrontation with Ken, and forcing him to tell her what they've planned.

"He's fucking insane," Tilly said, shaking her head. "They all are, they've gotta be, everyone who follows him."

Danny saw Laurence leave the compound. His sleek Lexus tore out of the opening in the trees and roared away down the road. She'd almost gone after him. It had taken all she had to stay where she was, to wait and hear from Tom, while worrying that she might not hear from him at all. That she'd let Laurence go, while Tom could be lying dead down in the compound. She hadn't been able to see inside the Lexus and so didn't know if Taylor was with him or not. Now there is no question. Had she seen Taylor, she would have gone in pursuit. It's best she didn't. Tom and the others would have been left behind.

"We could be too late already," Josh says.

Tom doesn't answer. Danny sees how his jaw is clenched.

"We'll get there," she says, trying to reassure Taylor's brother. "He didn't go by too long before you called me. Five minutes, tops."

"Five minutes could be all it takes," Josh says. He sounds defeated.

Tilly strokes his arm, tries to comfort him, but Danny can see her face. She's expecting the worst, too.

They've called the FBI. It was the first thing Danny did when Tom took over driving. They can't trust the local cops, but Josh and Tilly were kidnapped over state lines. Taylor was transported across them, too. Danny has sent them to the church and to the compound. Tom hasn't said much since he got in the car, but he did mention that they don't know how long the feds will take. "It's up to us," he said.

They reach Belleville. Danny hopes they're not too late. She's not thinking about the story anymore. She's thinking about a young girl – who knows how many young girls, how many 'brides' – whose lives are in danger. Tom speeds the car through the streets, not reducing their speed, taking the corners so tight they go skidding across into the other lanes. It's late, and they haven't come across anyone else on the road. Danny wills it to stay this way.

54

As soon as they reach the church, Laurence grabs Taylor by the hair and drags her from his car. With his other hand, he keeps checking his phone. "*Shit*," he says, skimming messages on his screen. Taylor's body is twisted, and she can't see what any of them say. She *does* see who he's dialling, though. It's Bill. It rings for a while. No one answers.

Laurence makes a noise, then puts the phone away. "He's not coming," he says, shaking his head, talking to himself. "It should be done by now. It should all be dealt with. He isn't coming." He shakes his head again, with finality this time, and continues on into the church.

Inside, there are people already there, waiting for them. They stand down at the front, on the stage in the auditorium. There are six other men present, each of them with a young girl. Taylor recognizes some of the girls. A couple of them look like they've just woken up, are still half-asleep. The others are wide awake, and they are worried. Their wide eyes dart around the room, see how Laurence has Taylor by her hair. He lets go of her, takes her by the hand instead.

"Where's Bill?" one of the men says. They are all holding on to their girls, too. Have them tightly by the hands or the wrists.

"He's coming," Laurence says. He snaps the words. He's on edge. His usual diction, his cultivated accent, is slipping. This is not how he usually presents himself.

The men see how his nose is swollen and bloodied. See the bruises on his neck. "What happened to you?" another says.

"Don't worry about it." Laurence looks around. "Where's Ken?"

"We haven't seen him."

"He should be here. He should have everything ready."

The men shrug, don't know what to tell him.

"We just got here about ten minutes ago, give or take," one man says. "You're the first other person we've seen."

Laurence keeps Taylor by his side while he searches. Ken is in the first place they look – Laurence's office. The door has been locked from the outside. Laurence has a spare key.

"What happened?" Laurence says.

"Your fucking secretary!" Ken says, rubbing his broken arm and looking pained. His face is bright red and blistered. "She knows! She knew about the cyanide!"

Taylor feels her blood run cold at the mention of cyanide.

"Danielle?" Laurence says, eyes narrowing. "She beat you up and locked you in my office?"

"That's exactly what she fucking did, the crazy bitch! She almost took my fucking eyes out!"

"Language, Kenneth," Laurence says, regaining some of his regular composure. "Where is she now?"

"How the fuck should I know? I've been locked in here for Christ knows how long!" He looks upon Taylor, as if suddenly realizing she is there, by Laurence's side. "*You*," he says, sneering. "This is all *your* fault –"

He takes a step forward, but Laurence places a hand upon his chest. "Behave yourself, Kenneth. Is everything else prepared?"

"Almost," Ken says, still glaring at Taylor. "The drinks are ready, and the dresses."

"You said *almost*."

"I don't have my bride. I didn't have a chance to go and get her –"

"There's no time," Laurence says.

"What?" Ken says, his blistered face dropping. "But they could have brought her along for me, they could've –"

"You can find one on the other side," Laurence says, showing his teeth.

"But I had the one I wanted picked out –"

"Then you shouldn't have let yourself get beat up by a fucking *girl*!" Laurence says. His composure doesn't just slip again – it is *gone*. Color rises in his cheeks.

Ken cowers under his roar. Laurence pulls him from the office and pushes him ahead of them.

The other men and the girls are waiting for them when they return. Ken rushes by everyone, into a door by the side, and when he returns, he carries dresses. Plain and white. He hands them out, giving one to each girl, his lip curling as he passes by Taylor. In the end, he is left with one dress spare. He looks down at it as he returns to the side door.

"Put them on," Laurence says.

The girls hesitate.

Taylor swallows hard. She can't look at Laurence. Can't look at the other men. She's too scared of them seeing her.

She thought she was tough. When she was on the road, alone or with Tom, she thought she was tough. She imagined what she would do if ever she found herself in such a situation again. How she would stand up to them, the way she's always dreamed. But now the moment has come, and here in their presence she finds she's still the scared little girl she's always been. The scared, broken little girl that they have made her.

"Put the dresses on," Laurence says. "I don't like repeating myself." He clears his throat, forces himself to smile. "My dears, this is a joyous evening for us all. Let's not ruin it, hmm?"

Taylor can feel herself shaking. Tastes the blood in her mouth from when he hit her. Her scalp crawls from when he'd pulled on her hair, and her skin itches from his touch. She looks at the other girls. The two who looked sleepy are wide awake now. They're all of a similar age as her. Some are younger. They're all scared.

Taylor finds her voice. "Don't do it!" she says. "He's going to kill us!"

The girls freeze.

"*Taylor*," Laurence says.

"He's gonna fucking kill us!"

Laurence hits her. The other girls gasp. Laurence turns on them and on the men. "Put on the fucking dresses! Make them do it if you have to!"

The men do as they're told. Most of the girls don't try to fight them, though some of them struggle a little. They're too scared. Scared and broken. They're like Taylor. They know what will happen if they refuse.

Laurence takes Taylor by the face. "I've been patient with you for long enough," he says, his accent Southern. "I've waited for you to behave, and at every turn you've disappointed me." He bunches up the dress and holds it in front of her face. "You will wear the dress, Taylor. Soon – very, *very* soon – you will thank me."

55

Tom gets them as close to the church as possible. Danny has both hands pressed on the dashboard, bracing herself. "Jesus!" she says as he slams on the brakes. "I thought you were gonna go *through* the church!"

Tom doesn't respond. There's no time. He's already out of the car, running inside. He has Bill's gun – took it from Josh shortly before they reached the church. Behind him, Danny, Josh, and Tilly are following him in.

He doesn't know the church. Has never been in it before. Doesn't know where they could be. He runs forward, bursts into the auditorium, expecting to find bodies, dead, he's too late –

There are bodies, but they're standing. Seven men, six girls. Tom sees Laurence and Ken. Ken is looking worse for wear. Next to Laurence, one of his hands on her shoulder, is Taylor.

She sees him. "Tom!"

Laurence sees him, too. He holds Taylor from behind, an arm wrapped around her throat. There's a chalice in his right hand. Tom pulls out the Beretta, points it at the stage.

Danny, Josh, and Tilly catch up with him in the auditorium.

All of the other men have chalices, too. They grip the girls by their shoulders, like Laurence was before his hold became more aggressive. The girls, including Taylor, are all wearing white dresses. They're barefoot.

Tom points the gun at Laurence. He's trying to shield himself behind Taylor. "Let her go," Tom says.

"Don't drink, whatever you do!" Danny says. She's addressing the girls. "Don't let them make you drink! It's cyanide!"

One of the men is panicking. He starts to move the chalice toward the girl he's holding, to her mouth. Tom jerks the gun in his direction. "Nobody moves," he says. "I will put a bullet in your brain. Drop the chalice. All of you – drop the fucking chalices."

The man's hand is shaking. He does as Tom says. The others promptly follow suit.

"Clive *Buck*," Danny says, as if realizing something. "The mayor. And that's Bob Rhodes and Stan Allanson."

Tom turns the gun back to Laurence. "*Drop it*."

Laurence doesn't.

"Let her go, asshole!" Josh says.

Tom takes a step closer to the stage.

"Not another fucking move, Rollins!" Laurence says. He lets go of Taylor's neck and squeezes either side of her mouth, forces it open. "I wanted you here to see this," he says, "and now here you are."

He grins. He looks insane. He moves the chalice toward Taylor's lips.

56

Taylor tries to close her mouth, but Laurence holds her firm. She struggles against him, but it's no good. The chalice is getting closer. No one moves. She sees how Josh and Tilly, and the woman she doesn't know standing with them, how they all watch with wide eyes, wishing they were closer, wishing they could do something. The other men and the girls nearby, they're all staring. Some of the girls are crying.

"Taylor."

It's Tom's voice. He hasn't lowered the gun. She looks at him.

"I promised I'd never let him hurt you again," he says.

He fires.

For the first time in a long time, Taylor feels no fear. The bullet is coming towards them, and she's not scared. The chalice, with its poison, is near her lips, but she's not worried.

The chalice flies from Laurence's hand. Taylor sees his index and middle fingers separate from his hand. There's a red mist, and then the stumps squirt blood. Laurence cries out, lets go of her, clutches his wrist. Tom lowers the gun, but only a little. He's still ready to use it.

Taylor turns. Laurence is cursing loudly. He feels her eyes. Turns to her.

"*You*," he says. He looks like Ken now, earlier, when Laurence had to hold him back. "You're not worthy – you never were. You're a snake. You tricked me – you tricked me and lured me in with your –"

"Shut the fuck *up*," Taylor says. She takes a step forward and kicks him between the legs. Laurence screams, and it's the most satisfying sound Taylor has ever heard. He falls. He curls into a ball and clutches himself.

Taylor steps back, away from him. Out of his reach. She closes her eyes. She takes a deep breath. She smiles.

Now.

Now she is free.

57

Tom races onto the stage, to the fallen pastor. With his left hand he pins him to the ground by the back of his neck, then presses the Beretta to his skull.

"*Don't!*"

Tom turns. It's Danny. She's followed him onto the stage. Josh is by her side, though he's frowning at her outburst. Tilly is gathering the girls, leading them away from the defeated men lined up behind them.

"Don't kill him," Danny says. "Don't kill any of them."

"Why the fuck not?" Josh says.

Tom thinks this is a good question.

"Because the cops are on their way," Danny says. "And no matter how many friends they may have –" she glares at the men to her right "– there's no way they can cover this up. There's too many witnesses. So let them live, and let them get what's coming to them. It'll be worse than anything you can do right now. Inmates don't take kindly to pedophiles, and they're gonna be *especially* rough on cops and a *mayor*."

The one Danny looked at when she said *mayor* is shaking. He's breathing hard, and his face has turned red. Sweat runs from his temple. He drops to the ground and scrambles for his dropped chalice, clasps it in both hands, hoping to drain away the last few drops, hoping that these will be enough.

Josh is on him. He runs over and knees him in the face, then kicks the chalice away. The mayor is crying. Josh pulls him back to his feet, makes him stand. A dark patch spreads in the crotch of his trousers.

Tom looks back down at Laurence.

"Are you going to listen to her?" Laurence says. His tone is mocking. He laughs. "Are you going to listen to my *secretary*? What does she know?"

"I was never your fucking secretary," Danny says. "I was always your downfall."

Laurence frowns at this, not understanding, but then his eyes narrow in pain as Tom presses the gun harder against his skull. He wants to do it. Wants to pull the trigger. To put an end to this sick man and everything he's ever done or stood for. His finger is twitching on the trigger.

"Do it!" Laurence says. "Do it!"

Tom knows Danny is right. This would be too quick. Too easy. It's what he wants. He looks at Ken, too, standing meekly to one side, nursing his broken arm, looking like he's about to piss himself, just like the mayor. Tom wants to kill him, too. But, again, Danny is right.

Tom turns to Taylor. Silently, he puts the question to her. Is this what she wants? Does she want him to kill them right now – Laurence and Ken? It's up to her. It's her decision. This was never his fight.

Taylor understands. She looks at him for a long time. The FBI will hopefully be here soon. Every minute, they're getting closer. This building, this town, will soon be swimming with federal agents.

Taylor shakes her head, just once.

Tom takes the gun from Laurence's skull.

EPILOGUE

It's been a week since the incident at the compound and the church. Physically, everyone has healed. Mostly. Josh's face has returned to normal save for some new scars and residual bruising.

Taylor lives with her brother and Tilly now. Legally, Josh and Tilly are still applying for guardianship, but they've been assured this is just a formality at this point. Taylor will be living with them long-term.

Tom has been staying in the spare room. It's early morning, and he wakes to the sounds and smells of breakfast cooking. Tilly gets up early. Tom feels like he's put on ten pounds since he first came to stay.

He's been awake for a while. He's dressed, sitting on the edge of the bed, looking out the window. By his side, his bag is packed and waiting. Outside, he hears a car pull to a stop in front of the house. He recognizes the sound of the engine. Danny's. There's a knock at the door. He listens as it's answered. Sure enough, Tilly calls up to him, tells him it's Danny.

Tom heads downstairs. He takes his bag with him.

"She's on the porch," Tilly says. "I told her she could come in, but she said she'd let us eat breakfast first." She notices the bag on Tom's shoulder and raises an eyebrow.

Tom heads out. Danny leans against a porch railing, her face turned to the early morning sun. Tom puts his bag to one side, then leans against the railing opposite, arms folded. Danny sees the bag, too. "You moving on?"

He nods. "You're up early."

"I have news. Thought you might wanna hear it." She nods at the bag again. "Seems like a good thing I came as early as I did."

"You could've called. It's a long way to drive."

"I was already in town."

"How come?"

"I'm staying at a motel. It's not too far from here."

"There a reason for your being in Portland?"

She grins. "Researching my story. The far-reaching tendrils of the Temple of St. Philomena, from Belleville, Washington, down into Portland, Oregon."

"That's long for a subtitle."

She laughs. "Something to think about. I'm not gonna be able to publish the damn thing for a while yet, but I can keep myself busy writing and researching it."

"Why's that?"

"Because of the trial. Because I'm a witness." Danny and Taylor will both be witnesses. "The story, and my part in it, won't be allowed to be published until the trial is over. But the story can wait. What's more important right now is putting an evil man – hell, a whole bunch of them – away behind bars for a very long time."

"You're still going to write the story, though."

Danny takes a deep breath. "Did I tell you about my

priest? I don't think I did. Father Dudley. He told me about Scarlet. Told me something might be wrong in the Temple of St. Philomena. I went to see him after the FBI let us loose. I asked him what I should do. If writing the story was still the right thing. He said I should. He said it's the right thing to do. To tell people the truth. No, I don't see how I can't. Then no sooner had I started on it, I got an option for a book deal. I'm gonna take it, of course, but that doesn't feel all that important right now. It's weird, because it's everything I've ever wanted from my career, but now I've got it, it just kind of pales next to everything we found out."

Tom grunts. "You said you came here with news."

"Laurence tried to kill himself last night," she says. "He wasn't successful."

"How'd he try it?"

"Hanging. One of the guards checked in on him, though, cut him down. They've got him on suicide watch now."

Tom nods.

"Heard that from one of my contacts. I also heard from him that none of them are having a good time inside. Laurence isn't the first who's tried to kill himself."

"Good."

"*And* it's only been a week. They've got a long way to go yet."

They stand in silence for a moment. Danny is staring at his bag. "Have you told her?"

"Not yet," Tom says.

"Are you going to?"

"Sure."

"She'll miss you."

"I'll miss her."

Danny nods. She pushes herself off the railing and stretches her back. "I think they should be done eating now," she says. "I'm gonna head inside. You want me to send her out?"

Tom nods.

Danny turns to head inside, but she stops herself by the door. She turns back to him and offers her hand. They shake. They don't say anything else. Danny goes inside.

Tom looks up and down the road. It's quiet. He picks up his bag and throws it over one shoulder, then steps down off the porch. He stands in the pathway cutting up the center of the lawn and turns back to the house, waiting.

He doesn't wait long. Taylor is dressed, too. It's the weekend, but Monday is her first day at her new school. She's told Tom how she hasn't been sleeping so well the last few nights, anxious about her new start. "But it's not like a *bad* anxious," she said. "It's – I'm kind of *excited,* too. I mean, they're all gonna know who I am and what happened, but whatever. I'll just have to deal with it. I probably always will."

She wears the Santa Muerte pendant he gave her. She's smiling as she steps out onto the porch, but it fades when she sees where he is and his bag. She takes her time coming to him.

"You're going," she says.

Tom nods.

"I knew you would, eventually," she says. "I just thought we maybe had a little more time."

In just a week, she's already changed so much. She smiles more. She laughs harder. The tension has gone from her shoulders – from her whole body. She still bites the skin around her fingers, though, and Tom has noticed how she squeezes the pendant tight enough it must dig into her palms. But, in time, she'll heal. Maybe not completely, but she'll move on. She'll put this behind her, where it belongs. She's tough. She's always been tough.

"Do you want your necklace back?" she says, tugging on the pendant.

Tom shakes his head. "She's yours now. She's kept you safe this far. I'll feel better knowing you have her."

"*You* kept me safe," she says. She takes a deep breath. "Thank you, Tom. Thank you for helping me. Thank you for stopping when no one else would."

They smile at each other, but they're sad smiles. Parting smiles. Tom feels the sun beating down on the back of his neck. It's going to be a hot day.

"Take care of yourself, Taylor," he says, readying to leave. "I'll think of you."

"You know where I am," she says, motioning to the house behind her. "If the mood ever takes you, don't be afraid to get in touch."

"Maybe I'll send you a letter," he says.

She blows air. "Or, y'know, you could join the rest of us in the present and send an email."

"Maybe I'll ask for your email address when I send my letter."

"I look forward to hearing about what kind of trouble you find next, Kerouac with fistfights."

Tom laughs. "I'll be sure to tell you every detail. Goodbye, Taylor."

"Bye, Tom."

He smiles at her, then turns and starts walking down the road. He doesn't look back, though he knows Taylor is still there, watching him go. He hasn't heard her go back inside.

Then he hears footsteps behind him, coming up fast. Tom turns. Taylor is running to him. She slams into his chest, wraps her arms around him, squeezes him. Tom hugs her back.

"Bye, Tom," she says again, then she lets go, and she walks away now, back to the house, and she doesn't look back.

Tom watches until she's inside. Until the door is closed. She's safe. She's safe here.

He leaves.

The End

ABOUT THE AUTHOR

Did you enjoy *Road Kill*? Please consider leaving a review on Amazon to help other readers discover the book.

Paul Heatley left school at sixteen, and since then has held a variety of jobs including mechanic, carpet fitter, and bookshop assistant, but his passion has always been for writing. He writes mostly in the genres of crime fiction and thriller, and links to his other titles can be found on his website. He lives in the north east of England.

Want to connect with Paul? Visit him at his website.

www.PaulHeatley.com

ALSO BY PAUL HEATLEY

Blood Line

(A Tom Rollins Thriller Book 1)

Wrong Turn

(A Tom Rollins Thriller Book 2)

Hard to Kill

(A Tom Rollins Thriller Book 3)

Snow Burn

(A Tom Rollins Thriller Book 4)

Road Kill

(A Tom Rollins Thriller Book 5)

No Quarter

(A Tom Rollins Thriller Book 6)

Made in the USA
Monee, IL
27 August 2022